The Regency Switch

HELEN GASKELL

ONE PLACE. MANY STORIES

HQ
An imprint of HarperCollins*Publishers* Ltd
1 London Bridge Street
London SE1 9GF

www.harpercollins.co.uk

HarperCollins*Publishers*
Macken House, 39/40 Mayor Street Upper
Dublin 1, D01 C9W8, Ireland
This edition 2026

1
First published in Great Britain by HQ,
an imprint of HarperCollins*Publishers* Ltd 2026

Copyright © Helen Gaskell 2026

Helen Gaskell asserts the moral right to be identified as the author of this work.
A catalogue record for this book is available from the British Library.

ISBN: 9780008769574

Set in Sabon LT Pro by HarperCollins*Publishers* India

This novel is entirely a work of fiction. The names, characters and incidents portrayed in it are the work of the author's imagination. Any resemblance to actual persons, living or dead, events or localities is entirely coincidental.

All rights reserved. No part of this publication may be reproduced, stored in a retrieval system, or transmitted, in any form or by any means, electronic, mechanical, photocopying, recording or otherwise, without the prior written permission of the publishers.

Without limiting the exclusive rights of any author, contributor or the publisher of this publication, any unauthorised use of this publication to train generative artificial intelligence (AI) technologies is expressly prohibited. HarperCollins also exercise their rights under Article 4(3) of the Digital Single Market Directive 2019/790 and expressly reserve this publication from the text and data mining exception.

Printed and bound in the UK using 100% Renewable
Electricity at CPI Group (UK) Ltd

Praise for *The* Regency Switch

'A fun, fresh take on a Regency romcom that had me alternately cackling and swooning from the first page right up to the last'
Virginia Heath

'A brilliantly fun time-slip, Regency romcom that effortlessly weaves the lives of Etta and Hetty – despite their separation by two hundred years. The dual storyline was fresh and funny (chamber pot, anyone?), the characters flawed and lovable. Devoured in one happy sitting!'
Michelle Kenney

'Who hasn't dreamed about being transported back to Regency England? Nobody I want to be friends with. I had an absolute blast reading this funny and touching novel . . . I cackled out loud in places'
Emma Orchard

'Helen Gaskell's brilliant debut novel, *The Regency Switch*, is both charming historical romp and witty contemporary romance with just the right amount of spice'
Darcy McGuire

'What a fun ride! This magical debut from author Helen Gaskell hits all the right spots – funny moments, tender moments, body-swapping, magical realism, and some spice. I highly recommend this if you're looking for an escapist book which will leave you feeling warm, fuzzy, and believing in the power of love'
Dana Hawkins

Helen Gaskell is a freelance content designer who works primarily on GOV.UK projects. Recently, she led the content design for the government's first public-facing AI project. Helen spent the first decade or so of her career at the BBC and in 2016 spearheaded an award-winning body positivity campaign that garnered millions of views across social media. During the pandemic, Helen worked for Copenhagen-based Tactile Games as a writer for bestselling game *Lily's Garden* (with over a million daily players) and penned the first sapphic romance storyline for a mobile phone game. She has spoken on narrative design for the Romantic Novelists' Association and is the first games writer to be admitted as a full member.

Helen lives in Manchester with her daughter, cat, dog and husband (in order of precedence). When she's not immersed in romantic novels, she's usually halfway through one of many niche handicrafts.

In memory of Nana Joan

Prologue

2023

Lady Agatha Bainbridge found the box in the attic under piles of dusty old clothing and half-broken furniture. It was remarkably well-sealed, but eventually opened under the combined pressure of a letter opener and a hefty wallop.

'Jemima!' she called out. 'Come up here and look at this.'

A few minutes passed before she heard the creaking on the stairs and her sister appeared.

'What is it?' asked Jemima. 'You know I've got to head out to my Stitch and Bitch group any minute now.'

'Oh, shush now. You can afford to give it a miss this week. Look what I have found!'

Aggie angled the box forward to show what was inside: there was a bundle of notebooks tied together with a frayed-looking ribbon, along with a smaller box containing a delicate gold bracelet. Intrigued, Jemima untied the notebooks and they peered closer, inhaling the musty scent of old paper. The sisters might have had their differences, but both were old and wise enough to feel electricity crackle from the pages.

They opened the top book first – a faded red leather

diary – to find it filled with beautiful handwriting. Aggie put her reading glasses on and tilted the page towards her as Jemima gasped, already a line or two ahead.

Dear Descendant,

If you're reading this, my calculations were correct and these years of study have been worthwhile. I am unsure how to describe what it is that I have planned to do. The transformation, the metamorphosis . . . The Switch?

Chapter 1

2023

It was an ordinary day – much like the day before, and, Etta assumed, much like the next. A Tuesday. Etta hated Tuesdays.

She had a theory about them. Mondays marked a fresh new week in the office, hot off the back of a relaxing weekend spent eating paninis and embroidering woodland creatures for her Etsy store. She might not be getting up to much herself, but Etta liked listening to her colleagues talk about their weekends, their many friends and rambunctious families.

By Wednesday, it was the middle of the week – practically Thursday, and Thursday was practically the weekend. On Fridays she worked out of her tiny studio flat, with half an eye on *Judge Judy*. Then back to another quiet weekend lying in bed until lunchtime and poring over her friends' Instagram feeds while stitching custom embroidery orders for Etsy – when she ever got any, which was increasingly rare.

But Tuesdays – oh, Tuesdays were the worst. On Tuesdays, the week stretched out ahead like elastic ready to snap. Nothing good ever happened on a Tuesday.

Etta clutched her coffee cup closer to her chest as she

waited on the platform for the Tube to arrive. She liked living on the Circle Line. Not really central, but pretty close. It was worth the mice and the fact she could see both her oven and her toilet from her single bed. She'd be in work in less than half an hour. For most people, everything in London took forty-five minutes to an hour to get to. Not for Etta, though. On the Circle Line, it was thirty.

She found a seat between two man-spreading businessmen and opposite a pair of chattering old ladies. She dumped herself down, wedging her coffee cup between her legs. She could smell stale sweat from the man to her left. *Gross*. Trying to make herself as small as possible – which was difficult, given she was unreasonably tall – Etta opened up her favourite mobile game and started matching little blobs. The plot was getting exciting: her character had renovated the entire mansion and Etta was wondering what on earth could possibly be left to do.

She was just about to find out when the carriage jolted. Checking she hadn't missed her stop, she reached down to save her legs from getting covered in cappuccino foam and felt a prickle of awareness: the feeling of being watched.

The carriage had stopped in a tunnel. Alarming, but not as alarming as the fact that it was empty. Well, nearly empty. She looked across the aisle at the two old ladies, who were now completely silent and staring right at her. Etta became aware of the smell of petrichor on the air.

This can't be real, Etta thought. *I've fallen asleep. I hate horror films, but I bet this is what they're like.*

'Are you going to kill me?' she whispered.

The old lady on the right smiled widely. 'Oh no, dear! Quite the opposite!'

'You're . . . going to, what, *alive* me?'

The lady on the left was assessing her, beady-eyed. 'In a way, yes.'

Etta paused, horrified. This must be a joke. She dismissed the thought. She had very few friends left in the city to organise pranks. Her closest friend had been gone almost as long as her parents had, and the others had scarpered to the countryside after Covid. Work, maybe. Perhaps someone at work.

Etta studied the two women in front of her. They certainly didn't look like pranksters – or indeed murderers. They just looked like two – vaguely familiar – old ladies.

Rich old ladies, she thought. The one on the left was wearing an immaculate tweed suit jacket and skirt, with pearls. She could see the collar of a white silk shirt underneath the woman's buttoned-up jacket and patterned green scarf. Hermes, possibly. The woman was stately – almost too tall to be old. Almost as tall as Etta, in fact.

The clothing of the lady on the right looked as expensive as her companion's, but extremely brightly coloured. She was shorter, rounder, and far, far jollier than the aloof woman next to her, and reminded Etta vaguely of her own long-gone mother. She wore a patterned pink dress, underneath layers of cardigans, scarves and jewellery. Looking down, Etta saw a pair of Converse trainers.

Both women were wearing hats, which somehow felt about right. Etta thought people didn't wear hats enough nowadays, suddenly feeling quite jealous. The jolly woman's bright white feathery mess of hair was escaping from a battered Panama while the woman on the left wore a smart green cloche with feathers, with steely grey hair peeking out from underneath.

They both looked at her expectantly. Etta felt, as the youngest person present by perhaps fifty years, that she should probably say something helpful. She went through her mental filing cabinet, but found nothing under the 'stuck in an empty broken-down Tube carriage with two old ladies' tab.

'Um . . . I wonder what's wrong with the Tube? Do you know where everyone went?'

'I think we've got more important issues to cover, dear.' The lady on the left – cloche lady – was clutching a red leather diary, full of sticky notes and bookmarks. She turned to one of the last tabs in the book.

Etta's stomach did a strange sort of flip.

The lady in pink leaned forward excitedly. 'Ooh, dear, say yes! You're going to have the most remarkable time. I'm so excited for you.'

Etta blinked. 'What do you mean?'

'Don't tell her, Jemima! She won't believe us – a pair of total strangers. It's better we just get it over and done with.'

'Sorry, Aggie. I just can't help myself. I wish I could go, too.'

'Well, you can't,' Cloche Lady – Aggie? – replied. 'You're too old. Besides, it's Henrietta's name in the book. She's the one.'

Etta stared. 'Go where? How do you know my name? I'm supposed to be getting off in a minute.'

Aggie ignored her. 'Now listen up.'

Jemima leaned forward, a conspiratorial look on her face. 'Oh yes, dear, you really must pay attention. It's terribly important.'

Aggie glanced at Jemima, mild irritation showing on her

face, then back at Etta. 'You're Henrietta Moore, and it's 2023. But we're offering you a once-in-a-lifetime opportunity, right here, right now. If you take this bracelet, you'll be Henrietta Bainbridge, and it'll be 1817.'

Jemima leaned forward again, her Panama tipping slightly. 'Take it, dearie. A holiday in Regency Britain! How much fun would that be?'

These women are mad, Etta thought. *Completely mad.*

As if she could read her mind, Jemima interjected. 'Better humour us, hadn't you, dear? If we're unhinged. The safest thing to do.'

Aggie glared at her companion, then continued, her voice becoming urgent, 'When we put this bracelet on you, you will swap places with your ancestor. It's akin to, well, a blip in the universe. And you needn't worry about Hetty – we'll look after her.'

Jemima spoke up again, eyes twinkling. 'Yes, we will. But she was the one that started this – she knows what she's doing. Oh, my dear, how confused you are! I wish we'd found you sooner, but you're Charlie's descendant really, not Hetty's, so you can hardly blame us for taking a while.'

'Yes, thank you, Jemima. Now, the best tack is to roll with it. We know you've been reading those historical romances, so as long as you're careful you'll be fine. The only thing we need you to do – and this is very important – is to write a diary.'

Jemima leaned forward and patted the red leather book Aggie was holding. 'Every day, dear. And don't forget to tell us about the Marquess when you find him. Make sure you do. Every detail. We'll find it in the end, and it will lead us to you. I think so, anyway. This time-travel stuff is discombobulating to say the very least. But the Marquess . . .!'

'Never mind the damn Marquess, Jemima. The bracelet. She has to know how it works.' Aggie's voice took on a new urgency, 'Hetty – Etta – about the bracelet. Take it off, put it on, that's all fine. But break it—'

Jemima took a deep breath.

'Break it, at any time,' Aggie continued, 'and you'll come right back. Holiday over. Only, so will Hetty. The swap will end.'

Etta felt more confused than she had ever been in her life. This must have been written all over her face, because Aggie reached forward and clasped her hands.

'Best not to think too much about the how,' she said kindly. 'Just roll with it. By the end, you'll understand. If you stick it out, you'll have your happy ending. We know that for sure, don't we, Jemima?'

'Well, we think we do, Aggie. Not very feminist, mind, but that's 1817 for you, I suppose. Now, what was the last thing we were supposed to say?'

'Gosh, I don't know, Jemima. Something about that awful snake, I think. What was her name?'

Jemima was wrapping the thin golden chain around Etta's wrist as she said, 'Oh, Aggie, I don't remem—'

Etta blinked. It was an ordinary blink – the kind everyone does, thousands of times a day. She barely registered her eyelids flickering shut, but there was no way to miss what she saw when she opened them again.

Chapter 2

1817

Etta was struck by the sudden, jarring absence of sound. Darkness seemed to surround her; it took a moment for her eyes to grow accustomed to the gloom of, what, a cellar?

She felt cold, dampness clinging to her skin, and realised she wasn't wearing her coat. She was covered in a blanket. Or perhaps a shawl. And she could feel her hair, usually tied in a tight bun, brushing against her face, neck, and upper arms. Strange, given her hair was still growing out from the bob she'd experimented with earlier in the year.

She turned her thoughts to what was in front of her. She wasn't on the Tube any more, that much was clear. She was facing rows upon rows of wine bottles, neatly stacked in wooden racks, with hand-written labels on each shelf. A wine cellar, then.

The labels were illuminated only by a flickering light source, which came from behind her. She moved to wipe the dust from a label, only to find her wrists were strapped to her chair.

And then she freaked out.

At least, she thought she was freaking out. She'd never really lost it before – not even when her father died – but it felt like the rational thing to do.

'What the *ACTUAL* . . .? HELP! What the hell?!'

She tried kicking her legs, but the chair was surprisingly sturdy. Also, her legs were covered in long skirts, which weren't particularly conducive to kicking or in fact any kind of dramatic physical activity.

Etta took a long breath. It was all a dream. She'd done a mindfulness workshop at work one time. The woman had told them to notice each part of their bodies one bit at a time – Dave from accounts had fallen asleep. Etta started noticing, but it really, really didn't help. She noticed her feet, bare on a stone floor. She noticed the long skirts on her unshaven legs. She noticed she had no bloody knickers on. She noticed her small and completely uncontained boobs. She noticed the bracelet, which she desperately wished she could tear off right this moment.

She noticed she was strapped to a chair in a dark and musty cellar, and that she was probably going to be late for work this morning.

This was definitely not helping.

Before Etta had time to notice much more, she heard distant voices growing closer. Male voices, arguing: one stern, one defiant. She turned her head to one side, seeing a dim light coming from a corridor to her side.

'Charlie, it's not right. I do understand why you want to try and help, but you need to give up.'

'Just come with me and see, Max. I swear I saw her shudder.'

'With cold, probably. Or horror. It's wrong, Charlie. You shouldn't experiment on your sister.'

'Now hang on, don't you go pinning all this on me. She asked me to. "Charlie," she said. "It's time to go to the cellar."'

The men rounded the corner, still arguing, and Etta saw their faces in the flickering candlelight. One was stunningly, blindingly handsome, while the other looked like a young Hugh Laurie. The handsome one looked angry, so she decided he must be Max. He looked like he was called Max. Tall, dark, handsome. Like a hero from an historical romance, she reflected, right before she noticed what he and his companion were wearing.

1817, the old ladies had said. The Regency era, then. Knee-britches and shiny boots. Cravats and white shirts under dark evening jackets. She must be dreaming.

Roll with it, they'd said.

She cleared her throat. 'What the hell is going on?'

Etta's voice was dry, crackly from disuse. The two men turned their attention to her, looking as startled as she felt. This seemed unfair. Surely if anyone had the right to be shocked, it should be the person who was on the Tube in 2023 with two eccentric old ladies only minutes earlier, holding her smartphone in one hand and coffee in another. The one strapped to a wooden chair, surrounded by wine bottles.

Etta felt almost angry with it. Certainly indignant. 'Why the *flying fuck* am I in a cellar, strapped to a chair?'

The young Hugh Laurie impersonator's expression turned from mild consternation to full outrage. 'Why, Hetty Bainbridge! You harridan! If Mother heard you use language like that . . . My goodness! She'd have your guts for garters! Where on earth did you hear it?'

'That's not Hetty. You're not Hetty,' said the impossibly handsome Max.

His friend looked at him as though he were mad. 'Of course it's Hetty, Max. She's just where I left her.'

'No. That's not – you're not – you can't be Hetty. Your face. Your expression.'

'Looks the same as ever to me, old boy. Bit less gormless, perhaps. Must be, cursing like that. By god, Hetty, I didn't think you had it in you.'

Etta recalled that the old ladies had mentioned someone called Hetty. Swapping, they'd said. A blip. *Roll with it.*

She took a deep breath. 'Are you going to keep staring at me all day, or are you going to unstrap me from this chair?'

Max seemed to have been jolted out of his shock and had remembered himself. Etta watched him carefully as he unhooked the leather belts around her wrists. He was dressed more neatly than his companion and smelled of sandalwood and mint. Etta's stomach flipped as he looked down at her, confusion burning in his eyes.

'But what about my experiment, Stanhope?' the Laurie lookalike chimed in plaintively. 'I was only going to startle her just a little. Just to perk her up, you know.'

'Your experiment is no longer needed, Charlie. I think strapping her to a chair was enough.'

'Oh, but she's been strapped to countless chairs over the years, Max. I don't see what could be different about this one. Besides, this time she asked me to do it.'

Max looked at Charlie sharply. 'No more straps, Charlie.'

Free from her restraints, Etta turned in her seat and surveyed the scene. There was a table directly behind her, covered in a vast array of metal and glass tubes (full of what she assumed must be battery acid) and fabric-covered cables. Hand-written notes littered every surface.

'What on earth is going on here? What am I, Frankenstein's monster?'

Max jolted. 'Who's what-now, Hetty?'

'Frankenstein. You know, the classic novel by Mary Shelley. Mad scientist creates a monster with electricity and body parts.'

Charlie looked confused. 'I say, I don't know where you've been reading that stuff, Hetty. Father doesn't keep novels in the library. Thought you were more interested in staring at the sky and things, than reading those.' He paused, looking reflective. 'Besides, can't be that classic, can it? Never heard of it.'

Max found his voice again. 'I've met a Mary Shelley, though, abroad. One of the Godwins, no?'

'Oh lord, I dunno,' said Etta. 'Mary Wollstonecraft's daughter. She was bezzie mates with Byron. It's been bloody ages since my English GCSE to be honest.'

She stretched and stood up. Her muscles felt much weaker than usual and everything around her seemed . . . lower. Bigger, somehow. The two men seemed to tower over her. Despite the discomfort in her wrists and the freezing cold, damp stone under her feet, she felt detached from everything around her.

'This is such a weird dream. Why am I so short?' Etta looked down at her thin nightdress and plain wool shawl. 'Where are my clothes? I think it's time to wake up now.'

Panic was starting to take hold. 'Hello? Weird old ladies? Time to wake up!'

She felt her legs begin to buckle under her and Max started

forward to steady her. She looked up at him and found herself staring into a reassuringly concerned face.

'Oh, stop making sheep's eyes at Stanhope, Hetty. You've never paid him any attention until now, and I don't see why today should be the day to start.'

Max was examining Etta's face again. 'I'm really not sure this is your sister, Charlie.'

'Not my sister? Don't tell me you've gone queer in the head too, old chap. Clearly my sister. Look at her. My god, you've known her nearly as long as I have.'

Max paid no attention, still assessing Etta. 'What's your name?'

Etta looked up at him. This didn't feel like a dream, but he certainly looked like the kind of man she might dream about. In her very best dreams. 'Etta,' she said. 'Henrietta Moore.'

'Well, that settles it,' said Charlie. 'It didn't work. She might well be chatting away, but she's still mad as a March hare.'

'Be quiet, Charlie.' Max glanced at Charlie derisively, then looked back at Etta. 'Hmm . . . I don't know. What's the date?'

'Nineteenth of September 2023. The weather is terrible. Wet, miserable. I was on the Circle Line. Heading to work. I must have fallen asleep.' Etta was babbling now, she knew, but she needed to make sense of what was happening.

'2023? What do you mean, 2023?'

'Mad, I'm telling you,' Charlie interjected. 'She remains utterly mad.'

Max straightened up and started walking Etta across the room and along the corridor he and Charlie had entered from. Etta could see now that she was most definitely in a cellar of some kind.

'You know, if I'm not asleep then I think I actually must *be* mad,' said Etta. 'One minute I'm chatting to two old ladies on a train, the next I'm in a cellar with two posh blokes, dressed in only a nightie. I don't even have shoes on.'

'You seem pretty sane to me,' said Max. He looked down at her feet, then without saying a word, swept her into his arms and carried on walking.

Etta squeaked. 'You picked me up! How did you do that? I'm nearly six feet tall and . . . and plus-sized!'

'No, you're not.'

Etta tried to wriggle away, but he held her firm. 'Yes, I am. And it's fine. Hashtag body positivity. I don't need to be carried anyway.'

Max glanced down at her. 'Yes, you do. You're thin as a stick, freezing cold, and you have no slippers on. And your dreadful brother has been holding you in his wine cellar.'

He was right – the cold ran through her strangely unfamiliar body, right to her bones.

They ascended some stone stairs. Looking around, Etta saw she was now in a small room adjacent to the kitchen. Her only indication that it was a kitchen at all was that it looked like a period house she'd seen on a school trip once. Moonlight filtered through small windows; beyond the open door she could see a large wooden table covered in baskets of unprepared vegetables and, at the back of the room, a huge old-fashioned black stove, which looked like an Aga's great-grandmother.

'Charlie? How can we get her back to her maid without getting caught?'

'Servants' stairs. She sleeps next to the nursery.'

'Ah, yes. I remember the way.'

Etta looked up at him as they ascended another set of stairs, feeling as though every feminist bone in her body should be wailing with protest at being carried like a doll. She hated herself a little for liking it.

Attempting to orientate herself, she looked at the walls and tried to remember more of the school trip. She'd been down a set of stairs like this, but she could tell these walls were freshly painted. It seemed like a lot of effort for stairs made for servants to use.

'Where are we?' she croaked.

'Your country home on the Bainbridge Estate.'

'But not your home?'

'No. I live at Stanhope, nearby. We used to play together – don't you remember? I'm here for dinner with your brother.'

A vague recollection came to Etta. It floated through her consciousness like a ghost: a memory belonging to somebody else. A boy, with Max's dark hair and soft brown eyes, running past her as she watched the sky.

Etta was a brunette. Always had been. But from the corner of her eye, even in the dark, she could see blonde hair.

'I remember . . . but it's not my memory.' She paused, very much aware of his strong arms around her. 'You can put me down, you know. It's fine.'

His lips quirked in a smile. 'Don't you like being carried?'

'Well, it's not very feminist, is it?'

Confusion flickered on Max's face. 'Seems feminine enough to me.'

'No, I mean . . .' Etta paused, and took a deep breath. 'Oh god, I suppose you don't have feminism, do you? No pussy hats, no *Vagina Monologues*, no *Vindication of the Rights of Woman*. No contraception, probably.'

She knew immediately she'd erred when his surprised eyes met hers.

'Perhaps not, but I do, Henrietta Bainbridge, understand Latin, and I can take an educated guess at the last.'

'Well, it's not very independent, anyway,' Etta backtracked. 'To be carried, I mean.'

Max looked down at her as he finally reached the top floor of what felt like a massive house, yet he was barely out of breath. 'Humans aren't meant to be independent. We all rely on one another.'

Etta struggled to understand the expression on his face. Charlie had fallen behind, Max's long strides taking them quickly across the house.

'Your face. So different. I don't understand how Charlie can't see it. Your features are the same as ever, but every expression has changed.' His eyes roamed over her, curious.

They stopped by a door and Etta couldn't help but be a little relieved – she had no response to that. Max put her down and they stared at one another, still so close they were nearly touching, as Charlie huffed and puffed up the corridor behind them. Etta could feel the heat radiating from him and had to stop herself from snuggling back into his arms.

Charlie finally came into sight, and she realised she was still staring at Max. He broke eye contact immediately and stepped away, twisting the signet ring on his finger.

'Your room. Charlie, I can hardly believe your mother still has Hetty in the nursery. She must be very nearly twenty-one by now.'

'Better than the madhouse, Stanhope. That's where most people would have her, but Mother's too sentimental for that. Thinks they wouldn't treat her well enough.'

'She's right,' said Max. He gave Etta another curious look, arching one eyebrow, and opened the door for her. 'But, Hetty, somehow I don't think you'll be in the nursery much longer.'

She barely had time to register a plain, dark room with a couple of old school desks scattered in front of a blackboard, before a short, kindly-looking woman in her late fifties bustled up.

'Oh, Hetty, what on earth have you been doing? You should have been in bed a long time since!'

Charlie looked sheepish. 'Sorry, Nanny. I took her for . . . well, for a talk.'

'Now why would you want to be chatting with Miss Hetty, Lord Bainbridge? You know she barely says a word. And her in her nightdress, too! Why, it's past midnight!' It was at this point Nanny spotted Max. 'My goodness, Lord Stanhope. I hope you're well? Excuse me if I don't curtsey. My knees aren't what they were.'

'Don't worry, Mrs Cummings. I spent so much time here as a boy that you're practically my nanny too, and I wouldn't want Nanny Berkins curtseying to me either.'

Mrs Cummings blushed as she raced to smother Etta in a large and rather itchy blanket. Feeling it was time to say something, Etta stuck her hand out. 'Lovely to meet you, Mrs Cummings. I'm Etta.'

She had never seen a blushing woman turn so pale so quickly. 'Hetty! You . . . you spoke! Bless my days. Did you really speak?'

'Well . . . yes?'

Mrs Cummings looked at Max, and then over to Charlie, as though needing their confirmation. Charlie pulled a face, then nodded in a non-committal manner. 'Yes, well! I cured her. You're welcome.'

'Master Charles! Sorry, I mean Your Lordship. But – well, I never! You haven't been experimenting with your sister again, have you? You know your mama forbade it!'

Charlie shrugged again. 'I don't see the harm. She has no idea what's going on half the time. More! And anyway, as I said – I fixed her this time.'

Mrs Cummings looked cynical through her amazement. 'We'll see about that. Come, Hetty. Let's warm you up by the fire. Off you go, Your Lordships.' She shooed the two men out with the confidence of an old retainer.

Etta wasn't sure what to say to the older woman, but it turned out she didn't need to say anything at all. She found herself quickly ushered next door to a small bedroom, tucked into a rather uncomfortable bed and, although her mind was a whirlwind of confusion and conjecture, exhaustion soon overcame every other thought.

She dreamed of her last holiday – an ill-fated hen-do in Ibiza that happened too soon after her dad had died. The end of her family and the beginning of the end for her friend group too, before a global pandemic and romantic relationships had scattered them around the country.

If those eccentric old ladies were right and this truly was a holiday, then perhaps it would be more exciting than crying and watching a former friend shag her way through every nightclub on the island without even taking her engagement ring off.

Chapter 3

2023

Hetty was only very vaguely aware of the two older ladies next to her. Much more overpowering was the press of other bodies: the stench of humanity, the stinging light in her eyes.

And, of course, the noise. Oh, what noise. The roar of metal carriages bringing with them gusts of freezing air and waves of angry-looking people. The sound of feet pounding on steps, of metal staircases grinding. The bizarre intermittent noise that accompanied moving gates as the people around her seemed to flee onto the street almost as though for their own lives.

Hetty focused inwards. She knew she must breathe. She pressed forward and was grateful for the welcoming arms of her descendants.

'What are we doing, Aggie?' she heard the one who had introduced herself as Jemima hiss as bright sunlight hit her face. Hetty took large, grateful gulps of fresh air as they paused next to a wall and pulled her hair over her face. It was short, but it was at least thick enough to block out the confusing scene in front of her.

She felt Aggie's hand pat hers as the woman continued

to argue with her sister. They'd been quarrelling over the meaning of free will and it was proving a welcome distraction.

'Don't let's go through this again right now, Jemima. We've been through it more times than I can count.'

'Yes, but I *still* don't properly understand it,' Jemima moaned. 'And it's hard to know how it ends, isn't it, when the diary gets so patchy?'

Hetty peeked out from between her strangely dark hair. Aggie was glaring at Jemima in annoyance, but the sisters were seemingly unstoppable at this point.

'I'm just saying. The Switch, or whatever has happened, does seem to have worked rather well. You must admit it's quite the brain-fuck, isn't it?'

'Jemima!'

Hetty took a deep breath, steeling herself against the world, then pushed her hair back over her head. 'Where am I? What year is it?'

They both looked at her. '2023, dear. Central London. Oh gosh, you do look upset – let's call a cab.'

Aggie raised her arm, and they watched as a black carriage – missing any kind of horse but still, somehow, moving at quite some speed – stopped by the pavement.

The older ladies bundled Hetty into the carriage before she knew what she was doing, gave directions, then Aggie pressed some kind of button which cut off the driver's reply mid-sentence.

'Rude,' Jemima reprimanded, before continuing. 'So has this really worked, then?'

Hetty swallowed her fear. 'I'm quite sure . . . Fairly sure you were always destined to find me and my diary. I did all the correct calculations. I got my numbers right.'

'But how did you know it was going to work?' Jemima interrupted, fussing over Hetty's dishevelled locks. It was rather nice, being fussed over.

Hetty felt her shoulders hunch. Truthfully, she was as surprised as they were that her plan had worked – if indeed this was not a dream.

'Look, Jemima, you're not the theoretical physicist here. That would be Henrietta. Best not ask too many questions – let's leave it to the expert.'

'And according to the first page of that diary, if she breaks the bracelet, they both swap back? Well, either of you could break it at any time, right? And then what?'

Aggie hushed Jemima. 'You're not helping, dear. Come on, let's get Hetty home.'

She turned to Hetty, and only kindness and concern were on her face.

'Oh, how I wish we'd found Etta sooner – perhaps this swap could have happened years ago. You poor child. Both of you must be so scared. And we would have loved to have had a niece to dote on all these years.'

'Well, now we do, Aggie,' said Jemima, leaning forward. 'Don't worry, my dear. We're going to have such a wonderful time. Just you wait and see.'

Chapter 4

1817

The first thing Etta heard the following morning was birdsong, and the sound of a fireplace being scraped out. Her body was heavy with blankets and she knew immediately that she wasn't in her poky studio flat under her duvet.

For a moment, she lay still and went over the events of yesterday. Increasingly, against every logical fibre in her being, she was beginning to feel that something momentous had happened. That maybe, just maybe, *Doctor Who* was onto something – time travel was indeed possible.

Her every physical sense told her that she was not where she had been only hours before. These sheets felt different against her skin; her very skin felt different against her bones. The bed sheets *smelled* different – still clean, but not of cotton-scented non-biological detergent. Thicker, rougher, heavier. Etta took a deep breath, inhaling the scent of dried lavender and soap powder.

She'd breathed too hard and started hyperventilating. Etta rolled herself in a ball and counted in, one, two, three, four, and then out, one, two, three, four – an old pandemic trick, from when she'd strained at the four white walls of her flat – and finally managed to get her breathing under control.

Roll with it, she remembered. *Roll with it*, because let's face it, this can't be real.

She sat up, discovering the room to be much colder than she expected, and felt smooth wooden floorboards under her feet as she looked around.

She was sitting on a tall, metal-framed bed with an ominous-looking chamber pot by her feet which she was going to have to make immediate use of.

She shed the old-fashioned quilt and sheets, and looked around to try to distract herself from the fact she was crouching down, weeing into a little bowl, in the middle of a freezing cold bedroom, with no toilet paper in sight. She hadn't had to drip dry since a memorable childhood camping trip. Etta winced as she recalled being towed along on an interminable hiking trip with her dad who, unable to find childcare, had forgotten his daughter might need such luxurious amenities as toilets and showers. At least he'd remembered to take her along in the first place.

She could see a writing desk with piles of papers and notebooks next to it on the other side of her bed. A quill and inkpot sat on top. Etta looked down at her hands and saw ink stains on her fingertips which she hadn't noticed last night. So she was a writer, she thought. Well, that was going to be something she'd struggle to live up to.

If she was going to have some kind of historical adventure, writing was probably the last ladylike hobby she'd put on her list. Music she could do, and her embroidery was great – her last commission had been rather too obscene for yesteryears, but she could happily confine herself to throwing in the odd suggestively-positioned lily. But writing? Not her strong suit. The C she got in her GCSE had been one of the proudest moments in her scholastic career, and she was very much going to miss spellcheck.

Besides the writing desk, the room was sparse and cold. Paint flaked from the walls and a few threadbare rugs were scattered across the bare floorboards. The only adornment on the walls was a child-like illustrated watercolour alphabet and some framed pressed flowers. Etta was desperate to look in a mirror, but there wasn't even one of those. She'd read dozens of Regency romances, and this was not one of them.

She got up, finding a dressing gown on a chair next to her bed, and sat down at the writing desk. There was a brand-new red leather diary in the centre of the table, which she opened. She read the first page.

Dear Descendant,

If you're reading this, my calculations were correct and these years of study have been worthwhile. I am unsure how to describe what it is that I have planned to do. The transformation, the metamorphosis . . . The Switch?

Enclosed is a bracelet of my own design: please place on the wrist of the woman with whom I exchange my life.

To that woman: please, so we may find you, describe your name and direction.

Underneath was a space, and then the words:

I am sure this may seem strange, but then again perhaps in your time this is a commonplace occurrence. Either way, I hope you will indulge me. I have written some notes in the following pages in order that you might navigate this time, and I have contrived that if the bracelet is broken we shall switch back.
Yours,
Henrietta Bainbridge

Etta sat back and stared at the empty space on the page, unsure what to think, then unscrewed the top of the ink bottle and dipped in the quill. The nib spluttered, but she managed to scrawl her name and address well enough. In for a penny, in for a pound.

She flicked through the diary for a moment, seeing pages and pages of elegant handwriting and knowing she should read them, but now wasn't the time for homework. Yes, she was extremely curious about the previous owner of the body she was in, but right now her primary feeling was one of gnawing hunger.

Her golden bracelet knocked against the diary as she set it down, reminding her of her supposed get-out clause. The old ladies had said the same. In the unlikely event that this really had happened – that she really *had* time-travelled to Regency England – at least she had an escape route.

Smelling the welcome scent of toast, Etta padded into the next room. Mrs Cummings was there, sitting by a pile of sheets, which she appeared to be embroidering.

'Good morning, Hetty dear. It's a cold one today. You sit next to that fire and let Nanny sort everything out for you.'

'Hello. Morning.'

Mrs Cummings recoiled, blinking furiously, then appeared to collect herself.

Etta drew closer to the nursery fire as the older woman bustled around her, covering her shoulders in a shawl and bringing over a tray. It had a pot of tea and a plate with a slice of now-cold buttered toast.

Etta eyed it distrustfully. 'Mrs Cummings – Nanny? – is this what I always eat for breakfast?'

Mrs Cummings looked like she hardly knew how to answer. 'Why, yes, as well you know! Miss Hetty, I really can't think what's come over you. To hear you call me Nanny again . . .'

Etta saw tears building at the corners of the older woman's eyes. As confused and taken aback as she was, she felt compassion for this strange woman who clearly loved her very much.

'Please don't cry! I'm as confused as you are, but I'm sure everything will be okay.'

'Oh-Kay? What can you mean, child?' cried Nanny, looking at her in tearful confusion.

Etta mentally checked herself. She'd read enough Georgette Heyer novels and seen more than enough episodes of *Bridgerton* (if there could ever be enough episodes of *Bridgerton*!) to know she was going to have to think carefully about her language – and everything else, for that matter – if she was going to survive this odd dream-slash-holiday. Although she'd covertly pinched herself three times now.

'Fine. I mean fine, Nanny. I think everything will be wonderful.'

'It is wonderful indeed, my dear. I never thought to hear you speak to your old Nanny again, as though you were a grown-up lady. My goodness, what will your mother say?'

It began to sink in: in this version of her life, there was a mother. A family.

Until now, Etta had had no family left in the world. Her mother had died giving birth to her and she had only ever seen her face in photographs, while her dad – always somewhat distant to begin with – had been killed on the M6 by a sleeping lorry driver soon after she left home for uni. She never had siblings; she hadn't so much as a cousin to her name.

Luckily Nanny didn't appear to be expecting an answer. She poured Etta some tea, which she drank gratefully. Her throat still felt cracked and dry.

Eyeing up the toast with mistrust, she found it was delicious – fresh, solid, and quite different from the squishy bricks she was used to buying from the local corner shop. If an old lady with a tartan shopping trolley had inexplicably squeezed this one on the shelf 'for freshness' then at least it had held its shape.

Nanny was bustling around in a room next door to the nursery. Peeking through the open door, Etta could see her pulling clothes from a wardrobe. She sipped her tea and began to formulate a plan.

Clearly, in this dream, her character Hetty was being treated like a child. Etta recalled Charlie – her brother – treating her like an idiot last night. But she was clearly rich, or from a rich family, at least. This was a big house, and Charlie and Max had been dressed in very fancy clothes. Max, in particular, had been exceptionally well-dressed in those tight capri-style trousers . . .

Moving on swiftly from that distracting image, Etta thought about the books she read. Max had mentioned she was nearly twenty-one. That meant she should be in London, right? Probably should have been for at least three years, swirling around ballrooms in fancy dresses meeting potential suitors. But not if everyone thought she was some kind of billy no-mates who stayed in her nursery all day working out how to time-travel.

Well, that was going to have to change. Etta was absolutely buggered if she was going to be magically transported into a Regency fantasyland and then sit about in a draughty nursery all day. The old ladies had called this a holiday. Who spent their holidays barefoot in an attic? That was more Charles Dickens than Jane Austen.

Who knew how long this would last either? Perhaps until this strange gold bracelet snapped, like those two batty old ladies had said, or perhaps for a few hours. Or perhaps she'd fallen asleep and missed her stop and would wake up in Hammersmith any moment now. Either way, this was her dream-slash-life right now, and things were going to change. Pronto.

Etta looked down at her empty plate, her tummy rumbling still, then wandered into her bedroom. 'Nanny, are you there? Tell me, does everyone else in my family go downstairs and eat a nice hot breakfast?'

Nanny paused, smoothing down the plain-looking faded pink dress she'd placed on the bed. 'Well, yes, child. They'll be there any moment. But . . .'

'I wish to join them, Nanny.'

Nanny was clearly horrified by this development. 'Oh no, Miss Hetty. They won't be expecting you. And I think your mother would say we should call Mr Withings, the doctor. It's so strange, seeing you up and about like this.'

'No, Nanny. I'm going downstairs.'

Nanny looked dismayed. 'But, Miss Hetty . . . You don't even have any stays!'

Etta paused, then remembered a line from her favourite novel. The heroine had been so upset, the hero had had to unlace her stays. Stays must mean some sort of corset.

'Then I shall go without,' she said defiantly.

Nanny looked appalled. She was *shook*, thought Etta. 'Without stays! Miss Hetty! How could you think so? Well, I never!'

'You can say "well, I never" all you like, Nanny, but I don't see why I should be up here eating cold toast while everyone else is eating sausages and beans.'

'Miss Hetty, I don't think you're quite well. You're . . . You're not making sense.' Nanny was inches away from wringing her hands, so Etta softened her tone.

'Perhaps not, but I reckon you've got the gist of what I'm saying. And if I have no stays, then I will have to go without them.'

Nanny looked more astonished than ever, but Etta noticed something else in her expression. Something like pride. They really must have all thought Hetty was past praying for. But Etta wasn't. She stood quietly, watching Nanny rally from this unexpected conversation.

Recently, Etta had been forced to go on mandatory assertiveness training at work. At the time, it had felt boring and pointless – like her boss had been spending too much time on LinkedIn. But if there was ever a time to put what she'd learned into practice, it was now.

'Listen, Nanny. I need you to pretend with me. Pretend that I am not Hetty, but someone else. A woman who is perfectly well. Someone who can speak and think and dress like anyone else.' Etta watched carefully. Nanny was taking it well so far, so she continued, 'Pretend I have come out of nowhere, and don't know what to do or who anyone is. Now, what should we do? Let's work together.'

To her mild surprise, it worked. Nanny seemed to pull herself together, with a little shake of her head.

'Well, Miss Hetty. In that case, I shall go to your mother's dresser and borrow some of her clothing. I'm sure Lady Bainbridge won't mind. Or even notice, at that.'

The last comment was mumbled, as Nanny quickly bustled out of the room. Etta sat on her bed, fingering the dress there. The fabric was soft and well-worn. Looking more closely, she could see it had been hand-made with tiny little stitches. It had been mended many times around the hem. Hetty had nice clothes, she thought. Nice, but very old.

She got up and found a brush on top of a chest of drawers next to her bed. She could only assume she didn't have a maid of her own – it looked like it had just been her and Nanny. However, as she began brushing her surprisingly long, pale hair out of its tight braid, she heard the tea tray being moved in the nursery next door.

She got up to see who it was and found a determined young woman of about her own age wearing a black dress and apron. 'Hello?'

The woman's slightly fierce look completely deserted her as she stared at Etta. The metal tray made a racket as it hit the floor, the teapot smashing and covering them both in lukewarm tea.

'Miss— Miss Hetty?'

'. . . Kind of. Who are you?'

The woman gaped at her, astonished. 'I'm Bessie, your maid.'

Etta was relieved, despite the cold tea leaves on her feet. 'Thank goodness. Do you think you could help me do my hair? I have absolutely no idea what to do with it and I want to go down to breakfast with everyone.'

'Certainly, miss. I'll ring the bell for someone to come and clean up this tea first. I'm so sorry about that.'

'Oh, not your fault. I can't imagine you were expecting me to be a whole different person this morning.'

Bessie continued to look stunned, even after the bell had been rung and a housemaid had come in to clean up the spilt tea. She took a heavy, silver-backed brush, and started brushing out Hetty's long blonde locks. There was an awkward silence as she finished detangling it and began plaiting.

'Bessie, I presume you're not used to me talking or, well, doing much at all really. But can we pretend that I'm completely new here and don't know anyone? That I've . . . I don't know. That I've hit my head and am perfectly back to being a normal person, but have forgotten everything?'

Etta couldn't see Bessie's expression, but could almost feel curiosity radiating from behind her.

'Yes . . . Yes, miss.'

There was more silence. Bessie coughed, clearly trying to work out what to say next.

'Have you forgotten *everything*, then, miss?'

Etta nodded. 'Yes. Everything. I don't suppose you could, well, fill me in?'

Bessie's brow wrinkled in confusion. 'Fill you in what, miss?'

'You know, tell me what's going on. Who's who, where I am?'

Bessie paused, then whispered. 'So it worked, then, miss?'

'What?'

Etta quickly turned to look at Bessie but just at that moment, infuriatingly, Nanny bustled back in. She was carrying a large pile of clothes.

'Now then, Miss Hetty. I see Bessie has nearly finished your hair. A lovely job, too, especially with all that braiding! Oh, you do look so grown up with your hair off your neck like that. All that fancy London training coming in useful at last, Bessie!'

Etta watched Bessie's eyes narrow. She said nothing, but tweaked at an errant strand as Nanny laid out the pile of clothes on Hetty's bed and kept talking.

'Miss Hetty, I've brought you some old clothes from your mother. They won't quite fit, of course, but you're only a little taller than your mother after all – and just as trim.'

Yes, Etta thought. *Unnervingly short and slim.* She let her strangely small, light body be pushed and pulled into the clothes. She was going to have to get creative about knickers, because going commando was not her style, but besides that it was all a lot better than expected. The chemise was thin and delicate and the stays, while far from ideal, weren't as tight as the corset Etta had worn for her Halloween costume last year. Plus, they made Hetty's otherwise small-ish tits look *fabulous*. Like oranges peeking out of an overloaded shopping bag. Well, maybe tangerines.

Hetty's body really was far smaller and slighter than Etta's. Almost wraith-like. Etta had been meaning to lose weight for a long time, but on reflection her new light, weak body was not quite what she had imagined.

By the time they were done, the nursery clock read half past ten. 'You'd best get going, then,' said Nanny, looking tearful. 'Bessie, take Miss Hetty to the breakfast room.'

At the very last moment, Nanny touched Etta's arm. 'Miss Hetty, are you sure this is right? Are you sure it is what you want to do?'

Etta felt a wave of sympathy. The older woman looked extremely anxious. She tipped her head to one side and smiled. 'What's the worst they can do, Nanny? Shut me up in my room?'

Chapter 5

2023

Hetty stood with her aunts in the door of Etta's cramped studio flat and surveyed her belongings.

'And this is all she has?'

'Things are different, my dear. Very different. This flat is rented and was almost beyond Etta's means.'

'She was lucky to have something so central, she really was. And so close to the park!' Jemima added.

Hetty hesitated. 'Is that a privvy? Right next to the kitchen?'

Aggie pursed her lips.

Clearly not the right question, Hetty decided to try another. 'Where does the maid sleep?'

Hetty started in surprise as a snort of laughter made its way out of Jemima. She looked between her aunts. 'No . . . no maid, then? Very well. I think I have much to adjust to. Perhaps you could be so kind as to point me towards a contemporary etiquette book or pamphlet?'

Aggie stepped forwards. 'Hetty, no. You shall live with us.'

'But, Aunt! My intention was to live independently and freely. To make a small, peaceful life for myself, without becoming a burden on others.' Hetty saw her aunts were both ready to interject, but she continued. For once, it was time to stand up for herself. 'I need very little, truly. Food, shelter, that is all.'

Her aunts looked at each other, and then back at her. She noticed with horror that a tear ran down Jemima's cheek. She produced a brightly patterned handkerchief from one of her many pockets and sniffled into it.

'Really, truly,' said Hetty. 'I need nothing. I will be fine. I am here merely to calm and refresh my spirits a while. But I would be truly grateful if I could have your direction, so perhaps I might write to you for advice . . .?'

'Oh, Hetty. You poor little thing.' Jemima stepped forward and before she knew it, Hetty was pulled into a soft hug.

Hetty stood awkwardly, unsure what to do. She hadn't been embraced like this many times before and rare hugs from Nanny and Mother had slowly become more, well, business-like, as she'd sunk into increasingly low moods. Being hugged by Jemima was like falling into a feather bed of emotion.

Aggie put an arm out and pulled Jemima back, sensing Hetty's discomfort.

'Hetty. We can tell you're clever, but you might not be able to walk into Etta's office and keep on doing— Oh, Jemima, what was her job again?'

'God knows, Aggie. Who knows what anyone does for work any more? Computers, probably.'

'Exactly,' continued Aggie. 'You have a lot to learn, but you're still young.'

'I feel I have lived an entire life already – I'm already so tired.'

Aggie eyed her thoughtfully. 'How are you feeling, Hetty? Do you often feel low? We should discuss that, you know.'

Jemima was pulling clothes from a chest of drawers and stuffing them unceremoniously into a suitcase. 'Come on. No arguments. You're coming with us. Let's grab as much as we can and go home. You can come back for more later.'

Hetty stood by what she realised must be a modest cooking station and opened a cupboard. It was filled with small metal cannisters and odd little jars.

One low cupboard was different to the others, with a heavy, shiny white door. A wash of cold air rushed out at her as she prised it open with her new, strangely robust arms.

'What is all of this? Is it . . . food?'

Jemima wandered over, looking mischievous. 'If you think that's odd, watch this.'

She twisted something on the complicated-looking metallic plate next to them and suddenly, of all things, blue flames shot into vision. Hetty leapt back with a faint scream, then felt rather silly as her aunts both stared at her.

Aggie was the first to speak. 'Yes, you're definitely coming with us.'

Jemima shoved a large bag into Hetty's hands, and just like that, there was no more arguing.

'And where do you live?'

Jemima almost vibrated with excitement. 'Oooh, Aggie, do you think she'll recognise it?'

Aggie rolled her eyes. 'Oh, I'm sure she will, Jemima.'

Chapter 6

1817

As they headed down the corridor, Etta could see Bessie shooting her quick, curious looks. As hungry as she was, there was no chance at all she was going to breakfast without getting Bessie to spill the tea.

'Bessie, we need to talk. Where can we talk?'

Bessie looked behind them apprehensively, then back at Etta. 'Not now, miss. You're expected at breakfast – Nanny sent a maid to tell them. But yesterday evening you bade me give you this today.'

Furtively, Bessie handed Etta a piece of tightly folded paper. Unsure of what to do with it – and to Bessie's evident dismay – she quickly tucked it into the bosom of her dress.

'Bessie, Nanny mentioned you trained in London. Do you come from there?'

'Yes, miss.'

Etta smiled. 'Bit too quiet for you here, I imagine. I think we might go back to London, don't you?'

'Depends on your mama, miss.'

'I suppose it does, doesn't it? Ugh. Bloody 1817. Anyway, call me Etta.'

'Not on your life, miss,' said Bessie, casting her a disapproving look.

They had passed through several corridors, down some fairly ordinary-looking stairs and then through wider, more lavishly decorated corridors. It was like visiting a stately home, but everything was . . . new.

Etta smelled beeswax as they stepped into a corridor, the walls lined with colourful portraits of what were presumably Hetty's relatives. Hers, even? Although surely Hetty had hundreds of relatives in the intervening two hundred years.

She took in the portraits as they passed by, blinking at the freshness of the paint, then at the panelling below it. It was wood – not the dark wood of the stately homes she'd visited on school trips, but bright, polished wood that reflected light across the room. It hadn't been painted, either. It had never occurred to her that wood panelling might not have started off dark and forbidding. The more you knew, Etta mused, and hurried after Bessie who led her to a huge, wide staircase, looking up to high ceilings. There was marble everywhere, and even though summer light streamed in through large windows, Etta found herself gathering the shawl Nanny had put around her shoulders and pulling it tighter.

She was in a full-length pale blue dress, just like the ones in her favourite period dramas, but with even less stretch than she had imagined. Mercifully, it was short around her ankles by a good few inches. Nanny had muttered about that, but Etta was glad of it as she carefully picked her way down the stairs in Hetty's leather boots. Her mother's dainty shoes had not fit.

As she navigated the stairs, Etta noticed a passing footman stumble with a silver salver of letters. Openly staring at her, he stood to one side of an open door and briefly bowed his head.

Etta realised he was making room for her to enter and looked back at Bessie. Bessie nodded encouragingly towards the door and said, 'The breakfast room, miss.' It was clear Etta was now on her own.

Thankfully there were only two people sitting at the mahogany table in the elegant room and both were already known to her. She nodded at them as they stood up. 'Max, Charlie. Good morning.'

At this her brother Charlie gasped. 'Oh no, Hetty! You can't call him that! Lord Stanhope – or at least my lord!'

Etta looked over at Max. 'Does that mean you have to call me "my lady" then?'

Her brother looked vaguely appalled. 'Hetty! You aren't a lady! Not yet, at any rate,' he reflected. 'Maybe you'll pull it off, if Mother finds you some new clothes.'

Etta rolled her eyes. 'I suppose you mean I need to get married to a lord to be a lady. So I must be Miss – oh, what is it again?'

'Bainbridge. Miss Bainbridge. May I help you to some breakfast?' Max moved to a sideboard loaded with hot chafing dishes, their contents kept warm by lit candles.

Etta strode over for a look. It was an eclectic mix, but all good stuff. 'What have we got here? Ooh, bacon! And sausages, and all sorts. One of everything, I think.'

Max looked at her speculatively. 'One of everything?'

'Except the fish, yes.'

As he placed her plate at an empty place setting, Charlie looked over and rolled his eyes. 'Hungry, are we, Hetty?'

She glared at him. 'Why yes, Charles. Must be all of those *experiments* you've been doing on me. Good thing Lord Stanhope was around last night, wasn't it?' She turned to Max. 'And don't think you're escaping from this one, *my lord*. You're practically his co-conspirator.'

'Me? I was the one who rescued you, Miss Bainbridge!'

'Perhaps, but you're still a close ally of my tormentor.'

Max seemed to relax slightly when he saw the twinkle in Etta's eyes. Charlie, however, was oblivious.

'Tormentor? By god, Hetty, taking it a bit far there. For heaven's sake, don't say that to Mama.'

This last sentence came out in a rushed undervoice, as movement could be heard in the hallway. Within moments a middle-aged woman quietly entered the room. She was short, gaunt and delicately featured, wearing what Etta thought was the most elegant and expensive-looking dress she had ever seen; trotting at her heels was a tiny, extremely fluffy white dog.

Etta didn't have to guess for even a second what Hetty's relationship was to this woman – what she'd seen in the glass windows she'd passed earlier was a close reflection of the lady standing in front of her. As Etta and her companions rose up to greet her mother, she saw golden hair, a straight and neat little nose, a plush rosebud mouth and wide, innocent blue eyes.

'Oh, Maximillian, I see you stayed overnight? I'm glad to . . .'

She stopped, her eyes having registered Etta, and looked at her in complete bewilderment.

'H-Hetty . . . ?'

Etta quickly searched for the right title to use for her

mother. 'Mum' felt too modern. Mama. That's what Charlie had just said.

'Yes, Mama?'

'So, it is true! Hetty, have you truly come back to me?'

Before she had any time to answer this question, Etta found herself being almost crushed by the older woman. She didn't think she'd ever been so earnestly hugged.

A sweet, fragrant smell of rosewater washed over her and suddenly she realised she was clinging back. She had never been hugged by a mother before. For so long it had just been her and Dad, and he'd not really been one for outward displays of affection.

As Lady Bainbridge pulled back to examine her, Etta noticed that both of them had tears in their eyes. As she became aware of her surroundings again, she noticed the ridiculously fluffy dog yapping at her ankles.

'Hush, Hercules! It is only Hetty.' Lady Bainbridge grasped Etta by the shoulders. 'Hetty! Oh, Hetty. Look at you. Speak to me! Are you truly yourself again?'

Charlie interrupted. 'Mama, she has *never* been herself.'

Etta glared at him, then turned back to her mother and racked her brain for a suitably banal, non-giveaway phrase. 'Mama, I am perfectly well. Will you have some breakfast? The sausages . . . um, the sausages are very good.'

Etta quickly realised that she could have said pretty much anything at all and the woman still would have been delighted.

'Oh, Henrietta. It is as though all my dreams have come true! To see you here, offering me breakfast as though it were just an ordinary day!'

Etta wasn't sure how to respond to this. Luckily it seemed

she wouldn't have to. Catching and visibly suppressing her tears with a beautifully delicate, lacy handkerchief, Lady Bainbridge drew herself together. Her face sealed itself back up into the very picture of mild good-humour, almost as though she were pressing the lid back onto her own personal Tupperware box of emotions. The transformation was remarkable.

'And . . . and in time for the Season!'

If it were possible, Charlie looked even more startled.

'Mama, surely not! You can't . . . You can't possibly mean to parade Hetty around as though she weren't utterly dicked in the nob! Why, she's – she's a complete imbecile!'

Etta wasn't having any of it. 'No, Charlie, *you're* an imbecile. Mama, he had me strapped into a chair in the cellar!'

Lady Bainbridge sank onto a seat at the end of the table, looking faint. 'I— I must think. It is all too much.'

Etta racked her brain for more romance-novel info-gems. 'Should I fetch you some smelling salts?'

'Oh no, Hetty, how could you? Not that disgusting stuff. Even Great Aunt Matilda won't touch them. No, but do pour me some tea, please.'

They went back to quietly eating their breakfast, all watching Lady Bainbridge carefully as she added sugar and milk to her tea and then sat thoughtfully at the other end of the long table, stroking her little dog.

Charlie eyed his mother impatiently and whispered, 'I do wish she'd get rid of that awful bloody dog. I still can't believe she called the little beast "Hercules". I don't think I've ever seen such a ridiculous animal.'

Max looked over at Etta with mischief in his eyes. 'I don't

think he likes Hetty all that much. Is the feeling mutual, Hetty?'

Charlie interrupted. 'Oh, they love one another to the ends of the earth. Always prancing around Hetty, he is. Probably because Nanny feeds him scraps up in the nursery. Not sure why he's acting so off today. Stupid creature, I suppose.'

'Etta,' Etta said. 'I'm not Hetty. I'm Etta.'

She saw Max watching her carefully, but Charlie pulled a bizarre face that simultaneously made him look stupid while indicating that he found her stance to be hoity toity. Together, they smiled at him, and Etta realised she was going to have trouble holding a grudge against Charlie.

'Is that the face you plan to make when you present me in Society, Charles?'

He groaned. 'Oh no. I can imagine it now. Escorting you around the park in front of the *Ton*. I'll believe that when I see it.'

'Oh, you'll see it,' Etta whispered under her breath. She had finished her breakfast by this point and was trying to work out where she should take her plate.

Before she could decide, her mother finally spoke.

'Henrietta, dear, you must wait for me in the Yellow Room. I must think.'

'Yes, Mama. Remind me where it is, again?'

Her mother jolted. 'Oh yes. I suppose you're not accustomed to the lower rooms of the house. Oh dear, how mortifying! Charles! Accompany your sister to the Yellow Room.'

As they began to leave, her mother seemed to have another thought. 'And, Charles, you mustn't call her Hetty any more. Hetty is a name for servants. We should never have started calling you that, Henrietta. I am so sorry.'

'No, Mama. I understand. I wasn't myself, was I? Anyway, it's quite a sweet nickname in the overall scheme of things.'

Lady Bainbridge's face took on a stubborn look. 'No, Henrietta. It is not appropriate. You are yourself again. You must not be known by that name any more.'

As vague and as polite as her new mother seemed to be, Etta saw she could also be stern. She filed that thought away for later.

She stared at Charlie's arm, stuck out like he was expecting a bird to land on it, before realising she was meant to grab it. They went back out into the hall and she tried to calculate how many times her studio flat would fit into the cavernous, gilded entrance to the Bainbridge's mansion.

How on earth was Hetty going to cope in 2023? She hoped the two old ladies had something lined up because, man oh man, she was most certainly not missing that flat right now.

Chapter 7

2023

Hetty was still shaking from her second terrifying cab ride when she registered her surroundings. The three women stood together, facing a house Hetty vaguely recognised from childhood trips to London doctors.

'Oh, goodness. How . . . enlivening.'

Aggie was amused, now. 'Oh yes. The neighbours hate it. But the colour was very much Jemima's choice.'

'Goodness me, Aunt Jemima. The family townhouse is transformed. Most . . . Most unique.'

Jemima rubbed her hands together mischievously. 'Thank you, dear. There have been petitions, you know.'

Hetty smothered a smile. 'I can't think why.'

'Well, you know, it surprises me too. But apparently lavender isn't in keeping with our historic environs, or some such crap.'

'Oh. Goodness.'

Aggie smiled broadly and turned to Hetty. 'Well, Hetty, there's no point in standing around. Grab your bags.'

'My own bags?'

'Yes, dear. Welcome to 2023.'

The Bainbridges' London townhouse was absolutely not decorated in the same fashion as it had been in the early 1800s. As she entered the hallway, Hetty could only stare. Black and white striped wallpaper – 'zebra print', Aggie called it – clashed with a huge ornate mirror in a shade of pink that Hetty couldn't have dreamed up. Meanwhile, paintings of bold shapes and lines contrasted with the more traditional portrait paintings Hetty was used to seeing, some of which she recognised from her family's time there.

Ornaments could be found on every surface: china shepherdesses, black marble statues of naked men, brightly glazed vases, ill-made bowls and golden lamps.

'Leave your bags there. We'll show you your room later,' said Aggie, shepherding Hetty towards the vast kitchen at the back of the house. There was not a servant to be seen, Hetty thought, as she registered gleaming surfaces everywhere. Everything in 2023 was so . . . shiny.

Suddenly feeling exhausted, she inelegantly flopped into a reassuringly un-shiny kitchen chair as her new aunts bustled around. A plate of what could only be biscuits appeared in front of her.

'What is this coating? A preserve?'

'Solid chocolate, dear. Try it – it'll change your life,' said Aggie.

'And your waistline,' added a cheerful Jemima, holding a tray of oddly shaped bread. 'Sandwiches,' she explained, as the tray clattered onto the table. 'Thought we'd start you off on something familiar.'

Hetty poked at one. 'Ham. In between two slices of bread? I suppose one could eat it with one's fingers and have both ham and bread at once. How ingenious!'

She looked up and saw the aunts looking at each other. A whole conversation seemed to happen, in complete silence, before they looked back at her.

Aggie delicately picked up a sandwich, placing it on a small plate, while Jemima stuffed hers straight into her mouth and chewed loudly. Hetty decided to copy Aggie and pushed the boat out a little by selecting one of the crispy, thinly sliced potato wafers from a bowl. It was delicious, if oddly sweet.

'Prawn cocktail,' Jemima announced, as though this was a perfectly adequate explanation for everything that was happening to the inside of Hetty's mouth at that moment.

'So, tell me, Hetty. What has happened to our other distantly related niece?' asked Aggie.

Hetty hesitated. 'Well . . . She's probably . . .'

How to explain?

'Spit it out, dearie,' said Jemima, though a mouthful of sandwich.

Hetty sighed. 'Well, I expect that by now Charlie will have found her. I anticipated she might be a little . . .'

'Surprised?' supplied Jemima helpfully.

'Indeed. So I thought I would conduct things in a remote part of the house where she could be safely discovered after a few moments to . . . adjust.'

Aggie smiled wryly. 'Attics?'

'The cellar. My brother Charlie helped me down there and left briefly to fetch his oldest friend, who always treated me kindly. They will have found her within perhaps ten minutes.' Hetty decided not to add that she'd instructed Charlie to strap her to a sturdy-looking chair, in the event that Etta was so overwhelmed she fainted or went into complete hysterics.

It had been a close-run thing for her and Hetty herself had been relatively well-prepared.

Or she thought she had, anyway.

'What next for Etta, then?'

'I daresay we could find out from the history books, couldn't we?'

'Not quite, dear. There's your diary, of course.'

'Yes, I suppose we could look at that more closely,' Hetty added, suddenly hit by another wave of exhaustion.

Aggie stood up. 'Bed,' she commanded.

Hetty was too overwhelmed and tired to do anything except take her bags, be led through confusing surroundings and sink into an unusually comfortable bed. But this was more than any ordinary physical fatigue which might be expected from the act of travelling through time. She might have left her home, her family, even her body in the past, but her troubles had followed her all the way through two centuries: she knew the feeling of it deep in her bones. The familiar darkness was spreading through her again, like a black cloud pressing her down into the mattress.

The last thought that ran through her head was a desperate hope that she had done the right thing.

Chapter 8

1817

Charlie dumped Etta at the door to a room full of extremely elegant antique furniture. Alone at long last, Etta retrieved the letter Bessie had given her from her bodice and unfolded it.

Dearest Descendant,

I am sorry for what I have done, but only a little. I hope that this age will benefit immensely from your presence in it, and that you shall, too.

I have suffered from a darkness that has threatened to overtake me over the past years. It has become insufferable to live, and yet I feel certain my fate is not to die. Discovering a solution to this dilemma has been the focus of my life's work, and if you are reading this I must have succeeded. I hope you shall humour me as we live out the consequences; at least for a while. I hope you can find it in your heart to take pity on me and give this era a try.

For the sake of posterity and so that you may be found, I request that you complete the diary. I feel convinced that you shall be braver than I: that you will achieve great things.

You will find it is safe to remove the bracelet, so long as you do not break the chain. Break it, and we will both be instantly returned. But I beg you to give this life a chance. For my sake, but also for yourself.

Yours,
Henrietta Bainbridge

Etta folded the letter carefully, feeling a wave of immense pity. She felt so sorry for this poor woman: a time-travelling genius ahead of her time, yes, but also clearly showing symptoms of what would be recognised in her time, she felt sure, as depression. 'I have suffered a darkness', Hetty had written, and Etta remembered her father, in his worst moods, talking about the black cloud he always felt on his shoulder.

It would explain a lot – why everyone was so stunned at Etta turning up to breakfast, even her ability to speak. After all, so far nobody seemed to be able to label what Hetty had been suffering from; did depression even have a name in 1817?

She knew some people – her own poor father included – felt that weight every single day. Poor, poor Hetty. Perhaps Etta had landed in the middle of something a little more serious than some fun Regency romp.

She carefully smoothed the letter out, resting it on a table as she walked over to a huge, ornate mirror over the fireplace which was reflecting late morning light across the room. It was the first time she had looked directly at her reflection, and she was surprised to realise she recognised her face.

Her nose was still straight and her face still oval. Her eyes were still a vague greenish-blue and her mouth still small and plump. Her wild shock of freckles was still there, she was relieved to see, and she traced her fingers over her skin as she admired them. She vaguely recollected that her father had told her once, in one of his better moods, that they were where fairies kissed her as she slept. And freckles were so in right now that her hairdresser drew them on his face every morning.

Her eyebrows could do with a good plucking, though. They were lighter than before, to suit her new blonde hair, which was a good thing given how unruly they were. And she could do with having her fringe back.

If this were a dream, it was certainly the strangest one she'd ever had. She'd usually be at work by now. Long ago, in fact. Was it Wednesday? She'd be halfway through her tedious weekly team meeting, discussing the upcoming forestry management conference in Norway. But in this reality, her life as a major gifts officer felt unreal. This should be a good thing, shouldn't it? There was very little upside to wrangling euphemistically titled tax refunds for bland-faced CEOs, after all. But she suddenly felt unmoored. What would her life be like here? And how long would she be here for, anyway? This was so much more serious than a solo holiday in Spain or a date with a dodgy Tinder match. This was real life, two hundred years ago, when women didn't have the vote and nobody had invented stretch cotton knickers.

A floorboard creaked, breaking her reverie. She turned to see Max staring at her, his wavy dark hair nearly falling over one eye. My god, she thought, the man's got bloody good hair. Then she noticed he was clutching Hetty's letter.

'Why are you reading that?'

She sprinted over, grabbing it from him and re-folding it.

'I'm so sorry. I thought I saw . . .' He paused, looking at her thoughtfully.

'Well?' she demanded, examining him speculatively, deciding whether or not she could trust him. 'Slightly ungentlemanlike, isn't it, to read a lady's personal correspondence?'

Max stiffened at the accusation.

'Perhaps I might make it up to you by asking if you will let me have the first dance at the ball your mama shall no doubt wish to hold for you.'

'And what if I don't say yes?'

Max paused. He clearly hadn't thought of that.

Etta decided to step into the breach, hauling out one of her favourite romantic novel wish list locations from what she liked to think of as her Georgette Heyer mind palace. 'How about you take me to get ice cream at Gunter's? I'm sure I've read about that.'

His mouth twitched again. 'Gunter's? A flavoured ice?'

Etta was horrified. 'Have they not invented ice cream yet? Oh my god, this is terrible.'

'I'm sure you'll get used to it. But yes, I shall happily escort you to Gunter's, where we can discuss iced cream.'

'Ice cream, not "iced" cream. Although it's more like a frozen custard, I suppose.' She paused, starting to freak out again. 'Oh god, how on earth am I going to get through this wild adventure without a big tub of triple chocolate fudge caramel?'

Etta was too devastated by the realisation to pay any attention to Max's face, but she heard his laugh with dismay.

'It's not funny! At least there's coffee, I suppose. Ugh, I

bet there aren't even flushing toilets yet either! Or running water!'

'Oh, there's running water, don't worry. I'm sure water will always run.'

'You have no idea what I mean,' she said. 'Oh, I don't know how this is going to work at all. And I'm trapped! Unless I break this bracelet, I suppose . . . Oh, I don't know what to do!'

Max paused, taking one of her hands in both of his. 'Calm yourself, Miss Bainbridge. Your family will be back at any moment. You are perfectly safe, with many people to help you.'

She looked at him despairingly, wondering how much of Hetty's letter he had read. 'You think I'm mad, don't you?'

'No, for some strange reason I can't quite explain, I don't. But I do think I shall see you in town any day now, rigged out in the latest fashions, ready for me to take you to Gunter's for strawberry ices.'

His reassuring tone calmed her more than she liked to admit, and she found her hand tingling under his warm, calm fingers. He took her other hand and clasped them both together, giving her a firm squeeze.

She forced herself to focus. 'Okay. Okay. Yes. I can do this.'

'You shall. And you must. We both know your mind is sharper than it has ever been. It is time for you to go to London and take your place in the *Ton*.'

'Well, I definitely can't stay here and keep writing my diary and floating about in my nightie and stuff, can I? What on earth would be the point?'

She looked up at him and saw determination, mixed with

something else she couldn't recognise. He gave her hands another, final, squeeze and let her go.

'Precisely, Henrietta. Ices and dancing.'

Etta sighed. 'Only if you promise me one thing.'

'What's that?'

'Introduce me to whoever does your hair.'

Max's laugh was broad and deep. She knew she couldn't steal his barber – my god, how did people even get their hair cut in 1817? – but it was worth it to make him laugh.

Chapter 9

2023

Hetty squinted against the light. The noise had woken her up early. London in 2023 was the noisiest place in the world, but also pleasingly warmer. The metal grille in her room was hot to the touch and even the privy had one. It was all the very height of luxury.

The aunts had been quite thoughtful in their preparation of her room, too. Light blue stripes, blue and cream curtains and furniture she recognised from her mother's bedroom back in 1817. She had a large room with an opulent four poster bed – not a single feather sticking into her.

Hetty had spent the last couple of hours agonising over how long it might be before the bracelet was broken and she was dragged back to 1817. She had spent years working out how to achieve this. A shared item, shared ancestry, messages into the future, a little magic, and excellent timing . . . All for . . . what? A moment's escape? A day? A week, perhaps?

Or perhaps longer, given that Etta had clearly stayed at

least long enough to jot down enough information to set her descendants up financially.

Was Etta 'appropriate', though? Was she the kind of woman to take a liking to life in 1817? It was impossible to know.

She examined her golden bracelet forensically for any warping, any loose links in the chain which might indicate it had been broken once and then mended. Nothing so far, but then again she was no jeweller.

And what if she broke her own bracelet? So far, 2023 felt unknown, scary, overwhelming – but did she really want to return to an age where she did not fit?

The grey clouds began to gather again. Hetty wondered if she'd ever escape the darkness that had started to envelop her life in childhood.

She could barely recall when it had first begun to creep up on her. Sometimes it felt as though she had been sad forever, but she knew that had not always been the case. No, once she had been like any other child – and then inch by inch, as she slowly left her girlhood behind, a terrible mantle of despair had settled over her.

But no, she would not let sadness ruin her trip. Not today. This day could be all she had. Time to get started on her list.

She was pleased to find a water closet in an adjacent room with a huge freestanding bath, which was a very welcome upgrade. She climbed back into bed to await . . . To await whom, really? Bessie was left behind, along with Nanny. And her mother.

Before she could worry too much about what Bessie and Nanny and Mama must be thinking about their new arrival, and just in time to stop her from missing them, she heard the sound of pounding feet along the corridor.

Hopefully it was Aggie and Jemima bringing tea and toast, to draw her a bath, to help her into her clothes for the day. Anything, really. She could do with a distraction – any distraction – from the gathering darkness. Perhaps they could even help her shake it off?

The anticipated knock had hardly sounded before Jemima's face peeked around the opened door.

'Oi-oi! Morning, Hetty!'

She opened the blinds and they both blinked at the dim light pouring through the windows. It was raining.

Jemima put voice to what they were both thinking. 'Nice day indoors for us, then.'

Hetty examined the grain of the kitchen table. She wondered idly if it was the same one their chef had worked at two hundred years before. Probably not, she decided, but it was certainly well-worn. It looked how she felt.

'So come on, then. You're here – you've made it. So what next?' Jemima asked.

Hetty glanced up, then gripped her mug of what had turned out to be coffee. It was a most odd vessel. It had the words 'Sexual at 60' on the side and chips around the rim.

'I have a list. A statement of my heart's desires.' Hetty felt a thrill of excitement, of daring as she uttered the words out loud. 'I must admit, I have focused primarily on getting here,' she continued. 'But I do have a few things I should like to experience during my time here.'

Aggie was leaning forward in anticipation. 'Do go on, dear. I do love a wish list. I can't wait to hear it.'

Hetty bit her lip, delighted to share her plans with somebody at last.

'I should like to learn more about the nature of time, and what has been discovered in these intervening years. How time can be bent and travelled through. So much progress must have been made.'

The way her aunts looked at one another made Hetty begin to feel uncertain.

'Have scientists not yet learned to travel through time?'

Aggie winced. 'Not quite yet, as far as we know, dear. I'm sure we can try to find out though. What next?'

Hetty sighed. The next, at least, would surely be achievable on some level.

'The second on my list is to be able to converse with fellow students. To learn from others. To create bonds. As a young woman in my past environs, I was very much discouraged from academic exploration with peers.' She hesitated. 'Although, I suppose if humanity has not yet discovered time travel, my options might be limited?'

This time, both her aunts winced. 'You might need to catch up on your studies,' explained Aggie. 'Nowadays, you have to get quite a few exams out of the way to get into those circles.'

'But we can try and help you,' added Jemima. 'It'll take a few years, but I'm sure you can manage it. A very smart girl, you are.'

Hetty continued, trying to stay positive. She blushed furiously, but forced herself to press on regardless.

'Finally, I should like . . . Please do not suppose that I lack a moral compass, but I should like very much . . .'

Jemima and Aggie leaned in, gripping their mugs tightly.

'If it is not too outrageous, I should like to experience my first kiss.'

The aunts leaned back again.

'Yes, I reckon that one's doable,' said Jemima.

Chapter 10

1817

That first day was a long one for Etta. Nobody quite seemed to know what to do with her. A doctor was indeed called – one clearly well-known to the family and familiar with Hetty since childhood – and had pronounced Etta 'remarkably well-recovered' and 'completely sane'. Good-oh, she thought, as Dr Withings gathered his ominous-looking metalwork back up into his huge leather bag and shuffled off. Always good to have confirmation.

With this miraculous news, her brand-spanking-new mother found purpose. It seemed the house had been shrouded in gloom since the last Lord Bainbridge, Hetty's father, had died the year before. As the oldest male, Charlie had become the de facto head of their household – but the widowed Lady Matilda Bainbridge seemed to require very little input or permission from her son, barring access to the family coffers.

Charlie, seemingly stunned by his mother's new zest for society (or perhaps from general lack of desire for anything approaching responsibility), just continued to do as he was asked.

And he wasn't alone in this approach. The servants of the house seemed shaken by the energy Lady Bainbridge now possessed. Notes were frantically written and sent to all sorts of people; boxes of fabric and ribbons were unearthed from the attics.

They were to take Etta to London, just in time for the Season.

And yet at the centre of the storm, all was relatively quiet for Etta. Having reappeared and been determined suitable for display, nobody seemed willing to ask any difficult questions of her – her mother didn't seem to want to jeopardise their collective good luck.

Etta spent the afternoon being measured and excitedly quizzed about her favourite colours over various drawings of stick-like elegant ladies in fancy dresses. It wasn't until much later in the day when Etta found herself free to hunt down Bessie, who, thankfully, was more than willing to be found.

By this point Etta had a mental wish list. Right at the top: knickers.

Oh, there were so many other questions, but knickers rose to the surface every single time.

'Bessie. Where are my knickers? I didn't want to ask Mrs Cummings, but I can't carry on like this.'

Bessie frowned. 'Your whats, miss?'

Etta felt dread seep through her very soul. 'Knickers, Bessie. Pants. Underwear. I don't know . . . "Unmentionables"?'

Bessie continued to look confused, before a look of horror began to creep across her face.

'Do you mean . . . drawers, miss?' she whispered. 'Oh no, Miss Henrietta. No, no, no. Them's not – *they're not* – for the likes of you!'

Etta drew up a nursery chair and flopped herself down, already exhausted by the conversation. This really was turning out to be quite the experience. 'Drawers? Are we talking about the same thing? Is there a pen and paper anywhere?'

Half an hour and a stick of charcoal later, an outraged Bessie was watching on with her arms crossed as Etta cut out some old sheeting to her new pattern. Not one more day would pass, she decided, without her wearing some version of knickers. If this was a dream, it was turning out to be an extremely odd one. But no version of her life, whether dream or reality, would involve her nether regions flapping freely in the breeze.

She'd always wondered how Elizabeth Bennett had dealt with her period. It was bad enough risking pale leggings during that time of the month, but the thought of leaking through a white muslin dress was frankly appalling.

Thank goodness, then, for Bessie. Bessie who might be, yes, definitely was, quite horrified with her at this moment, but whom she was quite sure she could work on if given enough time.

Three very dodgy pairs of knickers later (spares carefully hidden from Mrs Cummings' view), the sky was slowly darkening and Etta was more than ready for some food. Charlie had left for London ahead of them, clearly keen to avoid any more difficult conversations about the cellar, but Lady Bainbridge was waiting for her eagerly in a small dining room.

She picked at an elegant dinner of soup followed by roast chicken and green vegetables – the full *Pride and Prejudice* experience was clearly reserved for fancy parties and not cosy dinners for two – followed by what was, quite frankly, the best raspberry trifle she'd eaten in her entire life.

Her mother had so many questions for her, and Etta felt awful not to be able to provide any satisfying answers. Why had she stopped talking? Etta had no idea – the letter hadn't given her any insights clear enough to pass on to her mother. What had she been studying in her diaries all those years? Who knew – 'time travel' could hardly be a satisfactory answer.

Etta was beyond curious about Hetty herself, so she felt immense sadness for the poor woman in front of her who had clearly loved her daughter but had simply not been able to get through to her.

Who did, in fact, love her still. It seemed Lady Bainbridge's heart had been waiting for a crack in Hetty's defences for many years. Now Etta had arrived, her love flowed in.

'Darling, you're going to love London this year. We have so many entertainments lined up! I've been planning your debut for years. This will be your moment!'

Matilda Bainbridge had so many ideas, especially about Etta's coming-out ball. Coming out as a young lady, that was, and not the 2023 version of coming out – something Etta supposed would probably go down somewhat less well with her mother. Her dress would be yellow, she thought – did Etta agree? Etta found she did. They would do more shopping together in London.

Had Hetty had this mother, too? Or had she given up on her? Etta would have done anything for a mother growing up, even one with an annoying, yappy little nightmare of a dog beside her night and day.

'Goodness, what *are* you doing, Hercules! Do stop bothering Henrietta!'

Etta shook the little dog off her leg.

'I don't know what's got into him. I really don't!'

Etta was more exhausted than she'd ever been when her mother finally led her up the stairs to a new part of the house. 'Where are we going?' she yawned sleepily.

Her mother took her arm and patted it. 'Your room. Your *proper* room, Henrietta.'

Etta leaned into Lady Bainbridge slightly, inclining her head. 'No more nursery, then?'

The older woman smiled. 'No, no more nursery. There's a nice little cottage awaiting Nanny just a moment's walk away once we go to London. Until we need her again, of course.'

Yes, Etta thought, when I marry Prince Charming and start popping out my Regency babies, and Nanny comes to coo at them while I sew samplers and dance at balls and wear lace tippets, whatever they are. Because belief could only be suspended for so long – just like there were only so many pages in a romantic novel, or minutes in a film. This had been the longest episode of *Bridgerton* in history, and Etta had watched a *lot* of *Bridgerton*.

But she was too worn out to keep questioning reality. Once again, Etta was dreaming before her head hit the pillow.

Chapter 11

2023

It wasn't the most noble instinct she'd had, but Hetty had noted a new tendency towards curiosity. She decided to exercise it on her way to top up her water glass that evening after a long bath when she overheard the aunts talking in their sitting room.

'Do you think she's missing her mother and brother?' Jemima asked Aggie.

'No, Jemima, I think she's overwhelmed. And I suspect there might be more – I am wondering if she's been experiencing depression?'

'Well, then, we need to get her to a doctor pronto,' Jemima said.

'And out of the house. Some fresh air will do her a world of good.'

'That's very old-fashioned, you know, Aggie.'

'And true. You and I both know it's not healthy, her just sitting around indoors reading the papers and looking out of the window.'

Jemima harrumphed, but appeared to concede the point. 'So what do we do?'

'I've got her a phone. Going to set it up now.'

'What, shove her in at the deep end? That's so like you, Aggie.'

'The sooner we can help her get her head around it all, the better. Now I'm not having the telly on if you're just going to speak over it all evening.'

Hetty had heard enough. It was all rather uncomfortably like the advice the family physician Dr Withings had given her mother before she was dragged all over the countryside for a long, cold, miserable year. Hetty had breathed fresh air from nearly every part of Scotland and none had solved her problem.

The problem of her future.

It would have been so much easier, Hetty thought, if only she'd given up on her experiments with time. Perhaps things would have worked themselves out.

But Hetty's heart dragged at the thought, snagged on the thorns of . . . Of what? She'd never managed to work out what it was. Why the time she lived in failed to fit in with how she saw herself. Well, perhaps it was time to look at herself in a new way.

Aggie and Jemima were squabbling over something called a Wi-Fi password when she walked in and dropped into a high-backed armchair.

'Hetty, dear! We were just talking about you. We've got you a nice little present. Still setting it up, though.'

Jemima's excited face was lit up by a smooth black rectangle. Aggie looked more wary, leaning forward in her chair.

'How's it going with that wish list?' she asked. 'We've been talking about it, and we've got some thoughts.'

Hetty sighed, feeling defeat pressing her down again as she remembered her first two, unachievable wishes, and her terrifying third one.

'It's hardly a list, is it, with only one probable item?'

Aggie's eyes were twinkling. 'About that. How about we, as your beloved aunts—'

'Descendants, technically,' amended Hetty.

'A mere technicality. Anyway, as your aunts, we each have one wish each to add.' Aggie leaned back, smiling. 'Jemima, you go first.'

Jemima huffed, frustrated with the rectangle, and attached a white cord to it. 'No, you first, Agatha. She won't like mine.'

'Very well. Well, my addition to your list is that you should attend a computer class. There's one down the road. Once you've got your head around how to use modern tools, you can move on to other types of formal education.'

Hetty considered this. It would take her closer to her original desires for learning.

'Yes, I agree. An excellent addition.'

Hetty looked at Jemima expectantly. The older lady placed the flashing object rather precariously on the arm of the sofa, lowering her brightly coloured reading glasses.

'Boring, Aggie, but I suppose yours was always bound to be practical. Mine's much better, in my opinion.'

Aunt Aggie smiled. 'For once, Jemima, I find I must agree.'

'Of course you do. Here you go, Hetty – your challenge, should you choose to accept it, is this. You will go dancing.'

Hetty blinked, feeling an icy thrill flash down her spine.

Terror or excitement? She couldn't be sure. 'Go dancing?' she repeated blankly.

'Yes, dear. Etta is probably out there dancing her little heart out, isn't she? Feels like all they get up to on those Regency TV shows.'

Aggie coughed.

'Well, besides the fucking, of course,' Jemima added.

'The what?'

'Never mind that,' interrupted Aggie, putting a reassuring hand on Hetty's arm. 'If you are to be kissed, it can't hurt to dance first.'

'I can teach you. Dancing, that is,' added Jemima.

Hetty considered this. 'And I suppose dancing here, alone, doesn't count?'

The aunts only laughed.

'But I have felt such a darkness. A bizarre heaviness that defies description – a cloud hanging over me. And it seems it has followed me, even here.'

Hetty sighed, twisting her fingers together on her lap.

'I have never met anyone who has been able to understand it, and I fear I shall never, ever escape it.'

Aggie reached over, stilling Hetty's anxious hands.

'Darling child. It was like this when I was much younger, but we have much better understanding of these things nowadays. And ways of escaping them, too. You will dance again, Hetty. You really will.'

'How could I ever expect to dance, when at times I have struggled even to move?'

Aggie squeezed her arm. 'We can help you with that, dear. You must keep talking to us about it, when you're feeling like this, because we can do things to help.'

Hetty sighed, feeling immensely reluctant. 'If only you could. My family tried. I think I have seen every doctor in the country. No one could help me.'

'We have a name for this feeling, now – depression. We have new doctors now; new treatments,' Aggie said. 'At least let us try and help you. We'll do our best to get you dancing. Will you at least consider it?'

Hetty looked between them, at their earnest care for her. They really seemed like they wanted to try – what was there to lose? Surely things couldn't get any worse. She felt a shimmer of possibility run over her skin as she pondered it. If she had travelled through time, surely advancements even more striking had been made in other fields?

'Very well,' she said eventually.

Jemima leapt up excitedly. 'Oh, I'm so glad you said yes! I know some epic clubs, dearie. So many good ones have closed down now, of course, and our weed dealer died last month, but I'm sure we can still go on a proper rager.'

'Calm down, Jemima. First things first. Let her settle in for a while. Let's book that doctor's appointment.' Aggie leaned back, returning to her newspaper. 'Besides, I'm not sure we'll need Uzzy. It says here in the *Guardian* that Generation Z don't like to take mind-altering substances these days, even of the herbal variety.'

Hetty bit her lip pensively. What on earth had she just agreed to?

Chapter 12

1817

It looked like the last day of a long summer so, on the first free afternoon she'd had after several days of dance classes, table-manner lessons, shoe-fittings and other forms of manic preparation for her journey to London, Etta decided to take one of Hetty's notebooks outside to read. To avoid the heat, she headed for the woods just past the gardens.

As she wrapped herself in her shawl and spread herself under a tree to read, sunlight dappling her face through the leaves, Etta realised she might as well not have bothered. She had chosen at random and Hetty's handwriting was close to illegible. It was going to take her quite some time to decipher it and, having wrangled with it for at least an hour every evening so far, she decided today was not going to be the day she managed to crack the case. Time for a day off.

She'd promised the old ladies on the Tube that she would write a diary herself, so settled on that and tried to offload as much as she could. But Etta tired of that quickly, too – after a while she lay back on the grass and stared at the sky. It was idyllic, really. There was no sound at all, besides the wind in the trees and the birds calling to one another. Puffy clouds passed overhead peacefully, no criss-crossing contrails marring their beauty, and birds flew on their long journey to sunnier climes. Or were they returning for winter? Migration patterns were not in her wheelhouse.

The longer she lay there, the more connected she felt to the ground. The trees swayed lazily in the wind above her, scattering the odd leaf, trunks ripe with lichen and mushrooms. Life was everywhere.

Her mind wandered to something one of her colleagues had said once. She hadn't been friends with anyone at work, particularly. But she'd enjoyed listening to office small talk, even though she didn't partake herself. And once, Dave from IT had been sounding off loudly in the break room about, yes, mushrooms, of all things.

It had been some nonsense hot take on anxiety and depression, she remembered. Dave had really been on his hobby horse about it. In the olden days, he'd opined in the confident bellow of a middle-aged white man, livestock had eaten wild magic mushrooms. Then, said Dave, these hallucinogens had made their way into the food chain. This meant that everyone in history was microdosing. Of course, modern cows, sheep, chickens, etcetera, weren't fed 'naturally' any more so no more mushrooms, said Dave, hence the 'crashing tidal wave of poor mental health'.

He'd been laughed out of the break room, probably because his whole rant had been a response to their boss banning his 'totally not illegal' mushroom-based chocolate-flavoured protein powder.

Etta wasn't missing her office, not one bit. Not Miranda the nosy receptionist, not Pervy Colin, and certainly not Dave.

She smiled, feeling overwhelming relief as she closed her eyes against the warm sun. No more stifling commute, no more wriggling into too-small tights, no more microwave meals for one. All she had to do was try on beautiful dresses, help her mother decide how to redecorate the house while they were in London, and eat gorgeous, elegantly cooked fresh produce. Even the most anxious servant in 1817 was infinitely more relaxed than a typical 2020s office worker. She had never known such freedom.

'Miss Hetty! Miss! You must wake up!'

It was getting dark, Etta realised; she must have been asleep for hours.

'You've been missed! You must come inside straight away!'

Bessie managed to hustle Etta indoors without any fuss, squirrelling her earth-stained dress and petticoat away somewhere. She couldn't really believe that she would get into trouble just for reading outside, but Nanny, caught halfway through packing for her new abode in the village, was quite miffed.

'You can't go running off out of sight, Hetty dear. Not if you're to go to London.' She patted Etta's arm placatingly. 'Now don't be cross with me. I haven't told your mother and father. Just try and do us proud.'

It was hard to be cross with Nanny when the older woman looked at her with such pride and love. Besides, she might not have any of the pressures of 2023, but there were rules all the same. Ones she'd have to follow if she wanted to be part of life here in 1817.

The bracelet felt heavy around her wrist. She'd give London a try before making any rash decisions.

As Etta got ready for bed, she heard Bessie come in from her little room next door.

'We're all packed for London now, miss.'

'Etta! Call me Etta, please, Bessie!'

'I can't, miss. It wouldn't be right. Anyway, Miss Hetty warned me about this, but it hardly made any sense at the time. You're really not her, are you? Even Miss Hetty would never go off and sleep on the lawn!'

Bessie was staring at her, desperate for answers that Etta couldn't give. She looked scared.

'No,' Etta said truthfully. 'I am not her and I don't have a clue what's happened. I come from another place altogether, another time.'

'Another time, miss?'

'The future, I suppose. One moment I was on the— sorry, just going about my day – and the next moment I was here.'

Bessie leaned back slightly, looking surprisingly mollified. 'You – she – warned me this might happen, miss, but I really didn't understand. I thought maybe she was as mad as everyone said.'

Etta smoothed the blankets down either side of her. 'Tell me, what was Hetty like?'

'Well . . . quiet, miss. Her ladyship thought that if she brought me here from London as a lady's maid perhaps Miss Hetty would . . . perk up a little. It didn't work, but . . . well, the pay is good and I like it here.'

'Sounds like we're going back to London for a while, though? You gonna be all right?'

'Oh yes, miss. Much of the household staff is coming, including . . . well, everyone important.'

Etta watched Bessie blush as she retreated to her room.

There was clearly a story there, and one she would deeply enjoy teasing out of Bessie.

Only a few days ago, Etta had felt like she had nothing and nobody. Today all her stresses and responsibilities were melting away. No rent, no bills, no 9-to-5 job. All she had to do was wear nice clothes and try to fit in. She decided to enjoy it as long as it lasted. After all, didn't people always say a change was as good as a rest?

Chapter 13

2023

It turned out that in 2023, one's doctor didn't ride over on his horse within the day: one had to rise early, enquire as to the doctor's availability, and then visit the doctor's own residence. Not only that, but either the doctor would then be available that very same day or not at all for several weeks.

While they all waited to discover which of those options it would be, Aggie and Jemima had put her on a bright red bus, given her a colourful map, the small glossy black rectangle, and left her to her own devices for the morning.

A man in an amusing hat had told stories about London as she and the other passengers on the roaring, smelly contraption had been driven around the bustling streets. He had looked at her with increasing bemusement as she went round a second, then a third time.

Finally she alighted outside Buckingham Palace and made her way towards Hyde Park. This at least felt familiar. Grass was always grass, and pigeons were always pigeons.

She sat on a bench and poked at the shiny black thing in her hand until it lit up, scaring her enough to make her drop it. Thankfully it fell onto the grass and remained intact. After that, Aggie had somehow appeared to collect her, clutching two paper cups full of hot coffee. Apparently the shiny black thing could also tell people where she was. Quite miraculous.

Hetty had sworn she'd never see a doctor again after all those she'd seen in her childhood. She'd been poked and prodded, offered all kinds of potions and lotions (many of which had made her very seriously ill) and had, at one particularly low point, been given daily ice baths. Nothing had helped. Especially not the leeches.

So it was with extreme trepidation that she sat in the stark waiting room, with Jemima knitting a strange lumpy pink object to her left. Something about test . . . test-tic . . . well, some form of cancer? Hetty didn't dare ask any more.

The truth was, she'd decided on her bus trip this morning that it was worth a go. If she'd managed to find a way through time, surely she could find a way through the darkness.

Jemima had helped her fill in registration paperwork at the front desk, and as it crinkled in her hand she realised she was creasing it in her anxiety.

'Henrietta Moore?'

She jumped, belatedly recognising her new name as Jemima poked her with a knitting needle.

She followed a distracted-looking foreign woman into a small, bright, clinical room, unsure which plastic chair to sit in as the woman took Hetty's papers and dropped herself at a desk. Hetty began to feel immensely out of her depth.

'I'm here to see Dr Ansari. Will he meet me here?' she asked.

She knew instantly she'd said something wrong, as the woman's head whipped around angrily. 'I would hope so, since I'm Dr Ansari. Sit.'

Hetty felt her skin burn with embarrassment as she sat, unsure as to how to proceed.

'I— I'm so sorry.'

The doctor was typing away at what Hetty now recognised to be a computer, ignoring her completely.

'Henrietta Moore?'

'Yes. I really am so very sorr—'

'Date of birth?'

Hetty gulped. 'Um . . . Oh lord . . . the eighth of May?'

Luckily Dr Ansari didn't appear to require a year, because Hetty's maths had completely deserted her.

'What's the problem, then? Symptoms?'

Suddenly Hetty felt more afraid than she'd ever felt in her life. All hope of recovery from the darkness that had followed her was in the hands of a woman she'd just accidentally but gravely offended. She covered her face with her hands and burst into tears.

She felt something nudge her forearm and looked up to find Dr Ansari proffering a cardboard box of tissues. She was regarding Hetty with a mixture of pity and empathy.

'I'm so very, very sorry. I—'

'No, I'm sorry. It's been a long day and I've been working evening shifts all week. Now, why don't you tell me all about it?'

'It's . . . it's a heavy sadness, an oppressive weight on me at all times. It just won't dissipate, no matter what I do.'

'And have you been eating well? Exercising?'

Little by little Hetty bared her soul to this clever stranger, who seemed to accept her story unblinkingly as though it were in fact quite ordinary to wake up crying every morning.

In fewer than ten minutes – the most difficult ten minutes

of her life, but ten minutes nonetheless – Hetty was back in the waiting room clutching a green-and-white slip. She looked at her aunt, biting her trembling lower lip.

'Aunt Jemima . . . The doctor thinks I have that term Aggie used before, "depression". She says that it's a condition many others experience, in fact. And she has provided me with a modern treatment to try that she says works for many people.'

Jemima stuffed her knitting into her colourful fabric bag and stood up to give her a hug. 'Let's pick up that prescription, then go and get a cup of tea and a cream bun.'

Chapter 14

1817

Etta gazed out of the carriage's thin glass window and shivered in the cold air. She shot her somewhat anxious-looking mother a reassuring smile and returned to her thoughts, carefully fingering her golden bracelet.

It had been a very strange few weeks, but Etta was sticking with her 'holiday' for now. It was still better than Dave and his bloody mushrooms – and she didn't miss her phone at all. Endless doom-scrolling on Instagram watching all the friends she'd grown apart from nursing their babies and going to NCT classes? No, thanks.

Bessie sat next to her now, crocheting something or other; her mother was lightly snoring across from them. They'd been travelling for hours by now and Etta was bored as hell.

'Bessie, tell me about yourself. Where do you come from? How did you get to be my maid?'

'Pa won on the races, miss. Won big, he did. First and last time, mind. Managed to persuade him to send me off to Miss Wimslow's Academy for Household Staff, never looked back.' Bessie paused. 'Well, I look back enough to send the old man the odd bob or two now and then of course. Reckon I've paid him back a few times over by now.'

'And you got a job dealing with me, then? What on earth made you stay?'

'I don't mind looking after you, miss. You're no trouble.'

Etta winced, remembering her first major encounter with a chamber pot. As horrifying as the first had been, the second had put any and all dignity fully to rest.

It was hard, Etta thought, to be too formal around someone who'd seen you half-naked and covered in your own body fluids and who had immediately gone to your aid in the most kind and understanding way. They had laughed, they had cried, and then Bessie had told her about James the second footman.

'Do you reckon you'll stick around, if your bloke pops the question?'

Bessie snorted. 'Reckon I'll be too rich on his exorbitant earnings to bother working, do you? I earn more than he does, miss.'

Lady Bainbridge snorted, shifting in her seat, and a sharp look from Bessie told Etta their tête-à-tête was at an end. Etta had almost forgotten that Ladies Do Not take an interest in servants' private lives – at least, not in front of other ladies.

'Ladies Do Not' seemed to precede a great many statements from her mother. Etta's list of Things Ladies Do Not Do grew longer and longer by the day. Ladies Did Not:

- → Pull an appalled face when presented with a cod's head for supper
- → Comment negatively, or indeed at all, on digestive issues

- Hike up their skirts to above their ankles when going up or down staircases
- Go downstairs before their hair was arranged, even when the hairdresser was expected
- Disregard their mother's opinion on hairstyles of the day
- Swear profusely when pricking themselves with a needle
- Sew their own sets of underwear at the tea table, even if they considered their own designs superior
- Sleep during church services and then provide feedback to the vicar afterwards, however constructive it may be

What ladies *did* do, apparently, was traipse around outside putting flowers in baskets and looking pretty.

Her mother seemed determined to get her to smear various dubious-looking lotions and potions on her face to 'cure' her freckles, but Etta was having none of it. GCSE History had taught her quite enough about Ye Olde Lead Poisoning – and her freckles, along with her eyes, were almost the only thing to add any colour to her face. As she told her mother, she had never seen anyone with freckles like hers. Lady Bainbridge, knowing a lost cause when she saw one, sighed and reluctantly agreed.

Etta wiped away some of the condensation clouding her window and peered through at the darkening sky outside. The carriage was beginning to slow. She refocused her eyes and saw they were drawing into a courtyard surrounded by stables. Thank god. She longed to stretch her legs and eat something – preferably something not from the digestive tract of any animal. Nothing with eyeballs either.

As she was helped down from the carriage by a very earnest-looking young man in what she had come, over the course of her journey, to recognise as 'ordinary person clothes', she could hear music and singing coming from the very large pub-slash-hotel. It sounded drunken and fun, which meant she probably wouldn't be allowed to have anything to do with it.

She mentally shook herself, physically shook her skirts, and followed her mother, who was being led through the dark to a door of the building far away from the fun.

They were exhausted as they followed the servant down a well-lit and nicely decorated corridor towards what Etta was assured would be an excellent supper immediately followed by bed. Lady Bainbridge, however, could not have been as tired as she looked because as they approached an open door and saw a small group eating their own dinner she froze immediately, whipping around to face Etta. Her face was a mask of horror, but it was far too late for whatever she had to say.

'Lady Bainbridge! Well, what a delightful situation! Why, I need not ask what brings you here!'

A well-built woman enthusiastically greeted her mother before turning a somewhat unnerving, critical eye on Etta. 'Goodness me, could this be Hetty? Why, how changed you are, for sure! I am your mother's old friend, Lady Best.'

Etta's mother seemed to tremble at this description, but replied in a pleasant voice.

'Yes, Henrietta is joining me in London for her first Season. Better late than never, I feel!'

'Better late than not at all, I think,' said Lady Best, openly assessing Etta.

Etta turned her chin up and said nothing, smiling in what she hoped was a mildly polite manner. She didn't like the way Lady Best looked at her, like she was a distasteful museum exhibit.

A brunette about Etta's own age – perhaps slightly older – joined Lady Best. She peered timidly around the door frame at Etta.

'Do let me introduce my daughter. Like you, she too will be enjoying the Season. Clarissa, this is Lady Bainbridge and her daughter Henrietta.'

Clarissa Best smiled, seemingly inclined to be friendlier than Lady Best. She was short, plump, with warm brown eyes. Etta held out her hand, and then wondered too late whether this was how ladies greeted one another in 1817.

Luckily she was not too far off. Clarissa briefly took her hand, then bowed slightly. Etta quickly dipped back at her, about half a second too late.

'It is lovely to meet you, Miss Bainbridge. You must call me Clarissa.'

Etta blinked. She had honestly not considered any other option until this moment, but she knew there were far more rules than her mother had been able to fill her in on in the last week.

'Yes, please call me Etta. Henrietta. Or Etta. Whichever you prefer. Henrietta, probably.'

Her mother shot her a barbed glance, but thankfully Clarissa just laughed. Her laugh was tinkling and elegant, Etta thought, but she found herself unable to be annoyed. The girl in front of her seemed genuine. Etta liked her at once.

Lady Best cut in before Clarissa could reply. 'Well, Clarissa, let us leave Lady Bainbridge and her daughter to their supper. We must call on you when we're in town – after all, we are practically neighbours.'

Etta reflected on this exchange over her beef bourguignon. She hadn't even made it to London yet, but at least there would be one friendly face – albeit perhaps not one her mother wholly approved of. She was sure that, in time, she'd find out why not.

The city came on slowly, Etta thought the following day as they embarked on the last leg of what was the longest, most interminable journey she'd ever suffered through – more slowly than it had in 2023. At first, she thought she was entering a small town as she gazed through the carriage windows. But then the streets became increasingly crowded, and she saw the distant but unmistakable shapes of St Paul's and Westminster Palace.

Of course, there was no Shard or Gherkin or even the London Eye. No Tate Modern or BT Tower. But London was London, she realised. Even two hundred years in the past, full of horses and stinking of their excrement, it was still somehow the same.

Oh, there was dirt and deprivation. But London had dirt and deprivation in 2023 as well, albeit from cars rather than animals. The only real difference was the colour of everyone's skin; she had never seen so many white faces. Out in the Bainbridges' large country estate she hadn't really thought about it, but London without its visible multiculturalism was nauseating. It was one thing to see people in period clothing, she thought, but the thin, short, pale bodies were somehow much more jarring.

'Everybody looks the same here,' said Etta.

Lady Bainbridge looked at her quizzically. 'Whatever do you mean?'

'Never mind, Mama. Never mind. I'm sure there are all kinds of people in London, of course,' Etta backpedalled, seeing she'd put her foot in it. She belatedly remembered that no Londoners ever liked being told London wasn't the best city in the world, regardless of what century it was.

'Oh yes, people of all kinds reside in London. You know, the Bests even have a footman from the colonies! Think of that!'

'Which colonies?'

Lady Bainbridge paused. 'Goodness, you know, I'm not sure. We shall have to ask.'

The carriage came to a stop. As Etta was helped down from the carriage in her wildly impractical muslin maxi dress, wrinkling her nose at the stench of horse shit and body odour, she gazed up at an enormous cream stone building. It was, she thought, the kind of building she used to look at on Rightmove and dream about. In 2023, it would be owned by a Russian oligarch. She was almost certain of it. Or a Saudi prince.

But in 1817, it belonged to her.

Or, no, her brother Charlie. Because of primogeniture and anyway she, a woman, couldn't exactly just nip to the local estate agent. She pulled at her suddenly too-tight bonnet strings.

One of the coachmen/horse-type people had already knocked on the front door and a staid-looking man who had very much come out of the 'Butlers R Us' catalogue was standing by it ready to usher them in. Footmen appeared and began to unload the carriage and her mother stepped forward to greet the elderly retainer in charge of them.

'Good afternoon, Monsett. Do come, Henrietta. I expect there is a nuncheon waiting for us.'

Etta sighed and followed her mother. She very much hoped that a nuncheon was similar to a luncheon, because yet again she was extremely hungry. Perhaps she would try inventing the sandwich again. Last time her mother had been appalled to see her create one, never mind eat it, but Etta was nothing if not optimistic.

'What ho! Looking pretty smart there, Hetty!'

Charlie had appeared at the door, hat in hand.

'And you, I must admit,' Etta said, looking at his outfit. 'Off to a funeral, are we?'

He looked down at his black coat and breeches and then back up at her, puzzled.

'Oh, this old thing? Bang up to the nines, isn't it? Max doesn't like it either, mind.'

Etta perked up. 'Have you seen him, then?'

'Seeing him now, old girl,' Charlie said, planting his hat firmly on his head. 'Off to my club. Toodleoo!'

Ah, Max. She'd been looking forward to seeing him. She had enjoyed some extremely X-rated, frustrating dreams about him. X-rated enough that she wasn't sure she'd be able to face him without blushing.

Thank goodness for the lovely notebook Hetty had left her – without it, she might have forgotten them.

Chapter 15

2023

Hetty fingered the plastic and metal packaging carefully, pulling it from the flimsy box.

'It sounds to me like you're depressed,' the doctor had said. 'Let's try you on some mild antidepressants to begin with. We can set up another appointment in two weeks to review how you're feeling.' She'd talked to Hetty about how she might not feel better right away so she knew what to expect, and also put her on a waiting list for something called CBT.

It was strange to hear the doctor give a name to how she felt. Validating, somehow. But most of all, it made her feel hopeful.

The fact that her doctor had been a woman was still causing Hetty's mind to whirr with possibility. A woman – completely equal to a man, absolutely able and allowed to prescribe her this medicine. Presumably she even had a degree.

Aggie set a laptop and notepad down on the kitchen table and sat next to her.

'Don't mind me, will you? Just got this proposal to finish

off before the board meeting tomorrow. Musk's not exactly going to stop himself, is he?'

'Aunt Aggie . . . I don't know whether I should take these.'

'Whyever not, dear?'

'I don't know. I don't know if I should alter Etta's body like this, when she might break the bracelet at any moment.'

'Oh, but you can't live life like that now, can you?'

Jemima joined them, moving Aggie's notebook aside and replacing it with her latest project – a half-worked embroidery hoop with odd-shaped leaves and the words 'Smoke weed every day'.

'Oh yes, Hetty, nothing is forever. Not relationships, and not even tattoos. You just have to live life as it comes and enjoy the memories,' Jemima said. 'Here, take a look at my Hall of Fame.'

To Hetty's absolute horror the elderly woman lifted the hem of her flowery electric blue top to reveal a patchwork quilt of faces – male and female – each encased in a heart, and each graced with a signature. She twirled, then curtseyed as she left the room.

Aunt Aggie rolled her eyes, tutting at Jemima, then smiled at Hetty's appalled face.

'You should see her arms . . . Anyway. My advice? Try the pills, Henrietta. Nothing ventured, nothing gained. Besides, you can always stop if you don't feel like they help. And Jemima and I will be with you every step of the way.'

Hetty bit her lip, still slightly dazed, and nodded.

Jemima's voice echoed from the bathroom next door. 'Hang on, sweeties, don't go anywhere. Just taking off my tights so you can take a gander at Cher and Madonna.'

*

It had been several Sundays now that Hetty hadn't attended church. She was beginning to miss the quiet reflection of a conversation with God, despite being at times cynical about His very existence. She had much to tell Him – about her trip, her new home, and especially her new diagnosis. Perhaps He could even help her come to a decision about the medication in her reticule.

Aggie pointed her down the road to a small but elegant church hidden away between houses. And now here she was, empty-handed but for a few unfamiliar coins for the silver salver.

The familiar chill of stone walls made goosebumps prickle at her arms as she stood at the open oak door, peering in. It was unusually empty. Perhaps she'd got the timings wrong or something?

Before she could retreat, a woman in a flowery shirt and neat pink cardigan bustled up to her. She was holding a bible with a slim booklet sandwiched inside.

'Here for the service, love? I hope you'll join us for a prayer circle afterwards?'

'Well—'

Hetty hadn't really been sure what to say next, so was relieved to find she didn't need to.

'Are you one of the mums? From the primary? I didn't think it was that time of year yet.'

Hetty blinked in confusion, but the lady just smiled and placed the bible into her hands.

'No, I suppose you're not, or there'd be other parents, too. They only visit to get their kids into St Leonard's Primary, but the vicar sees right through them. Well, anyway, welcome, take a seat. Here, Horace, how's the hip?'

And with that the woman was greeting the elderly

gentleman who'd arrived behind her. Hetty took a deep breath and slipped into a pew at the back.

She'd hoped to zone out slightly, to think about things, but the sermon was even more confusing than her welcome had been. The vicar seemed to be even younger than she was – perhaps this wasn't unusual here, but the pastor who occasionally called at the chapel on the Bainbridge Estate had been, according to Charlie at least, 'older than the sun'.

This wasn't a pointed sermon on the lurking demons within or on the dangers of failing to fulfil feminine duty. Not today, anyway. Instead, the young man at the pulpit had greeted them with outspread hands and the words: 'As the youth would say . . . come and roll with Jesus!'

Hetty's heart had curdled in her chest in second-hand embarrassment as the vicar had counselled them through the terrible dangers of items she had never heard of before. By the time the rest of the single-digit congregation rose and headed to the ring of flimsy chairs in the vestry, she had learned to strictly avoid such temptations as 'Meow-meow' and 'Special K'. She also vaguely missed Charlie, despite having been lectured on the need to abandon him at all costs.

She was trying to work out where the most likely source of inner peace was to be found – staring at the carvings in the ceiling beams, or at the figure of Christ looking all too happy to be on the cross – when she was presented with a cup of tea by the woman who'd welcomed her earlier.

'Here you are. I wasn't sure how many sugars you'd want, so I only added three. Do come and have a chat, won't you? We'd love to tell you what the vicar has lined up for us this month.'

They both gazed over to the vicar, who was dancing very strangely for a smiling young man with a mobile phone.

'Oh, look at our Andy. He's ever so into his TikToks, he really is.'

'Andy?'

'Reverend Dickens, I should say, but he does insist on being called Andy. Great service, Reverend! I see you're at the TikToks again today!'

Reverend Dickens was sashaying their way in a manner that alarmed Hetty. This was no Pastor Simmons, that was a certainty.

'I am indeed, Delilah. And who's this new addition?'

They were both now studying Hetty so intently she could barely remember her own name.

'Um, Hetty. I'm Hetty Ba— sorry, Moore.'

'Well then, Hetty, why don't you come and join our prayer circle? We're always looking for more young, energetic people. Today we collectively dedicate ourselves to inner peace and healing.'

Hetty wasn't sure how to put her thoughts into words. 'Isn't that a bit . . . heathen?'

The whole group was staring at her now. The vicar paused, clearly unsure where to take this unexpected conversation, then appeared to find a straw to grasp.

'Well, what are we all if not essentially, in our bones, heathen?'

Hetty realised her eyes were so wide with surprise they'd gone dry, and blinked. It suddenly all seemed too absurd that she'd come here to these eager strangers for spiritual guidance when it was right there waiting at home with those who cared for her.

She bid the vicar a polite goodbye. Time to take the advice she'd already been given. Time to try the medication.

Chapter 16

1817

London Sundays were an even bigger chore than Sundays in the countryside had been. At their local village church, Etta had been able to hide in what was essentially a little wooden cubicle for her family, with only servants, a few local gentry and assorted farmers to stare at her. It had been nice – peaceful, reflective, even. But in London, church was an Event.

Of course, a church could hardly ever be a loud place, but Etta had felt a new, unnerving level of quiet sweep over the pews as she walked down the aisle with her mother. Bessie peeled off behind them to sit at the back, leaving Etta facing as many eyes as she'd expect at her own wedding. The eyes were not admiring, though. She caught looks of wonder, disdain and disapproval from the immaculately dressed ladies and gentlemen in the chapel, whispers spreading like wildfire as they worked out who she was.

News of Mad Hetty Bainbridge coming to town had circulated amongst the neighbours. Everyone probably knew by now, Etta thought. And this was probably representative of the reception she could expect during her morning visits and all the parties her mother had threatened her with.

Well, better to start as she meant to go on. She looked next to her at her sublimely unconscious mother and levelled her voice to be slightly louder than necessary.

'Mama, why are these people staring at me?'

Her mother looked startled – an increasingly familiar expression. 'Why on earth would anyone stare, Henrietta? That would be dreadfully rude.'

'Perhaps,' Etta declared, staring one particularly impudent-looking woman dead in the eye, 'they do not like my new bonnet.'

Lady Bainbridge tutted disapprovingly. 'Oh no, Henrietta. Impossible. That bonnet is delightful. It matches your complexion perfectly.'

Charlie, who had been dragging his heels behind her, caught the tail of the conversation. 'Smart as anything, that hat, Hetty. The first stare.'

'You what?'

'Fashionable. All the ladies will be asking you about it, you wait.'

They reached their pew and Etta slid in next to her mother, settling just in time for the vicar to amble in. She had taken the precaution of slipping the red notebook Hetty had left her into her reticule and settled in for another attempt at her elegant notes. Hopefully there'd finally be some useful tips about how to deal with life outside of the Bainbridges' country estate.

However, she was yet again in for a disappointing read. She'd just about got to grips with Hetty's handwriting style now, and the more she read, the more she found there wasn't really much of use beyond Hetty's initial letter. This time she deciphered a list of family members and descriptions of their various personalities. Nothing new here, really – she'd already got the measure of her mother and brother, and it was somewhat unsurprising to read that Bessie really had been Hetty's only friend – if you could even call her that.

Suddenly, a voice was in her ear. 'Hetty, old girl, drop the book. The vicar is watching.'

She looked up to see that Charlie was right and glared at the indignant vicar equally indignantly. Etta hadn't got a particularly firm stance on Christianity, but she definitely had a view on being judged by men with comb-overs.

'Rude,' she muttered.

Charlie's shoulders began to shake next to her and after one last vicious glare at the vicar, which made him cough and continue his boring sermon, she shot him a glance. Her brother was creasing up with contained laughter, and Etta couldn't help but smile at him. He looked at her, tears welling, and she caught the giggles.

An elderly woman in front of them with a fantastically ugly hat turned and shushed them, which compounded matters. Charlie bit his hand and Etta looked away, trying in vain to Think Serious Thoughts.

Unfortunately, the vicar had taken a detour from his sermon. '. . . And blessed be those who *pay attention to the Lord*, for only they shall reach heaven . . .'

Charlie snorted, the situation quickly devolving. At this point, Etta was fairly sure neither of them had any idea what they were laughing about. She prodded him, trying to remind herself that she was supposed to be angry with him but failing. She felt a flash of joy at the absurdity of it all. Who'd have thought she'd ever enjoy church? Sunday morning lie-ins might be a thing of the past, but this wasn't too bad.

Everyone stood up, and she realised it was time for a hymn. Good stuff. Tucking Hetty's book away, she joined them. As one, the congregation sang. '*We plough the fields and scatter*,' they belted out, but Etta's mind was more in 'All Things Bright And Beautiful' territory. She couldn't stretch to the idea of a God joining all things, not quite. But her and Hetty? Perhaps.

Chapter 17

2023

Hetty sat on a bench. It was airy and the space around her was vast, but in place of the sky was . . . white. So much white. And light – so much light.

This morning, a letter had arrived for her. Inside it had been a shiny, bendy plastic – she was very much still getting used to plastic – 'card'. Aggie had helped her 'activate' it (although it still looked no different to the moment it had arrived) and had sent her off with Jemima for a day out.

At first Hetty had hated the noise and busyness of it all, but she was starting to appreciate it a little more now.

Suddenly, delighted screams ricocheted against the concrete pillars and marble floors of the vast shopping centre. A group of women around her own age gathered by a nearby shop. A young man arrived to join them and the friends crowded around him, pulling down his hood and ruffling his hair until he grinned reluctantly. They turned to leave and caught Hetty staring, but before she could feel even an iota of shame for being caught spying, they all, as one, smiled and nodded at her in friendly acknowledgement.

Hetty felt awash with gladness as the group melted into the crowds. She had no idea where they might be going but felt a tug – an unexpected impulse to run and join them, to introduce herself.

She was shaken awake from a dream which had barely begun when Jemima, back from doing some 'errands', plonked herself down on the bench and immediately expanded to fit the remaining space. Hetty almost laughed at her aunt's ability to produce endless cardigans, scarves, tissues and anything one could want at any time. Now that Hetty could grasp how the screens worked, they had been watching films and Jemima's bag was eerily similar to that of Mary Poppins.

'Had enough yet, dearie?'

Hetty considered this question carefully. She looked at her heavy bag of books, then back at her kindly aunt. 'Yes, I think so. I think one could spend all day in such a place, however. What is it called, again?'

'Westfield, lovely. A shopping centre.'

'And can we get the Tube home?'

Jemima twinkled at her. 'Changed your tune, haven't you?'

'It's not what I thought, you know,' Hetty mused, prodding at her strange bubble tea drink with its ginormous tube and chewy lumps of goo.

'What, 2023?'

'No,' said Hetty. 'London.'

'How are you feeling, dear? I did wonder if this might all be a bit much for you, but you seem to be taking it all rather well.'

Hetty thoughtfully sipped at her tea, before nearly choking on a boba and coughing. Jemima slapped her on the back.

'I never thought I'd say this, but I'm feeling much brighter, you know. I wonder if I was perhaps just not in the right frame of mind, before.'

As she said it aloud, she wondered when things had started to change. Was it the medication, or was it being out in the world again?

It all felt so wonderful. Not so long ago, Hetty would have shuddered at the very thought of wandering through crowds of chattering people and loud traders, but instead of shielding herself against it she'd allowed the noise to run through her body and energise her; to power her heart.

Nowadays every morning felt full of promise. She was starting to wonder – was it finally time to start working on her wish list?

Chapter 18

1817

Sunday afternoons were immensely boring. After lunch and a family walk in the park with her mother, who stopped frequently to talk to her friends (all of whom looked beyond surprised to see Etta), it seemed they were all expected to sit around in contemplation, reading and sewing and thinking about Jesus and stuff. All respect to Him, but no thanks.

Etta had spent all week dying for some alone-time in the city. She knew it was not the 'done thing' but, well, what if something happened to the bracelet and she didn't have another chance? Now she was (according to her mother) dressed respectably, she figured there was no time like the present. With her mother holed up planning her coming-out ball with the housekeeper, servants running around like mad with bunches of flowers and chairs and things, and Bessie away somewhere having (Etta could only assume) illicit pre-marital relations – well, there wasn't even anyone to say goodbye to.

Excited to see anything that wasn't the inside of a carriage or the church, Etta grabbed her pelisse.

She'd been fascinated, having read about these so extensively in her favourite romances, to discover that pelisses were just long coats. Her mother had impeccable taste; she paired her beautiful, vivid blue one with a light blue bonnet.

Despite all regency novels maintaining that the 'Season' conveniently started in March, it was actually late October and therefore chilly and overcast outside. She'd had a quick scout round for an umbrella, just in case, but lord knows where Monsett the butler kept them. If they were even a thing yet, that was.

Nobody in the household seemed to be expecting anyone to come or go, so she only saw a gormless-looking footman carrying a huge vase on the way out. She waved at him and said goodbye, but he just gawped at her.

Looking around the neat square her parents lived on, she tried to orient herself. She jingled her reticule, hearing the clinking of the unfamiliar coins in it. Might as well go shopping. Ooh, maybe she could see what people were reading nowadays? The thought propelled her urgently in the direction of Bond Street. Surely Bond Street would have a bookshop?

She'd already been forced down the main shopping streets – or glimpsed them from the carriage, at least – and she knew she'd passed a bookshop somewhere. She retraced the route she'd been on and quickly found herself on a deserted shopping street.

She should have known. It was Sunday. All the shops were, of course, closed because it was 1817.

Etta stood forlornly outside a very elegant-looking bookshop and wondered what to do next. She tried to ignore the few passers-by, but felt a prickle of awareness across her body and heard a man clear his throat.

She turned around and there he was, in smart town clothes, looking athletic and, well, not a little surprised. His hair had a slight wave to it, she noticed, before gazing into his wide brown eyes. He squinted at her quizzically.

'Max?' she said, fighting the urge to step closer.

'Lord Stanhope,' he replied reprovingly. 'You're supposed to call me Lord Stanhope. Although, really, you're not supposed to be here.'

'What do you mean?'

'It's Sunday. And more importantly, where's your maid?'

'With James, the second footman, I assume.'

Max took a deep breath then rubbed his forehead in mild anguish. 'And what are you doing here, Henri— Miss Bainbridge?'

'Henrietta is fine, you know. Etta, even.'

'No, it's not,' he replied firmly. 'Miss Bainbridge.'

Etta rolled her eyes. 'I was vaguely hoping to buy some books, but it turns out all the shops are closed. Which is extremely annoying.'

He sighed. 'Well, yes, it *is* Sunday.'

She bristled with the injustice of it. 'Well, what are you doing out and about then if it's Sunday and we're all supposed to be sitting around praying to Jesus and stuff?'

Max rubbed his temples again and looked genuinely frustrated. It was a good look for him, Etta decided.

'Off to see your mates, maybe. Or . . . your lady friend?'

She'd taken it too far; he looked appalled. '*Hetty!*'

'You can call me Etta. I'm Etta.'

'Etta, then! Oh god – Miss Bainbridge, I mean. You can't— You can't say things like that!'

Etta examined him closely. She wasn't sure she liked this conversation. It was very much following the Ladies Do Not pattern her mother was so fond of.

'Aren't we childhood friends or something? Ugh. It feels like I'm not allowed to talk about *anything* in this place.'

Max had gone back to rubbing his temples. 'Miss Bainbridge, you must learn to behave. You can't go around asking about "lady friends" – which I do *not* have – and you certainly can't wander around London unattended. On any day of the week.'

'Well, I'm not alone now, am I? You're here. And since you're Lord something-or-other—'

'Stanhope.'

'Well,' Etta continued, 'since you're *Lord Stanhope*, can't you get this bookshop to magically open? My father's library has absolutely nothing worth reading, and the piano music here is just awful.'

Etta heard a mild groan escape his lips. Very manly lips, she thought, gazing at him. He was the most handsome man she had ever seen. So why was she not doing her usual thing, blushing her face off and stammering?

She'd absolutely never seen him before that night in the cellar – she knew for sure – but she felt comfortable around him. He just seemed . . . Right. Just right. Like the porridge Goldilocks ended up eating. Warm, comforting. She could be herself around him – a brand-new feeling, and one she had stopped hoping to find anywhere in life, let alone so far from home.

Etta felt a zip of excitement as she nudged him in the side. 'Come on. If anyone can get this bookshop open, it's you,' she cajoled, eyes shining.

For a moment, Max looked at Etta like he wanted to eat her up. Then he seemed to recall himself and ran a hand distractedly through his hair, completing the overall look of a deeply ruffled man. He took a deep breath. 'Oh, very well,' he said, in a vaguely desperate voice. 'I can't exactly leave you out on the street unchaperoned. I'm already here to meet Higgins anyway.'

Etta cheered, wholly inappropriately, as he knocked on the door. Higgins, who must have heard them talking from his rooms upstairs, was already hurrying through the shop towards them.

'Lord Stanhope! How excellent to see you. And . . . Miss—?'

'Yes, good afternoon, Higgins. I've brought Miss Bainbridge.' Max ushered her inside brusquely. 'I don't suppose you could help her find the books she's looking for, could you? And perhaps one of your sons might kindly run to the Bainbridges' London residence at St Peter's Square and alert her parents as to her whereabouts – I believe her maid has taken a wrong turn.'

The older man looked disapprovingly at Etta; evidently them being here together was not the done thing. Oh dear. But Mr Higgins took his cue from Max thankfully.

'Not a problem, my lord,' he said. 'Perhaps my daughter could help the young lady while we discuss that book you ordered. I've had a letter back, and it is all most mysterious.'

Etta loved a mystery more than almost anything in the world. 'Oooh, what's mysterious?'

'Miss Bainbridge, no,' Max said, goaded into mild exasperation. 'Stay here with Miss Higgins and choose your books. I'll be back for you shortly. Do not even think of leaving without me.'

Etta glared at him, turning pointedly towards a slightly intimidated Miss Higgins. 'Tell me, Miss Higgins. Do you have anything naughty?'

Max appeared to grit his teeth, but gestured to Higgins to lead the way.

Etta turned back to Higgins' daughter. 'No really, though, do you have anything naughty?'

Miss Higgins giggled, and Etta instantly knew she had found a kindred spirit. She was blissfully piling armfuls of classic novels onto the elegant wooden counter when she next heard Max's voice emanating from Higgins' office in the back. The bookshop had exceeded her expectations; she had rarely been so excited – first editions of Jane Austen novels! – but her ears pricked up nonetheless.

'Going to be named? So you're telling me they haven't gone to print yet?'

'No, my lord. In fact, the publishers are over in Finsbury Square. Lackington and Co. They've asked where you've heard about the novel. They're quite curious about it, as Mrs Shelley is still making some last-minute changes before it goes to print.'

She heard Max groan slightly as Higgins continued, 'They are concerned it will not take. I imagine your enquiry will be quite reassuring.'

'Reserve me a copy, then, Higgins. And if you will, reserve a copy for Miss Bainbridge, chalked up to my account. I imagine she'll enjoy it, too.'

Could they be talking about *Frankenstein*? When had she mentioned that?

Oh yes, back in the cellar, when Charlie had her strapped into that chair like an experiment gone wrong. Oops. Would this alter the fabric of time and space or something?

The floorboards creaked as Max and Mr Higgins reappeared from the room behind the counter.

Etta felt the smooth leather covers of her pile of elegant books and smiled. 'You won't *believe* what I've found! First editions of *several* of Jane Austen's books! Fiona didn't think she had any, did you, Fiona? But we found them in a stock room out back. And so many other first editions! I don't know how on earth I'm going to carry them all!' Then Etta had a crushing, sudden realisation, as she looked at the piles in front of her. 'Oh! And I don't even know if I have enough money, actually.'

Etta hadn't earned a big salary at her job in 2023 and she'd had to budget carefully, but still, she'd had her own money. She made the choices on how she'd spend it. Her new Regency family were certainly richer than Etta had ever been, but she realised now that she didn't have any financial independence whatsoever. It was a strange feeling. Strange, and deeply unpleasant.

'Higgins, you might as well chalk this lot up to my account, too,' said Max.

Etta was appalled. 'You can't do that! There must be hundreds of pounds' worth of books here, even in old money.'

'Don't worry about me, Miss Bainbridge. I'll stand the nonsense. Send them round to Bainbridge House in St Peter's Square, Higgins. But perhaps you might get your man to deliver them anonymously.'

'Very well, your lordship.' Higgins picked up a pile of books and took them through to the back room.

'Anonymously, Max?'

'Lord Stanhope,' he corrected her, smiling. 'And yes. I'm not sure I'd like your parents knowing you've just managed to persuade me to buy up half of Higgins' bookshop.'

He laughed at her obvious dismay, but she was horrified by his generosity. Back in 2023, she felt bad even when a date bought her drinks. 'Then perhaps don't buy up half of the bookshop!' she said. 'I'm sure I can always come back for them later, once I've saved up or something.'

'Books are really quite expensive nowadays, you know, Miss Bainbridge. It might take you a while. Better let me get them. Call it a gift to the little sister of an old friend.'

Little sister? She wasn't sure she liked that.

'Well, okay then,' she agreed reluctantly. 'But only because I really, really, really need the books. You can't even begin to imagine what they'll be worth in— well, one day. In the future. Thank you.'

They left the shop and Max led Etta back towards home. 'In the future, you say. At which date do you feel they'll reach maximum profitability?'

She thought fast, or at least tried to. 'Um, I dunno. In, well, about two hundred years, maybe. If, you know, these authors become incredibly famous and well known and studied in schools and universities across the world. Which they could be.'

'Yes, I suppose they could well. And what might they be worth then, do you think?'

'Oh, thousands of pounds. Without a doubt. If we look after them.'

Max let out a strangled cough.

'Well, that would be quite something, looking at the size of that pile. We shall be millionaires.'

'Surely you're already a millionaire? You own a house in Central London, I bet. Even for a one-bed flat, you must have at least a million quid.'

Max looked gobsmacked. She was clearly going to have to google the price of things – oh god, no. Maybe she could ask Bessie.

She looked back at Max, biting her lip. 'Oops! Did I say millions? Gosh, that's a lot now, isn't it? Um, thousands? Hundreds? Yes, that's right. Or maybe dozens? Of . . . of shillings?'

He seemed to be trying to take it all in. *Oh god*.

'Ices.' She cut through his confusion with a sudden, determined statement. 'You promised me an ice.'

Relief flooded his face; ices were safe territory.

'Not today, Miss Bainbridge. You have forgotten it's a Sunday. Seeing as nobody has come for you yet, I shall take you back to your mother and we shall both hope nobody shall mind you walking out without your maid.'

'Oh, but look, I'm absolutely fine. It's all fine and dandy. Anyway, you're walking me home, aren't you?'

'We'll both be lucky to escape this episode without the gossipmongers having – oh! Is this her?'

A harried-looking Bessie was running down the pavement towards them, her skirt pulled up and hair flying in all directions. 'Miss! What on earth were you thinking?'

'Oh, Bessie. Is it really all that bad? Look – Max found me.'

Bessie continued to scold her for the rest of the brief walk home. He left them both at her door, with a promise to attend her coming-out ball a week on Monday.

A week on Monday felt worryingly soon, given half her dresses hadn't even arrived yet. She was going to have to make sure whatever she chose was absolutely spectacular.

Chapter 19

2023

Hetty had taken the bracelet off. It was the only item in a small jewellery box on her bedside table. It had been a few weeks, and as she'd said to a smiling Doctor Ansari on her follow-up visit, things were decidedly looking up. In fact, it was as though a weight had been lifted from her chest, her back, even her legs.

That evening, in a continuation of Hetty's introduction to the culinary delights of the modern age, they were assembled around the kitchen table in front of a large bucket of KFC.

'I've been thinking, Aunts. It's possible Etta will keep the bracelet on indefinitely. Since I've decided to give this age a go, I need to decide upon a course of action.'

Aggie put her cutlery down while Jemima paused, drumstick halfway to her mouth.

'Well, let's brainstorm,' Aggie said, as she took a sip of Sprite from her elegant high ball glass.

'Brainstorm? That sounds . . . somewhat alarming . . .?'

Aggie snorted. 'A turn of phrase. I think we should get you across some idioms.'

'Out of the house, too,' added Jemima, carefully selecting a fourth drumstick.

'Hmm,' Aggie continued. 'It's not like you don't have enough money to keep you going, dear. So you need to decide on your field of study. But whatever you do, you *will* need to start near the bottom I'm afraid.'

'Yup,' interrupted Jemima, mouth half full of chicken, slurping from her paper straw. 'No degree. No O-levels, even.'

'Yes. That seems like Step One, then.'

Hetty was confused. 'What are you referring to? My education?'

'Lack thereof, yes, my dear,' Aggie said. 'Without being able to use a computer, everything is difficult.'

'I can use this "mobile" contraption. I can speak to it correctly now and it tells me the weather and I can purchase things.' Hetty paused, not feeling quite as strong in her defiance as she would have liked. She rallied. 'And it looks up terminology I don't understand in the newspapers. So I am very well aware of the definition of a . . . compt-eur.'

Jemima snorted on a chip while Aggie took another sip of Sprite before replying. 'Let's start there. Perhaps it's time for you to start those classes we talked about?'

'Ooh, yes, Aggie,' Jemima said. 'You saw that one at the adult learning centre down the road, remember, when you were doing your Advanced C++ course? Computer Beginnings for Basics, wasn't it?'

'Computer Basics for Beginners. Yes, I think that will do just fine. And when you can use computers properly, my dear, we can have you study for your O-levels at home – or you can go to a local college. Get you out of the house, like Jemima said.'

'And into those dancing shoes, Hetty!' added Jemima.

And with that, it was decided. Aggie and Hetty picked up their cutlery again and jointly waited for Jemima to make fun of them, but thankfully she was deep into a bag of spicy chicken wings.

'Never make these spicy enough, do they? I swear to god, Aggie, I'm so sick of KFC. The jerk shop is only around the corner.'

Aggie sniffed. 'Yes, and when they can adequately replicate a Zinger Tower burger, I'm quite certain they will gain my custom.'

Hetty's trembling index finger pressed the button on the dirty white door next to the jerk chicken shop. She tried to peer through the glass around the sign saying *iLearn IT: Taking you from D- to C++*. This was the most afraid she'd been since the terrifying morning she'd first found herself on the London Underground. That seemed like a lifetime ago now.

Before she could worry for too much longer, she heard thumping on the stairs and the door was flung wide open. A cheerful, cherubic face surrounded by a riot of tight black curls peeked around the doorframe.

'Nice to meet you. I'm Stella. Here for the computer course?'

Hetty had no idea what to say, but thankfully it seemed like she didn't need to say anything. Which really was very lucky, she thought, as Stella was quite the most beautiful woman she'd ever seen. She was used to the pale, slim, fashionable, insipid young ladies her mother had tried to get her to befriend. Women with nothing to say, and to whom she had nothing with which to reply.

Stella, on the other hand, spoke loudly without even opening her mouth. Short and plump and delicious, she looked like the juiciest pear on the tree she used to sit underneath in her father's orchard. She wore a scandalously tight green dress and equally scandalous sleek high heels.

Hetty breathed in the scent of lemons and freshly picked mint as Stella stared at her.

'You're here for the computer course, right?'

Hetty nodded dumbly.

'Great.'

Stella closed the door behind Hetty, still looking intrigued.

'Must say, you might not have much in common with the other students. Are you sure you've got the right day? It's beginner level today.'

'Yes, quite . . . quite sure.'

Stella shrugged, then led Hetty up the narrow set of stairs and down an even narrower corridor to a small white room. It was covered in grey carpet tiles, with a huge table in the centre crowded with screens. Elderly people of various shapes and sizes were already sitting in front of them.

She sat down in front of the screen Stella gestured towards and waited until Stella showed the class where to press the small boxes to make the room light up with beeps. Hetty struggled to keep her eyes away from the woman who inexplicably seemed to take all the oxygen from her lungs, as she tried to get to grips with the small grey device she was expected to scrape across the desk.

Hetty was transfixed by Stella's dazzling hoop earrings, which swung as she laughed with an old man making an incomprehensible joke about hard drives. By her bracelets, which jangled and rattled as she stooped to pick up a lady's fallen mouse. She forced herself to focus on anything, anyone else, and her eyes met those of the woman next to her instead. She had a knowing look in her eyes, which Hetty decided to ignore.

'Now then, ladies and gents,' said Stella. 'Computer Basics for Beginners. Let's talk. I know a lot of you might have phones, but how many of you have used a desktop computer before?'

More than half of the class raised a hand. Hetty was not one of them. She felt her heart sink as she read the collective confusion in their eyes.

'Right,' Stella began. 'Why don't we go around the room and introduce ourselves? I'd love to know what you're hoping to do after these lessons. Go online shopping, maybe, or pay your bills? Give me an idea of what you're looking for.'

Hetty breathed out as the man opposite her started talking. She would have hated to have gone first.

Bill was hoping to Skype his daughter in Australia. Mickey wanted to be able to look up crossword answers. Ruth was looking for bargains, while Nigel wanted to pick up a new language ('Never too late'). And then, finally, it was Hetty's turn.

'I'd like to gain an education. My aunts suggested I study for . . . O-levels?'

She looked around, expecting judgement, but found none.

'Called GCSEs now, I think,' Nigel piped up.

Hetty smiled tremulously. 'Thank you.'

Stella's expression was one of curiosity as she moved on to Elsie, the last person in the room, who wanted to find free knitting patterns. As she gave them all headphones and put videos onto their screens, she stopped behind Hetty's chair.

'I teach this around my Comms degree course and can definitely help you sign up for uni, too, or the local college or whatever, no problem, Hetty – you could be getting started next week if you'd like. Is there anything else you'd like help with?'

Hetty looked up. 'I . . . I'd like to write a diary. I see there is a device here with printed letters. Is it as fast as writing by hand?'

Stella blinked, clearly baffled, and then smiled. 'Oh, yes, it's much, much faster. The class is quite short today – but if you'd like, I'd be happy to talk you through how it all works? Help you set up a Substack or something?'

Hetty nodded. 'Thank you – that would be awfully kind of you.'

Stella's smile brightened. 'It's a date.'

Hetty waited in the café next door, pot of tea ready and waiting, as Stella locked up the classroom. She'd never been so nervous in her life – not even when she'd placed the bracelet around her wrist.

She'd sat with her back to the door in an attempt not to worry too much, but it seemed to have exacerbated her anticipation. She picked out one of every cake on the menu. She hadn't realised they would come in quite such large slices, but it was far too late now. The table was covered in cake.

And then, a jangle of the bell at the door and the most beautiful woman in the world was sitting opposite her. Hetty could barely speak.

Stella seemed to have forgotten about the 'Substack' thing that she was meant to be explaining. Instead, she narrated her way through every cake on the table, noting the pros and cons of every slice, wondering and laughing good-naturedly at Hetty's extravagance.

Hetty realised Stella was waiting for a reply, and blushed. 'I'm so terribly sorry, but I was wool-gathering for a moment. What were you saying?'

Stella's eyes twinkled. 'Don't worry, it's pretty hard to offend me. I said, I'm sure they've got boxes so we can take some of this home with us. Or are you just dead hungry?'

'I didn't know what you'd like,' she said, cheeks burning, 'and I didn't want to get it wrong.'

Stella laughed. 'It's cake – it's hard to get it wrong when it comes to cake. C'mon, let's try a bite of everything and you can tell me all about yourself.'

Hetty wasn't sure how to start. 'Well, I am newly arrived in town.'

Stella lit up even brighter at this news. Her enthusiasm was infectious. 'Ohmygod, you have so much to look forward to! Let me be your guide!'

'I would be terribly grateful if you would. I really have no idea how to go on.'

Stella looked quizzical. 'Bit posh, aren't you? In a nice way, I mean,' she added quickly. 'Been watching a lot of *Downton Abbey*, maybe?'

'What – what's that?'

Stella's eyes widened, and she reached across the table impulsively and grabbed Hetty's hand. As quickly as she'd grabbed it, the touch was gone; they both stared at where they'd connected, where the crackle of electricity remained.

'It's . . . it's really good. Um, you should watch it. It's . . .'

Stella coughed, breaking eye contact; although the moment was over, Hetty found herself tucking it into a little pocket that had formed in her heart. A heart that already felt so much bigger than it had been yesterday.

'Well, it's pretty heterosexual, really, but it's got its moments.'

Heterosexual. A new word, but one Hetty felt she was expected to know. She had taken to writing words down on her phone for times like this, and made a mental note to add this one to the list.

'I haven't watched much television, really. I could do with some recommendations. I do feel a little like I'm . . . stuck in the past, you might say.'

Another person might have ridiculed her, Hetty thought, but not Stella. They laughed, they chatted, and laughed some more, and Hetty found herself opening up like – well, more like a book than a flower, she thought, marvelling at the pure wonder of it all. Stella was just constantly amazed – Hetty hadn't tried sushi, hadn't been to the cinema?! – but she didn't laugh at her, no matter what.

Hetty felt new bookmarks being placed through her pages as Stella gleefully planned a host of activities. As Stella leaned across the table, planning dinner at a famous local pizza place that 'has the best pepperoni you've ever tried, Hetts', Hetty breathed in her heady mix of lemon, mint, and hope.

Chapter 20

1817

Etta didn't think at all about Max while she was being told off for her trip to the shops, first by Bessie, and then half-heartedly by her mother. She didn't think about him as she walked in the park the next morning, or the following day as she walked around checking flower arrangements for her 'coming out' ball. She didn't think about him over lunch and she certainly didn't wonder whether he would like her beautiful light-blue silk and lace dress.

But she really, actually, didn't think about him as she stood by the door ready to meet her first guests a week later. For some reason, as the first carriages drew up and people started stepping down, reality hit her.

Until now, when meeting people in this age, she'd let her mind wander. She'd detached herself from reality, as though she were cosplaying at being a Regency lady. It had felt like being in a strange immersive play where everybody was just really, really great at method acting.

But now, as she watched a stunningly beautiful young brunette woman approach her up the steps, she found herself taking an involuntary step to the side – as if her body simply didn't want to get in the way of such elegance. This woman looked too immaculately put together not to be real, her silken yellow cloak shimmering in the candlelight as though made from spun gold.

Lady Bainbridge greeted the woman and her mother first. 'Mrs Marley, Miss Marley. How lovely.'

Mrs Marley seemed very pleasant and ready to pass by, but Miss Marley's face contorted into a rather false smile as she studied Etta.

'Miss Bainbridge. How . . . surprising . . . to finally meet you,' said Miss Marley. Not waiting for a response, she swept past into the ballroom, smelling faintly of roses and malice.

Etta's confidence crumbled. She looked up at her mother, who was greeting more guests and felt remarkably alone. She really was in 1817, she realised. This wasn't a dream. For the first time, she really felt every one of those two hundred and six long years.

She curtseyed again and again, barely looking at her guests and feeling like she shrunk an inch with every passing dignitary. Her family must be important, she thought. And real.

She was fingering her bracelet as she registered her mother's hand against her bare arm. 'Why, Henrietta, you're chilled to the bone! You should have said! Well, it is time to go inside now anyway. The quartet will be setting up.'

Her mother swept her inside and Etta grabbed a cup of champagne from a passing footman on her way in. Lady Bainbridge gave her side-eye but, typically, as they were in public, said nothing. The pursing of her mother's mouth, however, indicated that Ladies Did Not get drunk. She made a mental note not to get too wrecked, however tempting it was – Hetty's body probably couldn't take as many negronis as hers could back in 2023 – but she needed a little Dutch courage.

As she made her way across the ballroom, on a mission to eat her feelings at the buffet table, she heard Miss Marley's voice wafting towards her from a crowd of giggling women who all seemed around their age.

'The audacity! Remarkable, truly remarkable. I suppose Lady B is happy to think her daughter's not a loony, but I'm not convinced just yet.'

To her surprise, Miss Marley was staring her dead in the eye. Etta tilted her head questioningly, but Miss Marley smiled maliciously and steadily returned her gaze. Audacity indeed – she had meant for her to hear every word.

Etta stepped towards Miss Marley and her little band of female admirers, who started in a mix of horror, fear and glee. Had she not been having a huge internal crisis, Etta would have been angry as hell. As it was, she was backfooted and confused.

Etta cleared her throat. 'Miss Marley, is it? Nice to meet you.'

Miss Marley looked at Etta contemptuously. 'We met at the door. It seems it's true, then. Hetty really is unfit for company. Her brother was right.'

'My brother?'

She smiled around her at her acolytes. 'Oh, yes – we know all about poor Hetty Bainbridge. "Dicked in the nob", I believe he likes to say in his club. Well, how lovely that your mother is finally letting you out.'

Etta was absolutely stunned. Not even the biggest bitch in high school had been as much of a bitch as this Marley woman. There was nothing in Etta's armoury for this kind of attack. Then fate came to the rescue.

'Miss Bainbridge! I don't think you recognised me and Mama when we arrived earlier. It's so overwhelming, isn't it, one's first ball?'

Etta whirled round and was immensely relieved and grateful to see Miss Best, the young woman from the inn, standing behind her.

Miss Marley let out a cruel laugh. 'Oh, you have an ally, I see? Well, a friend in need is a friend indeed – and Miss Best, what age are you now? Twenty-five, is it? Truly a friend in need.'

Etta knew this would be a moment she'd be thinking about later, once she'd come up with a dozen cutting replies, but frustratingly she found herself grappling for a comeback.

Miss Best's bottom lip fluttered, but she had obviously dealt with Miss Marley in the past. She took Etta's arm and turned away. 'Come, Miss Bainbridge. Do tell me where you got your dress. The trimming on the flounce is quite lovely.'

As they walked away together, Etta heard the words 'Too bran-faced to wear white, of course . . .' recede into the background.

She pulled Miss Best into an alcove. 'Thanks for rescuing me – my god, what a bitch!'

Clarissa giggled, eyes wide. 'Henrietta! You mustn't!'

'Well, she is, though. And at my own party!'

Clarissa sighed. 'Yes, well. Miss Marley isn't the easiest person to deal with, I must admit. And she does lead the pack, rather.'

Etta paused, mentally taking stock of the encounter. 'And has Charlie really been going around telling anyone and everyone I'm off my trolley?'

Clarissa looked confused. 'Off your trolley?'

'Dicked in the nob,' Etta clarified.

'Oh.' Clarissa looked at Etta assessingly. 'Yes, I'm afraid he has been rather . . . active. But you don't appear insane to me. Perhaps . . . eccentric. But your family is thought of very highly, you know. Miss Marley may well come to regret her treatment of you.'

'You bloody bet she will.'

Etta was not a violent person, but right now she badly wanted to hit Miss Marley in her smug little face. She leaned into the wall and pressed her hot face to a cool marble column next to them. The room seemed to be rammed with posh people pretending they weren't there solely to see what Mad Hetty looked like and Etta's dress felt tight and sweaty. She could feel every whalebone in her stays pressing against her chest.

'Ugh, it's so hot in here. I need a sit down.'

Clarissa grasped Etta's arm. 'Not now! Lord Stanhope is approaching! He's a friend of your brother's, isn't he?'

Etta saw him immediately. He was like something hot off the pages of *Vogue* or *GQ*. His hair shone in the candlelight and his immaculate clothes only accentuated his masculinity. It was his expression, though, that was most arresting. Etta thought his eyes might bore into her very soul.

It was exciting and thrilling and slightly too intense. Did he not realise she was halfway through an existential crisis? She felt irrationally cross with him, then looked down. She coughed out a bubble of laughter as she saw his feet.

'Miss Bainbridge, I've been looking for—'

'Max, your *shoes*.'

'Lord Stanhope,' Max said. 'What of my shoes?'

'Your *shoes*. Look at them. They're like ballet slippers or something.'

Clarissa stepped into the breach, nudging her gently. 'Miss Bainbridge, Lord Stanhope's shoes are quite appropriate, I must tell you.'

Max looked at Clarissa quizzically and Etta remembered Miss Marley's earlier venomous attitude towards Miss Best. Well, nobody could accuse Clarissa of being anything but lovely.

'Lord Stanhope, delightful to see you,' Clarissa said demurely. 'Miss Bainbridge is still learning the ropes, as you see.'

Max raised an eyebrow. 'Oh, please don't worry. I'm sure she'll be fine under your tutelage. If,' he added, looking rather pointedly at Etta, 'you decide to take her on, Miss Best.'

Clarissa smiled and murmured some form of agreement, while Etta continued to take stock of his shoes and pleasingly well-cut britches.

Her gaze lifted to his face and she found he was smiling at her.

'Miss Bainbridge. Have you had your dance lessons yet? Will you dance with me?'

Etta pulled a face. 'Okay, then. I've been learning non-stop, so I might as well give it a bash.'

Poor Miss Best looked appalled at Etta's lack of graciousness, as Max guided Etta towards the dance floor.

She did well enough, she thought. Hetty would probably have floated like a fairy. But Etta barely bothered to mind her steps as she romped around the room. She knew people were probably staring, but at this point, what had she really got to lose? She may as well have fun, she thought, narrowly avoiding stepping on another set of toes as she rounded a corner.

Perhaps others were disapproving, but Max seemed more than happy to match her energy. Slowly, she felt everyone seem to perk up. At first she thought she was imagining it, but she saw young women smile a little wider, their partners swinging them slightly more enthusiastically.

The dance ended and Max led a somewhat out of breath Etta off the dance floor.

'Wow. That was way more fun than it looked in *Bridgerton*, and certainly more fun than that old dancing teacher at home made it look. More like a ceilidh dance,' she said.

Max manoeuvred her towards the edge of the room. 'Well, you certainly brightened things, I must admit.'

'Do you think? I thought they all had sticks up their arses, but I don't care. It was fun.'

'Etta! Miss Bainbridge!'

Etta smiled. 'Yes, I know, I know. No swearing. Sorry, I forgot.'

Max looked like he was wrangling with what to say next. 'Miss Bainbridge, we need to talk and we don't have long. You're not Hetty, are you? So what has happened to her?'

'If I tell you, you're going to think I really am Mad Hetty Bainbridge.'

He looked at her seriously. 'Try me. I promise to hear you out.'

Etta took a breath, considering this. The party all around her seemed to blur out of focus. *Oh well*, she thought. *In for a penny, in for a pound.*

'I think . . . I think Hetty and I swapped lives. One minute I was heading to work and it was 2023, and then these two old ladies appeared and told me I was about to swap with her and that . . . That it was about this bracelet. Then I was in a cellar strapped to a chair and it's 1817 and it's not a dream . . .' Etta's voice caught. 'I know I probably sound crazy, but it's not going away. It's been weeks and I haven't woken up.'

Max rubbed his temples. After a moment, he leaned forward, his face fixed, his voice low. 'Miss Bainbridge, there is clearly more to this story than can be told here. I am aware this is a scandalous proposal, but . . . do you think your maid could arrange a correspondence between us?'

'Bessie? Oh yes. I daresay she can have a word with her close friend James, the second footman. Can't I just write to you like a normal person, though?'

Max raised his eyebrows. 'I don't know what it's like where you're from, Miss Bainbridge, but a lady does not openly write to a gentleman. And your letters will most likely go to your brother to be franked before leaving the house.'

Etta sighed. 'Ugh, okay. I'll talk to Bessie. You're right. I hate using the bloody feathers to write though. My mother says I'm terrible at it. She won't let me write any invitations. So I hope you're all right with pencil.'

Their time was up. Miss Marley was approaching with the awful, arch Mr Smythe. He'd refused to so much as touch her hand when they'd been introduced at the door, so she'd taken special care to remember the toad's name.

'Why, Lord Stanhope, how lovely to see you. We were just remarking on your kindness to Miss Bainbridge,' said Miss Marley, who slowed her voice to a patronising crawl. 'How are you, Hetty? Enjoying your first dance?'

Max didn't react. 'Miss Bainbridge was just telling me about her interest in . . . Calligraphy.'

Etta knew she had a dangerous look on her face, but

before she could say anything they heard the odious Mr Smythe's smarmy, patronising tones. 'How delightful. You *can* read and write, then, Miss Bainbridge?'

'Oh yes,' said Etta. 'Can you?'

It seemed Mr Smythe wasn't accustomed to quick retorts. His face blank, he sputtered, struggling to know what to say.

Max cut in. 'As a matter of fact we used to call you Wobbly in school, didn't we, Smythe? Wobbly was never all that strong in Composition class. Or Comprehension, come to that.'

Smythe looked burningly angry. 'Oh, very amusing, Stanhope.'

Etta screwed up her face mock-thoughtfully. 'I think it's *Lord* Stanhope, isn't it?'

A burst of laughter surprised itself out of Max. He cleared his throat, signalling it was time for an entente.

'Miss Marley,' he addressed her graciously. 'I believe a dance is about to begin. Is there room for me on your dance card?'

He led Miss Marley to the dance floor, while Smythe pointedly strolled away from Etta, leaving her on her own. Etta didn't care. She watched Max make polite conversation with Miss Marley for a moment, who despite her acid tongue to her was certainly being pleasant enough to him, and then went off to find the food. Hopefully there'd be eclairs, because she could do with more than a little bit of comfort eating right now. Miss Marley might be more than a little tart, but – much like Lady Bainbridge's little lemon curd-filled pastries – she was also beautiful.

Chapter 21

2023

Hetty hadn't done as much theoretical physics as she would have liked yet, but at least her computer classes were progressing well. She'd started writing a daily diary on Substack and had even managed to open something called an Instagram account, thanks to Stella and her favourite classmate Elsie, a former photographer.

Hetty had never been able to get to grips with painting, despite it being de rigueur amongst all fashionable young ladies in 1817. Photography, however, was a different matter. All it had taken was a pointed comment from Elsie to Stella about getting some practice in 'out of this horrendous lighting with someone who doesn't need new knees' and here she was at London Zoo staring at a real-life tiger.

More unnervingly, it was staring right back.

Stella chuckled. 'You'd almost think you'd never seen a tiger in your life before, Hetty. Not even in a book.'

Hetty bit her lip. Oh, how little she knew of the truth. She tore her eyes away from the tiger and into the even more entrancing gaze of Stella, who was holding two sticks of—

'What . . . what's this?'

Stella's face twisted into utter disbelief, before she turned her head and took a huge bite out of one of the pink clouds next to her. 'Candy floss, silly.'

Hetty was still exploring the mysterious qualities of the candyfloss – what little there was left of it – when they reached the zebra enclosure.

'They're . . . stripey. Stripey horses? How completely bizarre.'

She'd given up hiding her astonishment now, and to her immense relief Stella had likewise seemingly given up on astonishment at Hetty's constant astonishment.

'You're hilarious, Hetty. It's like you're some posh old Tudor lady in the body of a cute brunette.'

'Tudor?! And . . . you think I'm cute?'

Stella laughed and nudged Hetty in the side. 'Obviously you're cute. Especially when you let me steal your candyfloss.'

Hetty grinned, feeling daylight flooding her as she handed over the rest of her bright pink miracle, and then started awkwardly as Stella linked their arms.

'What next?' she asked, her voice shaking slightly.

'Hmm. How do you feel about meerkats?'

'Good. Great. Wonderful. I feel just excellent about meerkats. Lead the way.'

'You don't know what a meerkat is, do you?'

'Not a clue.'

There was some invisible bond pulling them together, Hetty thought, and it seemed to pull tighter as the day went on. *Bessie wouldn't believe her eyes if she saw me now.* Oh, how she wished she could share these feelings with someone – and yet at the same time, they seemed too private, too precious to share with a single soul.

As a young girl, Hetty had never met handsome princes or dashing knights in her dreams. They had always been full of princesses instead. And even in the wildest ones, no warrior queen or ethereal angel had been quite so spectacular or blinding as Stella.

'Come on, we have to do this! I freaking love these!'

Stella was pulling her towards a board gaudily painted with cartoon animals – the faces had been cut out. Stella handed her phone to a confused-looking tourist. Hetty hesitated for a moment, but, though it was hard to explain, the pull of Stella's hand on her wrist wasn't just physical.

'Say cheese!' Stella called to Hetty.

'Cheese!'

They emerged from behind the cut-out and looked at their photos – Hetty as an elephant, Stella the giraffe – and electricity seemed to crackle between them. She'd never danced a waltz, never even attended a dance, but suddenly Hetty felt the desire to twirl and spin and dance until she was dizzy. The world seemed to shine around her in a new, vivid way which totally eclipsed the simple satisfaction she'd always found in her studies.

As they walked towards the lion enclosure – and before she even knew what she was doing – Hetty's hand brushed against Stella's.

Hetty pulled her hand back. 'Oh, I'm so sorry! I didn't mean—'

'To hold my hand?' Stella asked, taking Hetty's hand in hers. 'That's a shame, because I like it.'

Hetty stared at Stella and felt a sudden, intense urge to

kiss her, tingles running between their joined hands. She blinked it away.

'Is this a bit much for you, Hetty?' said Stella.

'Maybe a little. Only . . . only a very little, though.'

A crowd had appeared out of nowhere and they turned to see what was going on. To their surprise, a lioness had appeared at the window. Their hands gripped more tightly than ever.

The lioness watched them quizzically for a moment, before abruptly turning and calmly prowling over to her mate.

Hetty turned in delight, only to find Stella watching her. Stella reached over to push a loose strand of hair behind Hetty's ear, and Hetty found herself wishing she were a little braver – that she could embrace her inner lioness.

Chapter 22

1817

The morning after the ball was, according to Bessie, not to be spent doing anything other than resting after a long night of dancing. Lady Bainbridge took her own breakfast in bed, at about eleven o'clock.

Etta wasn't as exhausted as all that. Max's dance request had set the tone for the evening and she'd enjoyed several more dances until the waltzes started. She wasn't allowed to join in on account of not having been approved by someone or other at something called Almack's, which had been a blow, but overall she'd had a surprisingly successful evening, socially.

But the number one most surprising thing about her first ball had been the *smell*. The 1995 adaptation of *Pride and Prejudice* had absolutely not warned her about that aspect of things, with its rose-dotted intro sequences and woodland walks, but then again how could it? Things had started off relatively sweet-smelling, the ladies giving off a delightful odour of either rosewater or lavender and the gentlemen of sandalwood or mint. It didn't last long, though, as people started getting drunk and dancing more energetically. By the end of the evening, the whole place had begun to absolutely hum. There was only one flushing toilet in the vicinity, so rooms had been created for guests to relieve themselves in chamber pots. This was, apparently, the norm. Nobody blinked an eye.

Etta hadn't seen Max again after their dance, but her promise to explain things with a letter never really left her mind. And now she had an entire morning to write to him. The biggest question, of course, was what she dared put in writing in the first place. Then again she instinctively felt she could trust him. She sat at the writing desk in the family morning room at the back of the house, clutching a pencil, desperate to be interrupted.

The piano looked at her. She could almost feel its woody little eyes. It was so long since she'd played and the one at the Bainbridges' house was beautiful. When she played nowadays, it was at the old uprights found at various train stations. She'd lost her piano along with her family, her dog, their home and everything else when her father died. There was no room for a piano in the tiny studio flat she'd ended up in after uni, all alone and frantically job-hunting.

But once upon a time she'd hoped she might be on track for a career as a musician. As a teen she'd played at every school event she could, backing up the school choir and teaching younger students for extra cash. She once even optimistically applied for a place at the BRIT School, although the family finances would never have stretched far enough to relocate if she'd got in.

But she hadn't got in, and she'd focused on other things at school, keeping her playing for herself and Dad. She'd always sung for Dad, but then one day he wasn't there to listen – and after that it had all seemed so pointless.

Perhaps it was time to see if Hetty's fingers and voice were as strong and agile as Etta's had been. She took her paper and pencil along with her, placing them on the stiff padded leather piano stool next to her. She could compose the letter in her head as she played.

Etta picked up the easiest piece of music she could see and flexed her fingers. The piano keys were far softer than she was used to so the lack of strength in her fingers wasn't too much of a problem, and her new voice – thin from disuse – was going to need some work, but even so it was a rush to be playing again.

As she learned this new piece, she formulated her letter to Max one line at a time, pausing between pages to get her thoughts down as they came.

Max,
 I am not Hetty Bainbridge, as you've guessed. I am Etta Moore, and I was born in 1998. Hetty might be 21, but I'm actually 25.

Yes, that seemed like a good, strong opening. She took a moment to try some vocal exercises. Her lungs weren't even half as strong as her old ones. Hetty hadn't used them even a fraction as much as Etta had, and it wasn't as though Etta had been sociable.

I was on my way to work one day in 2023...
 (How to explain the Tube, Etta thought? Pointless.)
 ...when two old ladies approached me. They told me

I would be swapping lives with Hetty and put a bracelet on me. The next moment, I found myself looking out of Hetty's eyes, in Hetty's cellar, and you were there.

She'd been thinking carefully about this next part. Who in 1817 would possibly believe what 2023 was like? They barely had decent toilets here. The house in London was better than Bainbridges' country estate in that regard, but only just.

I daresay you'd like to know what the future is like, but I'm not sure you'd believe me if I told you. I myself can barely believe that I'm here and keep wondering when I'll wake up. They did say I could break the bracelet if I wanted to and Hetty and I would switch back, but I'm not sure I do yet TBH. to be honest.

Thinking of Max's broad shoulders, intelligent eyes and cynical smile didn't encourage Etta to think too much about waking up. Waking up would be far more attractive if she woke up next to him, she thought, as she practised her arpeggios.

Etta gave herself a shake. It had been too long since she'd slept with anyone, never mind a boyfriend – the last time had been with a one-night stand, and the time before that was with an over-earnest but short-lived friend-with-benefits called Ken. Sadly, much like his beige, more plasticky namesake, Ken hadn't exactly been blessed in the lower abdomen. Lord knows what kind of cobwebs Hetty would find if she decided to give Etta's ladyparts a test run. Yes, back to Hetty.

I think Hetty made this happen. She has left notebooks outlining various scientific methods and theories. But obviously it could be the old ladies, too – who knows what they have planned?

She was beginning to write like a proper Regency Miss. Oh well. Inevitable, really. She stopped to flex her fingers, then moved on to the next section of music. Her fingers would ache all afternoon if she continued like this.

What next? Max was an old friend of Hetty's, she thought. If she'd had any friends, they might have been wondering where she was right now. Max would no doubt be wondering the same of Hetty.

The old ladies told me it was a swap, so if they are to be believed then Hetty is now in 2023, in my body. Personally I lived alone and had few (she couldn't quite bring herself to write 'no') *friends or acquaintances, but the ladies told me they would look after her.*

I think I'm actually a distant descendant of the family in some way, so hopefully your kind gift of books will find their way to her – they will become extremely valuable, so hopefully they are looked after and passed down the generations. If not, I did have a small amount of money from the death of my father many years ago. So, overall, I believe Hetty to be safe and well. And perhaps, if she was as depressed – melancholy, I suppose you might say? Low? Anyway, if she was as sad as Bessie has insinuated, she will find modern medicine helps her quite a bit.

She'll have a lot to wrap her head around though, thought Etta. A lot.

If you have any questions, I'd be happy to answer them. I'm still working out what all the rules are – we didn't have so many in 2023. Plus now I think back, the old ladies mentioned I have to find a marquess and lord only knows where I'll find one of those.
 Yours
 Etta

There, that would do. The piece was played, and so too was her letter. Etta took the letter over to the desk and folded it up. There was some sealing wax and a stamp, but she had no idea how to light the wax candle thingy, so she decided to leave it at that. Anyone reading it would think she was mad, of course. But then, didn't everyone already think that?

Chapter 23

2023

It felt like Hetty had been talking about Stella for the whole week leading up to her trip to the zoo, but now she was too quiet as they waddled down the street together towards a famous local bakery. Hetty thought her aunts had sensed something and now they'd decided to take her out for something they called 'brunch'. A 'nice little trip', they'd called it.

Aggie and Hetty took a corner seat as Jemima brought a mixed selection of gigantic pastries to the table, closely followed by a waitress with a tray of tea. Hetty wasn't sure that she'd ever had quite as much tea as she'd had over the last few weeks.

They waited patiently. Not expectantly – Hetty knew the tension was all hers.

'I don't want to ruin it for you, dear, but I think you'll probably find it easier to just get it over and done with. It's almost certainly not as bad as you think it is, you know,' said Aggie, smiling and cutting off a small piece of apple pastry and lifting it to her mouth.

'We know it's not,' said Jemima, spraying crumbs across the table through a mouthful of pain au chocolat. 'You're forgetting we've read your diary.'

Aggie winced. 'Yes, and I'm terribly sorry about that, dear. But until we found your diaries and the bracelet under that floorboard, you know, we hadn't the slightest idea about any of this.'

Hetty swallowed, feeling a huge weight on her shoulders. Of course. Her notebooks. In her old life, writing things down had become such an important part of her life. These notebooks had become like her closest friend – her only friend. She had written tirelessly on her scientific theories and studies, of course, but she'd also confessed her deepest thoughts and feelings, too. About the darkness that engulfed her. About the other, more confusing feelings, the dreams she couldn't possibly admit to.

She should have got rid of those particular notebooks before she'd attempted The Switch. She'd never imagined others reading them.

Her cheeks felt hot, her throat tight. 'So you know? About my preference for . . .?'

The aunts nodded.

'I realise such things are completely unacceptable. My nanny always said—'

Aggie looked very stern. 'Your nanny was wrong, Henrietta. Even in your time, women lived together – loved together.'

Hetty wasn't convinced. 'Yes, I know, but that was platonic love. I mean, I do realise there were two ladies in the village who shared rooms, but they were very good friends. And the two of you—'

Aggie laughed. 'Are sisters, Hetty!'

'We're not spinsters, dear,' said Jemima. 'Well, Aggie is,' she added, ignoring Aggie's pointed cough, 'but I'm a widow, you know. Who knows about the ladies in your village, but women can marry nowadays.'

'One another?' asked Hetty incredulously. She took a sip of tea, unsure what to say. She was hesitant to believe that what she suspected was coming, was coming. But come it did.

'My wife Kate died just last year,' Jemima said. 'We were partners for forty years. Married for seven, from the month they made it legal.'

'Your wife,' Hetty asked, astonished.

'Yes, dear. The love of my life, really. It's still so hard to believe she's gone. Thank goodness I have Aggie, or I don't know where I'd be.'

Aggie handed her sister a tissue, squeezing her hand.

'Now then, Jemima, you're doing very well, you know. Kate would be so proud to see you now, and I do hope you'll continue living with me.'

Hetty felt a sob rise in her throat and swallowed it back down, quite overcome at how close the sisters were.

'I'm so, so sorry for your loss, Jemima. It sounds most dreadful.'

Aggie took one look at her and passed the packet of tissues over.

Hetty wiped the tears she found running down her cheeks. 'So you're saying it's fine? To feel this way about women?'

Her aunts spoke as one, still holding hands. 'Yes, dear.'

Jemima smiled through her tears and then signalled something to the woman behind the counter. A waitress carefully brought over a slice of cake. It had seven layers,

Hetty noticed – each a different shade of the rainbow. The smiling waitress set it down and used a small device to light some sparklers on the top.

'I had them do it just for you,' said Jemima, smiling through her tears.

Hetty gazed at the swirl of chocolate letters on the plate. 'Congratulations on coming out,' she read in a whisper, then looked up at their smiling faces. Acceptance shone from eyes where she'd expected to see judgement, and it felt as though her heart beat as loudly as the cake in front of her. There was nothing wrong with her – there never had been. Hetty's spirit soared as she felt unseen shackles loosen from her body. There was nothing wrong, nothing unnatural about her feelings. She was free.

Aggie grinned. 'Welcome to 2023, dear.'

'Now,' added Jemima cheekily, grabbing her hand across the table and giving it a squeeze. 'Time to address that "first kiss" entry on your list?'

Chapter 24

1817

Etta didn't have to wait long for Max's response, but it didn't come in the form of a letter. It was an invitation: she was finally going to Gunter's for long-promised ices.

She felt a flutter of anticipation as she entered the parlour, Bessie tagging along for respectability's sake. This was exacerbated by the sight of Miss Marley at an adjacent table. Etta had seen more of the delightful Maria Marley – more often than not with the odious Smythe – at the few other parties she had been to so far. Miss Marley might not be the daughter of a lord or lady, but her beauty seemingly won her entry to every house and hall in London.

Etta suspected that Miss Marley's prime goal, besides netting herself a rich husband, was to make her dread their every meeting. Now, in Gunter's, Etta saw Miss Marley's eyes gleaming. There were seats free at her table, so there would be no escape today. Except apparently there would, as she saw Max stand up at the far end of the room. Somehow, he had managed to remain unseen by the sharp-eyed Miss

Marley, his back to the door and his face in a newspaper. He gestured for her to join him as he folded it up.

Etta felt immense triumph as she and Bessie swished past, offering up an arch smile and a small bow as she passed, murmuring, 'Miss Marley. Don't let me disturb you.'

'So, where's Hetty?' Max asked in a low voice, as he watched Etta eye up a strawberry ice suspiciously after insisting on a spoon for Bessie.

'I told you. She's in 2023. Is this just strawberry syrup poured over ice? Like, a freaking slushie?'

'I'm not sure what that is, but probably, yes. So her mind is in your body and your mind is in hers?'

Etta took a tentative bite of the strawberry ice. It was okay, though she couldn't be entirely certain of the provenance of the ice.

She shrugged. 'I suppose so. I mean, there's really no way of finding out. I'm trying very hard not to think about it.'

'So when is Hetty coming back?'

She let the ice melt in her mouth for a second, then looked him straight in the eye. A shiver ran down her spine and she nearly lost her words as she saw the earnest look in his deep brown eyes. A girl could drown in those eyes.

'When . . . when is *she* coming back? If she breaks her bracelet, I suppose, or I do,' Etta said. 'The old ladies seemed to imply it was forever if neither of us broke the bracelet.'

Etta saw him looking at her wrists and touched the bracelet instinctively.

'And you're really from the year two thousand and twenty-three?'

'Yes, 2023. It probably sounds weird to you, but it's honestly not. Not when you come from there.'

At this, Max cracked the widest smile she'd seen from him. His face was completely transformed. It felt like the sun coming out from behind the clouds and Etta found she couldn't help smiling back.

'So . . . what's it like in 2023?'

'Well, we had better ice cream for a start. This is fine, but I'd die for a tub of Baci's gelato right now.'

Max started to laugh at her expression – the most delicious sound in the world – then she heard Clarissa Best's gentle voice next to her.

'Lord Stanhope, Miss Bainbridge, how lovely to see you. Might we sit next to you?'

Despite liking Clarissa very much, Etta felt a flash of frustration at the interruption, but Max was far too polite not to welcome Clarissa and her mother to the table.

If Etta had learned anything, it was that privacy was a rare commodity in 1817.

Since they hadn't been able to really get into much detail at Gunter's, Etta soon received a note from Max via Bessie. Bessie handed the note over with a warning as she started lacing Etta's stays. 'He's courting you, miss.'

'Etta, Bessie. Call me Etta. God, everyone is so strange about names here. You're literally putting a bra on me.'

'No, miss,' Bessie replied. She was incredibly stubborn over this point. She hadn't asked any more questions about the sudden transformation of quiet Hetty into outrageous Etta, and she certainly wasn't about to drop formalities.

Etta pulled a face at Bessie in the mirror as she broke the seal on the note. Max's handwriting was beautiful. Bold, thick strokes in dark ink. She wouldn't mind a few bold thick strokes herself, she thought wryly, then shook the mental image of Max's hands on her body from her head.

Bessie tutted and told her off for ruining her hairdo and Etta quickly apologised before going back to her letter.

Walk with me and Charlie in the park this morning, he'd written. *Don't forget to bring your maid this time.*

Brief, but to the point. She was grateful. After all, it was a relief she hadn't completely scared him off by telling him about The Switch – she had been worrying that she should have drip-fed the truth more carefully, if at all. But would she be able to get him on his own, with her ridiculous brother present?

In the end, it turned out Max knew exactly what he was doing. Donned in his very best finery, Charlie was very quickly meeting and greeting what seemed like every gentleman in the park. Left to themselves at last, they had plenty of time to have a long-overdue chat. As Charlie went into great detail about the embroidery on his new waistcoat with one of his equally vacuous chums, they sat on a nearby bench.

'I suppose you're struggling to believe me, aren't you?' Etta asked. 'About me coming from the future.'

But if she was expecting pity for Mad Hetty Bainbridge, she saw only curiosity.

'Actually, I do believe you,' he replied in a thoughtful tone. 'You see, I was looking up the latest exploits of one Mrs Mary Shelley.'

'Oh! You mean the author of *Frankenstein*?'

'Yes. You mentioned that, I believe, when we first met,' Max said. 'Did you know that *Frankenstein, or The Modern*

Prometheus is still at the printers? There is no possibility you could have known about that book. It seems the publisher and Mrs Shelley hadn't even considered "Frankenstein" as a potential title – although the main character does have that name, I believe. Along with everything else . . . Well, for some reason, I do believe you.'

Etta exclaimed. 'Good thing I mentioned it, then, really, isn't it?'

Max ran his fingers through his perfectly dishevelled hair. 'Well, I must admit it does move the plot along somewhat.'

Etta had rarely felt so relieved: He believed her. The secret wasn't just between her and Bessie any more.

'So, what is it like, in the future? How did you spend your time? Are there friends and family who'll be missing you?'

'Nobody special. I don't know whether to be upset or relieved, to be honest. I only had my job and my tiny flat.'

Max looked confused. 'Your job?'

Of course. Hetty had had no job, like the vast majority of Regency poshos. 'Yes, my work. I had to earn my rent somehow.'

He looked more intrigued than ever. 'But what kind of work did you do? You're clearly not a labourer.'

'How do you know that?'

He paused. 'Well . . . I suppose . . .'

She laughed. 'No, I'm not a labourer. But I could be. In 2023, women had equal rights. We did any job we liked. It wasn't perfect, and we weren't paid as much as men, but at least I was protected by the Equality Act.' Etta slumped against the bench. 'God, it feels weird talking about the future in the past tense.'

Max sat back with her, and their shoulders brushed against each other.

'I like it,' he said, shifting slightly along the bench so that there was a gap between them. 'Equals. It makes more sense.'

She nearly asked him what he did, but then remembered all those Georgette Heyer novels. 'I suppose you're dreadfully important and have a whole estate to run and a seat in the House of Lords and stuff.'

He laughed. 'Oh no. That would be my father, although I do have my own investments to manage, of course.' He paused. 'I suppose . . . Women in this age cannot hold bank accounts, can they? Or even property, really. It never occurred to me how odd that is.'

He looked dismayed and Etta liked him all the more for it. She'd been a good girl and read her feminist history as a teenager, paid attention during her History A-levels, but Max was only just considering the unfairness of it and had no idea of the relatively happy ending she'd lived in.

So she filled him in on Queen Victoria, and Emmeline Pankhurst, and the AIDS crisis, and Section 28. He sat gripped as she described the London she knew, with the Tube and buses and mobile phones, until Charlie's waistcoat had been shown to half of London.

'We'd better go,' said Etta, rising. She automatically took his hand as he stood up.

Of all the things he'd experienced that morning, this one action seemed to surprise Max more than any other; he stared down at their hands, then back at her. Etta herself was equally surprised at herself as she felt the warmth of his hand against hers, even through two layers of gloves.

She felt her face burn red for some reason, and his eyes seemed to darken as he looked at her, suddenly intense with focus.

'Sorry,' she rushed, starting to take her hand away, but Max stopped her.

'No.' He put her hand on his arm and led her back towards Charlie. 'Never apologise for taking my hand.'

Chapter 25

1817

The parties ramped up as the Season continued. If Etta was lucky, she'd see Clarissa Best who tolerated her forthright statements and continued to very kindly and patiently fill her in on etiquette.

At first, Etta had been quite confused as to why Clarissa hadn't been snapped up. Twenty-five was quite old to remain unmarried in 1817. However, her confusion was soon clarified. Lady Best was a crazy bitch. No, calling her crazy was offensive to people with actual mental illnesses, Etta decided. Lady Best was a termagant. Etta met many other older ladies with an inflated sense of self-worth, but Lady Best was deemed unacceptable and even vulgar. There was absolutely nothing soft about her underbelly, either: no vulnerability or hidden maternal instinct. If social climbing could be considered a sport, then Lady Best was the national bouldering champion.

Lady Bainbridge seemed laid back enough to countenance Lady Best with her usual smiling tolerance, but most of society found Lady Best to be the outside of enough. Lord Best must have powerful connections, Etta realised, for such a very awful woman to be invited to so very many parties. She soon discovered that Clarissa's papa was bezzie mates with the dissolute Prince Regent, so Etta didn't blame him for being conspicuously absent – in fact, she hadn't seen him even once. But then again she had yet to meet the outrageous Prinny, who was apparently down in Brighton overseeing the building of the Pavilion.

And so, lacking the ability to chastise her husband, Lady Best had turned her critical eye on Clarissa.

Clarissa sighed and wilted under her mama's scrutiny, but would say nothing other than that her mother only wanted the best for her. It seemed none of the earls, baronets, etc. would do – only a marquess or duke, or a future marquess or duke, was good enough for the daughter of Lady Best. So Clarissa remained unwed.

Etta wasn't on close terms with anyone other than Clarissa, but she soon found out the full story behind the *Ton*'s disgust of Lady Best's high-handed ways. It seemed being Maria Marley's enemy could yield as much information as it could being her closest friend.

'You might want to reconsider your friends,' whispered Miss Marley, as their mothers gossiped in the park one morning. 'Everyone knows Lady Best was an . . . *actress* . . . before she met Lord Best and got With Child. She is said to have *blackmailed* him.'

She sounded absolutely scandalised. Perhaps she even was.

'Well, at least she's done something *exciting* with her life,' Etta said. 'Acting is quite a skill. You can't even act like a pleasant person.'

Their mothers had finished their conversation, so Miss Marley was forced to depart before she could give any kind of reply. Etta smiled as she clocked her wide eyes. She would bet any number of first edition Jane Austen novels that Maria was seething.

She turned to her mother, to whom she was feeling closer every day.

'Mother . . . Mama. Miss Marley doesn't seem to like me very much, or Miss Best,' Etta began.

'Well, dear, there's not much to like about Lady Best, that's for sure. But I really can't be sure why she would have taken a dislike to *you*.'

Etta paused. They hadn't discussed Hetty's childhood at all, but this felt like the right time. 'Mama, the other women my age—'

'Hardly women, Henrietta. Girls, really.'

'Yes, well – they seem to think I'm . . . mad.'

Lady Bainbridge looked over at Etta, eyes suddenly sharp. 'But you're not, are you?'

'No, of course not. But before . . . Well, I suppose I can understand why people might think I was.'

Her mother seemed to relax at this. 'You've finally grown up, Henrietta, and come out of your shell. It was bound to happen eventually.'

Of course. Denial was not just a river in Egypt, as Etta well knew from these past few weeks. But there was one question she was determined to ask.

'But they said – they're all saying Charlie's the one who's been spreading it around. Why would he do that?'

Lady Bainbridge looked steadily ahead. 'That's a question I shall be asking him directly. Now look at these roses – aren't they beautiful?'

*

Etta spent a while considering how she was going to punish Charlie. In the end she decided to confront him head-on. Hetty had not deserved this, and Etta would certainly not tolerate it.

It took a random family dinner at the house of one of her mother's many interchangeable distant relatives for Etta to decide the exact form of her revenge.

They were at the modest (huge, by Etta's standards) home of someone who was apparently her Great Aunt Maude, and for once Charlie had been dragged along. It was a golden – and rare – opportunity to pin down her elusive brother, who seemed to spend the vast majority of his time out of the house.

It wasn't long until Etta discovered why he'd deigned to join them on this occasion. Great Aunt Maude was, despite her dusty and tattered house, 'rolling in lard' according to Charlie.

'Got to do the pretty every now and then so she doesn't forget us,' he said.

It was a small gathering – just her mother, her aunt and Charlie – and Etta, who was seated next to Charlie, soon learned that Great Aunt Maude was almost completely deaf, so Etta finally had her brother to herself.

As her mother made painstakingly slow conversation with Great Aunt Maude, who seemed far more interested in her meal than her companions, Etta turned to her brother and gave him a wide, dangerous smile.

'So good to be able to spend some time with you at last, you absolute arsehole.'

'Oh, of course – hang on, *what* did you say?'

'I called you an arsehole, Charlie. For that is what you are. A pestilent boil on the arse of my existence.'

'Now hold on here—'

'You've gone and run your mouth off about me being utterly mad to the whole of London, haven't you? You've had a huge amount of fun telling everyone about your bonkers sister, I dare say?'

'Hetty . . .'

'No, don't you Hetty me. I'm Etta to my friends and *Henrietta* to you. You are quite literally the worst brother anyone has ever had.'

'Well, I'm sure it's not all that—'

Etta's eyes flashed with anger. 'Don't you *dare* downplay this. I can't meet a single person without them looking at me like a turd on their shoe. How did you think this would play out for me? Did you even think about me *at all*?'

Charlie looked like a deer in headlights. 'You must know, old girl, we'd quite given up on you.'

Etta slammed her fork down next to her plate. 'Oh, perhaps *you* had. But our mother clearly never did. I bet it gave you loads to talk about in your little boys' club, didn't it? I imagine you needed it, because your head is hardly rattling about with conversation, is it, Charlie?'

She gazed at Charlie, feeling triumphant. She'd been looking forward to reaming him out for weeks, and she wasn't about to miss this opportunity.

'Well? Got nothing to say to me now, have you? How are you going to make it up to me, if that's even possible?'

That was when she realised the table had been silent for quite some time, as it was broken by a sudden cackle.

'That's you told, isn't it, boy?' said Great Aunt Maude, who didn't seem quite as deaf as advertised.

Etta looked around the table. Great Aunt Maude was

gazing at Etta with new respect, as though seeing her for the first time, while her mother, calm as always, showed no surprise but an air of smug pleasure.

She loved them, she realised. Her family. They were quite wonderful, even Charlie. She had been totally alone, stuck eating TV dinners in her tiny flat and now here she was arguing with a brother. An idiot brother, but a brother nonetheless.

Charlie coughed, and looked around as everyone turned their eyes to him expectantly. He was pink-cheeked and speechless.

Lady Bainbridge was the next to speak. 'Your sister is quite right, Charles. I believe she is due quite the apology for your despicable behaviour, which we shall be discussing in the library first thing tomorrow morning.'

Etta couldn't help but chuckle quietly as Charlie squirmed uncomfortably. It wasn't quite revenge, but it was a start.

Etta took one long, last look at her brother. 'You're going to make this up to me, Charlie Bainbridge, because hardly anyone will speak to me. You have turned me into a pariah. It is not fair of you, and you must know it.'

Charlie was now horribly pale and Etta was surprised to see his eyes shining slightly as he blinked at her. 'Hetty – Henrietta – I . . . I truly am sorry,' he said sincerely.

'Then show me, Charlie.'

Etta took a leaf from her aunt's book and returned to her pudding, which really was very good. As she tucked in, she felt her mother's hand search for hers under the table and gave it a quick squeeze.

'I think I shall leave it all to Henrietta, you know.'

They all turned to look at Great Aunt Maude, but she was deep into her gooseberry tart.

Chapter 26

1817

Charlie set to work on Etta's reputation immediately. Thankfully, it seemed her brother was popular for his generally good-natured personality and generosity – a good word from him went a long way with Society. She imagined it also helped that he was okay-looking, titled and unmarried. Most peers could have found plenty of company on the basis of their title and wealth alone, but Charlie had more than that: annoyingly, given how cross she was with him, he had charm. It helped that he'd started using the right name: no more Hetty. She was all Etta now.

Suddenly, quite pleasant young ladies and their less sour-faced mamas began to approach her and Lady Bainbridge on their morning walks. Invitations began to flood in and her dance card filled up faster at every dance and ball.

Etta was so busy she could barely keep track of who she saw or which party she was at, so it was a welcome sight one evening when she and Charlie saw Max from the family's box at the opera. He joined them during the first interval after he heard Charlie's hilarious impression of the lead soloist. They both convulsed in laughter as her brother's falsetto drew attention, good and bad, from every box in the theatre and much of the stalls.

She and Charlie had been making up their own lyrics to the tunes they'd heard, and were probably laughing in a manner inappropriate for an opera house.

'Charlie, I didn't expect to see you here,' said Max, 'and I certainly didn't expect to hear your dulcet tones murdering Mozart.'

Charlie laughed and waved him into their box. 'Oh, Etta, it's Lord Stanhope, come to ruin our fun.'

Max grinned at his friend. 'Not at all. I can't promise to match your impression of La Bellina, though. That truly was impressive, but I don't expect your mother will be particularly happy with you making pictures of yourselves at the opera. And poor Miss Best here must be wondering what she's got herself involved with.'

Etta had invited Clarissa Best to join them for the evening, thinking it would be a nice way to thank her for being, well, her oldest Society friend. But though Clarissa blushed and demurred, she wasn't fooling anyone.

'Oh, Clarissa, I really am sorry,' said Etta. 'Your mother will be so angry.'

'Please, Etta, don't be worried,' she said gamely, though her smile didn't meet her eyes. 'It's truly the most fun I've had in months.'

Etta vowed to be better behaved as Max took the seat next to her, his strong hands resting briefly on the back of her chair as he sat. No gloves today, she thought. She was acutely aware of his closeness as the performance resumed and suddenly felt lost for words. Max, too, was quiet. As the next aria began, she noticed him almost unconsciously lean slightly towards her in his seat.

She felt his gaze on her as she concentrated on the singers, and felt an urge to finish what she'd started in the park; to really, truly hold his hand. She didn't quite know how she found the courage to do it, but looking straight ahead so as not to attract attention – she nearly huffed with laughter at the ludicrousness of it – she removed one opera glove, finger by finger. Then Etta took a deep breath and tentatively moved her fingers ever so slightly, gently brushing his bare knuckles. The electricity jolted through them again; Etta could hear her heartbeat pulse in her ears. He froze for just a moment at her touch, and for that second she thought she'd lost it all, but then he started to trace the lines of her fingers with his.

Etta had never wanted to kiss a man as badly as she wanted to kiss Max in that moment, and now she thought perhaps he wanted to kiss her back. It was thrilling.

Neither of them knew how long they had been sitting there, electricity pulsing through their fingers, when the music ended. Before Etta had even realised the audience had stopped applauding, everyone was getting up and a good-humoured Charlie was sorting out their transport options. She hurriedly dragged on her abandoned glove, immediately missing Max's touch.

'Etta, I'm going to head out with Royston, but I'll escort you and Miss Best home before I come back out. Stanhope, you'll join us in the Goose and Swan, won't you?'

'Not tonight, Charlie. I've got a meeting with my solicitor tomorrow morning. Why don't I escort your sister and Miss Best home?'

'I say, that's terribly generous. You don't mind, do you, Hetty? Etta, I mean.'

Etta looked over at Max, a small smile playing on her face, and agreed to the plan. The short carriage ride was quiet at first, until they'd dropped off Miss Best. Max handed her down from the carriage and to her door, then returned to the carriage just as Etta's exhausted friend realised she was leaving them alone.

They both knew he should have seated himself opposite Etta, but she could see the exact moment he gave in to temptation and went to sit next to her instead. The carriage jolted as it started moving, and the sudden movement made him sit nearly on top of her. She put her hands up to steady him as he flopped inelegantly onto the seat, and they grasped one another.

'I'm so sorry,' he said, but couldn't seem to bring himself to move. Her hands lay still in his, and he pulled them to his lap unconsciously.

Etta bit her lip. She racked her brains, trying to think of something to say, but ended up staring into his eyes. It felt as though they were drawn together with every movement of the carriage; his face was now only inches from hers.

She knew a perfect Society Miss would pull away, but Etta had no such scruples. She bridged the distance between them suddenly, almost impulsively, and kissed him.

Every nerve ending lit up as Etta went straight for a deep, open-mouthed kiss, running her hands under Max's jacket and across his hard, warm chest.

It was clear Max was stunned by Etta's forwardness. He withdrew, hands still around her waist where he had unconsciously pulled her to him.

'So, in 2023 it will be quite ordinary for young women to kiss men in carriages, I daresay?'

Etta smiled. 'Not carriages, but apart from that you've got it spot on.'

'Remind me to ask you where people kiss in the future, if not carriages.'

'Hmm. Maybe we could try a few different places to kiss in 1817, just so I can remind myself.'

This time it was he who kissed her and Etta began to lift her skirts to straddle his lap.

The movement seemed to shock him awake. 'Hang on, Etta, Miss Bainbridge,' he said rather breathlessly. 'This isn't right. We'll be at your house any moment.'

Etta sighed and sank back into her seat. He was correct – the carriage stopped outside her house within seconds, just as he seemed to make the terrible realisation that he was in no fit state to see her to her door.

Etta looked at his lap and grinned. She leaned over for one last kiss and decided to go hell for leather. Her hand brushed his groin as she went to readjust her crumpled skirts.

'Your groom can see me to my door. Let's finish this another time.'

Etta took one last look at him, delightfully ruffled and disconcerted in his carriage; Max was both speechless and very obviously turned on. She beamed as a footman led her up the steps to her house. Hopefully that would give him something to think about for a while. She knew she'd be able to think of little else.

Chapter 27

1817

Unfortunately Etta didn't see Max again until she was at the latest fashionable exhibition at the British Museum – and when she did, as much as she'd been replaying their kiss every spare moment ever since she left him reeling in his carriage, she was hardly in the mood for difficult discussions. She was convulsed in laughter over what was possibly the most bizarrely formed tiger she'd ever seen when she heard what was unmistakably Miss Marley's pointed cough, only feet behind her.

'Lord Stanhope, while I'm grateful for your escort, I fear not everyone is as appreciative of these marvels as we.'

Etta ignored the outraged Miss Marley and her obligatory tittering hanger-on, not even minding that they'd somehow snagged him as an escort – primarily because this tiger was almost too good to be true.

'Max,' she gasped, 'is that . . .? What on earth have they done to that tiger?'

Miss Marley bristled beside him. 'Miss Bainbridge. Of course. Well, as I'm sure you know, this exhibition is considered the best in the world. Although I imagine many people might struggle to understand the majesty and wonder of these awe-inspiring beasts.'

If Miss Marley was trying to have a dig, it was wide of the mark.

'But look – look! Its face!' Etta was clutching her stomach in laughter.

'I fail to see the humour, Miss Bainbridge.'

'Look, though! Max – ugh, Lord Stanhope, whatever – look, one eye's looking at you and one's looking at Mama, over there by the window. And why—' Etta paused, gasping for breath, 'why is its tongue hanging out?'

Miss Marley looked ready to explode with irritation, but Etta was too far gone to gather herself. She'd also just spotted the tiger's tiny, splayed toes, which didn't help things.

'Miss Bainbridge, control yourself! Who are you to say you know the slightest thing about tigers?'

'Well, clearly I know more than the absolute moron who stuffed this poor thing. Look how fat its tail is! Like a huge sausage . . . Oh my god, I can't bear it. It's too much.'

Etta turned her back to the tiger, mopping her eyes.

'Miss Bainbridge, you should know that my brother has worked tirelessly with the museum to curate this exhibition,' said Miss Marley icily.

Etta snorted. 'He must be very disappointed, then.'

'I didn't realise you were a renowned tiger expert, Hetty. Maybe that's what you've been spending all that time in the country getting up to. Learning about tigers, and not being a lunatic and an embarrassment to your family. How wrong we were to assume you were locked in an attic wailing like a caged animal!'

Wiping her eyes, Etta couldn't miss Max's sharp intake of breath. He wasn't the only one. Miss Marley's pale companion was also clearly appalled, but was the first to break the icy silence.

'Maria, let us look at the next exhibit. Leave Miss Bainbridge to admire the tiger.' And before either of them could say or do anything, she whisked Miss Marley away.

Etta let out a strangled choke from behind her handkerchief and Max automatically stepped towards her.

'Miss Bainbridge, are you well? I'm sure Miss Marley didn't mean to—'

'Oh, I'm sure she did. I'd love to say I didn't think she had it in her. But tell me, is that tiger truly as ludicrous as it was the first time I looked at it?'

'You're not upset?'

Etta let down her hanky, her wet eyes were accompanied by a wry smile.

'Oh, upset at that horrid little cow? I don't care for her opinion. Come on, let's take a closer look at this – this tiger.'

Max looked puzzled, but his mouth flexed into a crooked smile as he looked at it again. 'Yes. I can't say I've seen one in the flesh, but I must say it's not quite like the illustrations in my library.'

'Oh, you've not seen one?'

He paused. 'And you have?'

'Henrietta?' Etta's mother's voice rang out softly from behind them. She must have heard them talking. 'How could you have seen one?'

Etta was lost for words. She stared helplessly at her mother and then back at Max. He finally took pity on her.

'Illustrations, probably. In your family's library.'

Etta felt a wave of relief. 'Yes. Yes! Illustrations. Just like you. Because how could anyone like me have seen a tiger? I'd have to have been to a zoo, and I've only just got to London, right?'

Max's mouth quirked. 'Illustrations, Etta. The tiger at the Tower of London's Menagerie died some years ago and was the only one in the country. You're looking at him.'

'This . . .?'

'The very same. Although I can't say I'm convinced that both of his ears were originally on that one side of his head. Most strange.'

He smiled at her stunned face, then turned and greeted Lady Bainbridge politely.

'I do apologise, Lady Bainbridge, but I see Miss Marley has moved on. Since I agreed to escort her, I will go and join her and her companion – but I'm sure we will see one another again soon.'

'I do hope so, Maximillian. You are always welcome at family dinners, you know,' said Lady Bainbridge, smiling kindly.

And just like that, smiling charmingly back at them, he followed the odious Miss Marley and her cousin towards the antiquities section. And Etta was left standing with her mother, remembering when that delicious smile had been pressed against her lips.

'He's had to give up his rooms, you know, and move back in with his old man,' said Charlie over breakfast, reading Etta's mind. 'Stanhope, I mean. Making him escort the likes of Maria Marley around town, too. I imagine the old tartar is worried about him getting leg-shackled to the likes of you.' Charlie had eyed her nervously, seeming to weigh his next words unusually carefully. 'Been mighty close with old Maximillian lately, haven't you, sis? Been hearing whispers that you're spending rather more time together than is proper, I understand?'

'I think you'll find you didn't hear anything, brother dearest,' said Etta nonchalantly.

Charlie looked as though he was taking the measure of her. 'Don't be concerned with what I heard. Just make sure Mama doesn't hear, that's all.'

She'd punched him on the arm and joined Clarissa for the morning.

As she followed Clarissa through the shopping thoroughfare, she couldn't stop thinking about Max. It was hard to know where they stood with each other. She'd kissed Max's face off in that carriage and here he was acting like it never happened. Mind you, she'd not exactly been all over him at the museum either, and it wasn't as though he could just ask for her phone number so he could WhatsApp her. Romantic liaisons in 1817 were even more difficult to navigate than Tinder.

She needed to look interested, but not desperate. She trailed alongside Clarissa, tuning in and out to her constant stream of chatter, as she kept coming back to the question of how to engage Max again.

'And of course, I can always embellish it with a monogram. That'll make it a much nicer gift – it'll take longer, but I could give it to her for Christmas, perhaps,' Clarissa said.

She appeared to be waiting for Etta's agreement. Listening to Clarissa tended to be a good idea – her kind and forgiving friend was always full of sage advice. If only Etta could bring herself to concentrate this morning.

'A monogram? You mean, get her initials sewn on?'

'Yes, Etta! Why, what else? But I shan't *get them sewn on*. I will sew them on myself. It will make it more meaningful.'

Clarissa was holding a beautiful lace handkerchief. Sewing delicate, regulated needlepoint samplers wasn't Etta's strong point – a fact which continually seemed to disappoint her very forgiving mother. Etta still missed her Etsy store, for which she embroidered colourful and quirky woodland creatures. She thought she'd been very subtle in incorporating the odd badger into her neat floral whitework, but sadly her mother spotted them immediately every time. The worst thing was, her mother didn't even make her remove them and start again. She just sort of smiled sadly, patted Etta's shoulder and said, 'So amusing, dear, but perhaps not one to show to visitors' in a slightly deflated manner.

Etta had, however, caught Charlie eyeing up her work when he thought nobody else was watching. She was quite certain she'd caught him chuckling over it and liked him all the better for it.

Clarissa had moved on to a new pile of hankies, rubbing the fine fabric between her fingers thoughtfully. Etta hadn't really thought about Christmas yet, but she supposed, given she had no plans to go anywhere anytime soon, it made sense to start thinking about presents.

'Clarissa, about Christmas. How many people do you give presents to?' she asked.

'Oh, my mother and father of course. Then my younger sisters, and I always send something to my uncle, who lives alone.'

'So it's okay, then, to send presents to men?'

'Oh . . . Oh-kay?'

'Fine, I mean. All right. Is it all right to send presents to male friends?'

Clarissa gasped. 'You mean, to send a gift to a man to whom one is not related?'

She sounded almost like her mother, Etta thought, and bit back a smile.

'I'm assuming not, then.'

'Absolutely not, Etta! Goodness, no. Surely you must know that?'

'Oh, yes, I'm sorry, of course. I was quite forgetting myself. So, do you always sew initials?'

Clarissa blinked, still looking slightly shaken. 'No, not I. I like to add a few flowers in satin stitch.'

'What about woodland creatures?'

'Goodness, that would be quite . . . unique.'

Etta sighed, knowing this was Clarissa Code for unacceptable. 'Yes, I suppose so. Where do you buy your embroidery threads? I've been using my mother's. I really should have some of my own.'

Back on safer ground, Clarissa recommended a shop around the corner and they set off, having both purchased handkerchiefs to monogram.

'Is there anything else you might monogram? I need to be thinking about Christmas, too, and I don't suppose I can buy everyone hankies.'

'Oh yes. I like to embroider my uncle a pair of slippers every other year.'

'But how do you know his size?'

'I don't. Gosh, I hadn't thought about that. For all I know, he might have a pile of them somewhere.'

They both giggled at the thought. Etta proceeded to buy one skein of practically every colour of embroidery silks in the shop. The colours weren't as vibrant as she used to prefer, but Etta was finding her tastes had changed since The Switch. Life was vibrant enough already.

Clarissa took her back to her own sprawling London mansion for tea – a cold, forbidding place, but without any sign of her mama. Clarissa grabbed her hand and towed Etta up to a more scruffy-looking room at the back, stuffed with worn armchairs, scuffed but serviceable tables and piles of sewing.

An older woman was sewing in the scarce light by the small window.

'Nanny, could you go and ask for tea, please?' Clarissa gave the older lady a hug, then welcomed Etta into a very comfortable armchair.

'Mama would be horrified to know I brought you here,' Clarissa continued. 'But although it's cold, it's the most comfy room in the house. Mama likes to keep the place impeccable for visitors, but we seldom receive any unless Papa is home.'

Etta frowned. She knew why – there was no point denying it, because Lady Best was a downright awful woman disliked by nearly everyone – but she felt bad for her friend.

Clarissa didn't seem concerned, though, and was clearly delighted to have her friend for tea. They chatted about their purchases as Nanny brought in tea then retreated into a corner to finish her sewing in the gloom. Clarissa lit a candle – it was a slightly stinky tallow one, unlike the sweet-smelling beeswax Lady Bainbridge preferred – and showed Etta some of her sewing. It was impeccable – they spent a good half an hour discussing the neatness of her stitches.

As she looked through Clarissa's stitch-perfect samplers, Etta reached for another biscuit, but the plate was empty. Clarissa was nibbling the last one thoughtfully, poring over an embroidery book.

Oh well. She liked a woman who knew what she wanted, even if it was the last bit of shortbread.

Chapter 28

2023

'What on earth are you giggling about now? So much for your O-levels. Come on, share with the rest of us.'

Hetty took her Bluetooth headphones off and gave Aggie an apologetic look.

'It's Stella. She's been sending me these brilliant video things on my phone. She calls them me-mes.'

'Memes,' chorused her aunts.

Hetty studied them from her position on the sofa. The two had been quarrelling over the remote control all evening, so she'd returned to her phone under the pretence of signing up to study for her GCSEs online. The call of social media notifications had been too much, however.

'I'm sorry,' Hetty sighed. 'I'm being anti-social, aren't I?'

'Yes,' Aggie replied, as Jemima opportunistically grabbed the remote.

'Maybe she's just not a fan of the *Antiques Roadshow*, Aggie,' chirruped Jemima.

Hetty grinned. She was much more relaxed around the aunts now – much more relaxed, in fact, than she'd been with anyone in her whole life. She found herself being sucked into the strong temptation to be cheeky.

'*Maybe* I have my own ideas on what to watch . . .'

The aunts visibly perked up. She found Aggie examining her curiously and pulled a face. Jemima laughed, delighted, and even Aggie smiled.

'My goodness, you really *are* feeling better, aren't you? Go on then – what do you want to watch? Has your *friend* Stella given you any recommendations?'

Hetty bit her lip, blushing slightly. 'Well, I've heard there's something called Bridger . . . Bridgerford.'

'Oooh, *Bridgerton*!' corrected Jemima. 'Bit . . . heterosexual, though, isn't it? But an excellent choice nonetheless, my dear.'

Aggie sighed. 'I don't know, Jemima. Watching *Bridgerton* with one's niece? Isn't it supposed to be more than slightly risqué?'

Jemima turned a cynical eye on her sister, nudging her pointedly with her macramé. Her current project was all in black, with the most fascinating bright red plastic ball attached. As usual, Hetty had decided not to ask questions about it.

'Don't pretend for one second you haven't watched it, Agatha. Not for one split second. You forget we share a Netflix password.'

Highly amused, Hetty watched her sternest aunt turn beetroot red.

'Very well,' muttered Aggie. '*Bridgerton* it is. But don't say I didn't warn you, Hetty. Now, let's order a pizza – I can't be bothered to cook.'

Jemima giggled. 'I think I fancy sausage on mine.'

*

The clock was chiming midnight and Jemima was stroking her hand reassuringly by the time Hetty had rallied enough to share her opinion.

'Is that really what people think we used to get up to?'

'Well, didn't you?' asked Aggie.

Hetty breathed out. 'To be quite honest, I don't wholly know. It certainly isn't reflective of my life in the countryside.'

'What about the costumes?' asked Jemima. 'People got quite cross about the costumes, you know.'

'Well, they're not right, no, but that seems of minor importance compared to the . . . the Bedroom Activities.'

She was blushing heavily, and so was Aggie, so Hetty decided to move on to other subjects.

'I'm not sure the timelines quite match up with what I recall, but then it is quite obviously a work of fiction. And there was no mention of the advancements of the time. Why, I saw not one flushing privy! Surely people would be interested in that? I was so excited to see my first one!'

Aggie leaned back, taking a sip of wine.

'You know, they never seem to think about things like that. I always wonder what everything smelled like, for example.'

'Oh, awful, but then everyone was used to it, of course. Just as you are all accustomed to some of the inconveniences of this age.'

The aunts both blinked at her for a long second.

'The inconveniences of *this age*?' repeated Jemima disbelievingly.

'Well, yes. I have noticed a few! I knew things would have advanced in some regards, but in others the world is quite behind where I had hoped it would be.'

'Do elaborate, Hetty,' said Aggie. 'Where did you expect improvement?'

'Well, while women of all classes do seem a lot more equal, we do also seem to still have much judgement on the way we look. Why, a gentleman – no, a scoundrel! – had the audacity to address me in the street just yesterday!'

Aggie delicately bit into a crisp, chewing thoughtfully. 'Medicine is better, though, no?'

'Oh, most definitely,' said Hetty. 'That really is excellent. But I must admit I am quite dismayed to see the advances made in the field of warfare.'

Jemima and Aggie were starting to look rather stricken. Hetty reached for another slice of pizza.

'The food really is much better, though, Aunts! Such a delicious abundance of fat and sugar, and available to nearly all! Pineapples and bananas in every shop and even in the flavours of children's sweeties! That's fabulous news.'

Aggie put her bowl of crisps down. 'I'm not sure that's entirely good news, you know.'

'No, it truly is,' Hetty insisted. 'I know not everyone has enough food to eat, and that is a real worry. But very few people are starving and malnourished, by comparison.'

'Not none, though,' said Jemima, frowning.

'And the television. That truly is a remarkable invention. So much better than the printed word.' Hetty backpedalled. 'Come, don't be cast down. Let us watch more of this *Bridgerton*. It really is most fascinating.'

Aggie picked up her wine glass, downing the lot in one, then picked up the remote.

'One more before bed, Jemima? I think I'll crack open another bottle of red.'

Chapter 29

1817

Etta sighed at her lamb cutlet. God, she missed takeout. She'd been secretly working with the chef downstairs to try to make a pizza, but the cheese just wasn't the same. Fried chicken wasn't the same either – she couldn't seem to get the spice mix right, or the oil hot enough.

She'd made a few more acquaintances now – insipid girls, largely, whom she carefully said hello to in the park. Clarissa didn't seem to have a great deal of friends, but they spoke to her, too. She had to watch her words very, very carefully around the lot of them, Clarissa included. It was exhausting.

Etta was vaguely aware that there were much more fun-looking twenty-somethings at the parties and dances she accompanied her mother and Clarissa to, but they didn't tend to stick around for long – quickly disappearing into what she suspected were raucous parties within parties in other rooms into which she was most definitely *not* invited. She was left with all the other respectable young misses and their mamas. It was just like VIP sections in night clubs all over again, except this time the red ropes were invisible.

At any rate, she had enough acquaintances to be fairly confident of a good showing to the dinner her mother was hosting this evening. She was very much looking forward to it, mainly because they'd apparently all be singing and playing the piano afterwards and she'd been practising harder than she'd ever practised in her life.

Etta generally had far more spare time than she knew what to do with. Regency ladies tended to spend a good part of their afternoons writing letters to each other, but given all the people she knew in this era were in town, this seemed a waste of time. Having already given her descendants what she figured was a clear path to financial success – she might not have memorised any lottery numbers, but 'Invest in Apple' was a clear no-brainer – she didn't feel the need to work out further ways to help them.

So now, most days, she spent her time doing what she'd always loved – singing, playing piano, making music. It was wonderful to finally let herself indulge in music again. She had spent a fair bit of time transposing her very favourite pop bangers into piano music and was immensely proud of her work.

Her mother would often come and quietly listen while she did her embroidery; although she remarked at her daughter's odd choice of song selection, she seemed extremely impressed. Her brother would often tell her how much he enjoyed her voice echoing through the house over family dinners in the evening.

And so here they were, chairs arranged, waiting for Maria Marley of all people to take her place at the piano. Etta could only hope the ogre didn't bash her poor piano keys in.

Miss Marley was with Smythe again, who was apparently

a childhood friend – the gruesome twosome, Etta thought. She had no idea why Marley and Wobbly kept gracing her vicinity with their odious presence, but she had noticed with grim delight that they too had the most exclusive doors closed to them at parties. She barely concealed her glee as she realised Smythe was about to sing and caught Max's eye across the room.

It had been days and they *still* hadn't spoken about the electrifying kiss in the carriage. She could almost see it hovering there in the air between them. But tonight was unlikely to provide an opportunity to talk about it. As Smythe warbled nasally through some kind of appalling folk tune, Etta's mind turned instead to more practical matters: what she'd sing tonight. Her mother had advised against any of the pop songs she'd managed to work out arrangements for.

But . . . Etta wondered. A few people had sung traditional folk songs which she personally had felt were chock-full of innuendos. Only a complete child would have failed to catch the double entendre in the song about the milkmaid's heavy jugs, surely?

Her mother's wine was good stuff and although the group was hardly rowdy – Great Aunt Maude was openly snoring in the front row – she began to feel that her audience was ready to be enlightened.

And before Etta knew it, it was her turn. Maria Marley, whom Etta had noticed poring through the Bainbridge's large collection of sheet music after dinner, handed her a couple of Etta's own neatly composed pages as she gave up her seat at the piano.

'One of your own . . . unique . . . compositions, Miss Bainbridge? Your turn to *entertain* us. I wonder what kind of entertainment we can expect?' Miss Marley raised a cynical eyebrow. 'This one looks a little complex for someone of your intellect, though.'

What a bitch, Etta thought, taking the sheet music off her and plonking herself down at the piano ever so slightly drunkenly. She looked at what Maria had chosen. For someone with such a crappy choice in singing partners, she had chosen surprisingly well. So Etta settled in with one of her favourites: Hozier's 'Take Me To Church'. She was fairly confident she'd got the lyrics right, but as she suddenly reached the line 'worship in the bedroom' she finally realised her mistake and looked up from the keyboard.

Great Aunt Maude had finally woken up and was watching intently. The rest of the room stirred uneasily.

In for a penny, in for a pound. Perhaps the rest of it wouldn't be so bad. It was about church, for heaven's sake. How offensive could it possibly be? Etta found herself carried along into the chorus and the song wrapped itself around her as she leaned into the melody.

Next time she looked up, her fingers froze immediately. The room was almost completely empty. A few stragglers were making their excuse to her mother by the door. The last thing Etta saw was the triumphant face of Miss Maria Marley, as a faux-scandalised Smythe led her away with her outraged mother. Even Clarissa was going, Lady Best frog-marching her away indignantly. Lady Bainbridge looked absolutely lost as her evening circled the drain. Etta looked around to find Max was still present, but he looked pained as he downed the last dregs of his wine glass and made his excuses to leave.

'Well, carry on, girl! Why've you stopped?' Great Aunt Maude called out. Her voice cutting across Etta's panic.

Etta turned her attention to the old lady, still sitting on the front row. 'Aunt Maude . . . Can't you see everyone's gone? I don't think my song – well, I don't think it was perhaps as appropriate as it could have been . . .'

Maude was having none of it. 'When you're as old as me, young lady, you'll find you won't care a jot for the opinions of insipid idiots like the ones your mother invited to this party. Now sing on.'

Lady Bainbridge came back from wishing the last of her outraged guests goodbye, crosser than Etta had ever seen her. Even Hercules seemed to be in a bad mood, yapping around her feet.

'You know, Henrietta, I do wish you'd played something a little less . . . heathen. Where on *earth* did you find such a song? You will retire for the evening *immediately*. We shall speak again tomorrow morning, and I strongly suggest you think very carefully about what you wish to say to me.'

Etta stepped away from the piano, feeling tears gathering in her eyes. 'Mama. It – it was Miss Marley. She—'

'I didn't hear Miss Marley singing an inappropriate song. I *did* hear you, however, Henrietta. Now, to bed.'

Etta barely heard Aunt Maude's exclamations as she gathered her skirts and ran upstairs. She'd clearly messed up far more than she'd thought.

Chapter 30

2023

'Um, Hetty, you did know everything you have written on Substack is viewable online?'

Stella and Hetty were sitting in the old morning room of the big purple house. After their first proper dinner, over jerk chicken which made Hetty's eyes water and lips tingle, she'd suggested they come back to hers for their next 'Netflix and Chill', Stella had called it.

Last time, she had wiped her eyes with her fingers, which had been a mistake that had involved being far too close to Stella as she fussed over her in the bathroom. Stella had smelled of her signature lemon and mint with added layers of jerk chicken and all manner of delicious things which Hetty just wanted to eat up hungrily like a starving animal. And her body had pressed up deliciously against her own in the tiny walkway as Stella had wiped away her hot tears.

So Hetty sat on the love seat this time, while Stella tried to look over her shoulder from the sofa. It wasn't working brilliantly well.

'Pass me the laptop a mo',' Stella said. Another delicious waft of citrus as she dropped down next to Hetty on the love seat, plump and soft against her.

Hetty's heart knocked against her ribcage.

'Yeah, look, see. God, you've had comments and everything.'

'Comments?' Hetty slowly blew out a deep breath she didn't realise she'd been holding and shifted slightly as she felt Stella's arm against hers. She moved her own arm to the back of the seat, realising too late she was almost cuddling Stella. Oh well.

'Good ones! "This is hilarious. Shared." Look, they love it! What on earth have you been writing about? Bloody hell – you've had ten thousand views already today!'

'It's just . . . just a diary, an online diary, that's all.'

Stella tapped at the laptop and focused intently. Hetty gripped her teacup, desperate to know her opinion and trying not to ask.

Stella started reading aloud:

'I stumbled across a forest of what I believe they call "sky scrapers" today. They were awfully shiny – so much so that they hardly seemed real. That would have been a preferable option, in my view. St Paul's Cathedral was quite enough for me, with its ugly bulbous mound. It reminded me of the time our dog got a boil on his neck and wouldn't let anyone so much as touch it.

'It defies all sense and reason that modern humans dine on such very spicy luncheons as a matter of course and yet seem incapable of creating anything but the most bland of buildings.'

Stella started to laugh. 'Hetty, this is *brilliant*! How the heck did you think it up? It's bang on. Just like Lady Whistledown got dragged into 2023. You're a genius!'

'Do – do you really think so?'

'Hell, yeah! Hey – you should connect your Instagram and make videos. You could dress up in Regency clothes and everything.'

'Like on the television?'

'No, silly, like reels. You're so funny. It's cute.'

Hetty had never had female friends before. She had certainly never been called *cute*, never mind twice in one week. Her skin had never tingled at another's touch; her heart had never beat so loudly. She had nothing to compare this with. Was it possible Stella also felt this connection?

She bit her lip. 'Can it be done? The video? Will you teach me?'

Stella stopped typing. 'Um, yeah. Sure. Hey, I gotta go, though.'

Hetty suddenly felt cold as Stella hauled herself up and out of their seat and stood, watching her.

'Hetty, I have to ask. I like you. Like, *like*-like you. If we're going to keep hanging out, I have to know if you like me, too.' Stella rubbed her temples. 'I've been burned too many times. I don't need my heart broken again.'

'Your heart?' Hetty repeated. 'This is all very new to me, but my heart . . . my heart feels fuller around you.'

She had no idea which words in the English language could articulate how she felt around Stella. 'I don't . . . I can't describe it. You . . . You are *remarkable*.'

She hadn't said half of what she wanted to, but Stella seemed to understand. 'You're not out, are you?'

'Out?'

'You haven't told anyone you like women – that you're a lesbian.'

'Only my aunts. But then, I have nobody else to tell,' Hetty said. 'I have had a hard time coming to terms with my desire for Sapphic love, but I feel I am getting closer recently.'

Stella laughed, then tilted her head at Hetty. 'Sapphic love. God, that's something only you would say, Hetty.'

Hetty took a deep breath, but Stella mercifully interrupted her. 'We don't have to talk about it. It's fine.' She picked up her bag and turned to leave.

'Yes, Stella, we do. I want to. You fill my heart, my head, my body entirely. You're all I think of at night and again when I wake. My soul sings out for you. So yes, I do believe I feel Sapphic passion toward you.'

Stella stopped in her tracks, dropping her bag, and slowly turned around. She looked taken aback, her eyes equal parts baffled and wild.

'Hetty.'

Hetty felt as though her lungs might burst from the tension, but she'd rather die than look away. 'Yes?'

'Have you ever seen that scene in *Pride and Prejudice* where Mr Darcy comes out of the lake with his shirt all wet?'

'No.'

'Okay, whatever. I think I know why everyone likes it now.'

Stella was in front of her, now, stooping down until her

lips met Hetty's cheek. A fleeting kiss, then Hetty felt breath tickling against her ear.

'You're freaking out, aren't you? Let's take it slow. See you next week.'

And then Hetty was all alone, not quite sure what had happened but knowing that her life would never be the same again.

Chapter 31

1817

It was a week after the Piano Incident when Max joined the family for dinner. Charlie jovially led in his guest, having found him at a loose end in their club, and Etta felt herself swell with happiness.

'His old man's home and he needs to get out of the mansion. Hard times, eh, Stanhope? I know Etta's still in the doghouse, but I thought you wouldn't mind if I brought him back to have some of your trifle, Mama.'

Their mother smiled at Max indulgently. 'It's hardly my trifle, Charles. Although it is true that Cook follows the family recipe. But you are always welcome to come and eat with us, as you know, Maximillian, trifle or no.'

'Thank you, Lady Bainbridge. And I'm very pleased to hear you're serving my favourite pudding.'

It had been a hard couple of days for Etta. She had yet to venture outside the house and nobody at all had called. It felt as though she were infamous. Even Max hadn't shown his face – not even a note through Bessie. The shame had felt like lead weights pressing down on her – and yet all she'd done was sing one of the biggest hits of her generation. It was so unfair.

She'd felt particularly melodramatic as the bracelet clinked against her diary as she wrote, curled up in the big bay window looking out into the garden.

But then her mother had gone visiting, and a few good family friends had put it about how delightfully eccentric the hilarious Henrietta Bainbridge was, and then to cap it all: Miss Morridge had been kidnapped by the Earl of Kinnock and taken to Gretna Green. 'How fortunate!' her mother had said.

Poor Miss Morridge had been a close friend of Maria Marley, thought to be being courted by Smythe. In a double blow, it transpired that she was quite a willing guest of the Earl of Kinnock – and visibly pregnant. The scandal had put the seal on things for Etta, who had been given one last final scolding by her mother and then reluctantly forgiven.

It had been a difficult two weeks of looking wistfully at her golden bracelet, but the fact her whole family had come together to get through the scandalous occurrence of a relatively obscure and unpopular damsel singing an inappropriate song at a dinner party had kept her from looking too closely.

And here they all were, eating dinner, as though nothing had ever happened. And Max too, wrapped into the welcoming arms of the Bainbridge family.

It was the first time that she and Max had any semblance of privacy since their carriage kiss. Though Etta was still left in limbo, particularly after the added fiasco of the disastrous recital, she felt him looking at her over dinner, and she couldn't help looking back.

When she wasn't studying his face, watching expressions flit across his strong brow and expressive mouth, she was watching his hands. She wanted him to touch her. Her skin almost crawled with need.

She'd never felt like this: drugged with lust, but also so very comfortable about it. She'd had crushes in the past – of course she had – but this was something different, with Max. Everything about him, from his smell to the taste of him, was like the ultimate cashmere jumper. Reliably soft and relaxed; welcoming, warming . . . Home.

Sexy home, though.

Etta wriggled in her seat as the servants took away the last dishes. Charlie was busy telling Max to come for Christmas. 'Good thing you're nearby, really,' he said. 'Even if you're tied to your bore of a father, you can at least pop over every now and again.'

Lady Bainbridge studied Charlie carefully. 'Now, Charlie, that's not proper. The Marquess is an old friend of mine, as you must know.'

A lightning bolt struck Etta to the very core, spoon halfway to her mouth.

The Marquess? If Max's father was a marquess, that meant . . . That meant that Max would be too, one day? Perhaps he really was the Marquess those two old ladies had been talking about?

Etta felt herself buzzing with excitement as she tuned back in, but Lady Bainbridge almost immediately coughed meaningfully. 'Perhaps we should withdraw from the table, Henrietta, and leave these two to their port.'

Etta pursed her lips and widened her eyes in the manner

of an offended but very proper young lady. 'Good idea, Mama. If they're planning to be improper, I want no part of it.'

Charlie barely repressed a laugh, while Max's eyes twinkled appreciatively.

'Very good, Henrietta,' said Lady Bainbridge.

As she sat with her mother, organising her new embroidery threads while the ever-present Hercules snored at her feet, Etta realised she was becoming a different person. A person she quite liked.

Back in London in 2023, she knew now that she'd been deeply sad and lonely. But here she had a family and friends. Not as many friends as she'd have liked, but a hundred per cent more than she'd had before. Two hundred per cent, if she could include Max.

Etta waited until polite conversation had been had in the drawing room and Max and Charlie had withdrawn to play billiards, then went to bed. After Bessie had put her hair up for the night, she peeked out of the window. Max and Charlie were most likely outside smoking cigars right now – and it had rained in the morning, leaving the ground nice and soft. Today was the day to make her move.

Her room faced the large back garden of the house and, as expected, when she edged the window up she could smell expensive tobacco smoke.

She quietly wrapped a dressing gown over her nightdress and grabbed her notebook and pencil, along with a bit of white embroidery silk. Etta crept down the back stairs and out of the back door, carefully avoiding the last few servants closing the house for the night.

The billiards room was to her left and candles were still lit, but it was now quite late. Charlie and Max would probably wrap things up fairly soon, or go out drinking.

She poked her head outdoors and looked around and, for the first time, up – first at the distant bark of a fox, but then properly up. And oh, the stars: even right here in the very middle of London. The whole Milky Way, laid out just like a tray of chocolates for her to choose from. It stole her breath away. Never in her entire life had she seen so many stars.

She felt the light chain of her bracelet against her wrist and knew it had to go. She must carefully remove it: wrap it in silk and push it to the back of a drawer where it could never ever snap and interrupt this beautiful, endless dream.

Brought around from her wonder by the reality of the cold, she scanned the ground for footprints. As she'd hoped, there were two sets outside the window where Charlie and Max had been standing. It might be elaborate, and even a little bit unhinged, but it was the only solution she could think of; she was determined to find out his shoe size. If she was going to spend hours monogramming Max a pair of slippers, no way were they ending up in a pile like the ones owned by Clarissa's unfortunate uncle. But crouching in the cold, chill winds whipping over her bare feet and ankles, she discovered a fatal flaw in her plan.

Two sets of footprints lay in front of her.

She tried to remember what boots each man was wearing. Thankfully it came to her quite quickly – less surprisingly than it should have, she reflected wryly. She'd spent more than enough time staring at Max's well-sculpted calves to know he didn't wear pointy boots, and one set of footprints was decidedly pointy at the toes. Like an estate agent's, she thought, and shuddered slightly at the thought.

Etta took out the strand of white embroidery silk and laid it along a footprint, marking the length with her pencil. She then laid it width-wise and marked it again. Then she sketched the shape of the foot in her notepad, marking the areas she'd measured, and slipped the thread inside. Very pleased with herself, she stood up and brushed off her hands. She felt pretty smart. Now all she had to do was buy some slippers and get embroidering.

Then she heard the double doors she'd come through opening and a figure stepped out into the dark. Panicking, Etta fled across the lawn as quietly as she could and hid behind a tree. She risked a peek and saw a man's figure stooping to pick something up from the ground. To her horror, she realised it was her diary. As the man sat on the bench outside the billiard room, he was lit from behind. Etta glimpsed dark hair and broad shoulders and knew immediately that it was Max.

She twisted her hands together in the dark, trying to stay silent.

He turned a page. It was all too mortifying. She was fairly sure she'd used that notebook to write some sordid fanfic about him at some point. It wasn't as though she could access erotic chick lit on her Kindle any more and a girl had to keep herself occupied at night somehow.

She shivered with horror as he turned another page. This was too much. She shifted uncomfortably, twigs prickling her bare toes.

Max looked up suddenly; Etta knew he'd heard her.

'You should come out, you know,' he called across the garden. 'Nobody's here, and you'll catch a chill.'

She crept out, looking around, and made her way across the lawn to the bench. 'People do not die from little trifling colds, I am sure,' she quoted flippantly, trying to hide her horror.

Max raised an eyebrow. 'I was just enjoying this fascinating tale you've penned. Or should I say, pencilled.'

Etta felt herself blush from head to toe, hot with embarrassment.

'Where's Charlie?' she asked.

'In bed. Where you should be.'

Etta bit her lip. 'I had . . . Well, I had something to do.'

He looked her straight in the eyes, a smile playing on his lips. 'Cooling down after writing these warm stories?'

She sank her head into her hands. 'Ugh, how embarrassing. How much did you read?'

'Not enough. You're a very good writer. Very . . . imaginative.'

Etta raised her head, hearing amusement in his voice, and dared herself to look him in the eye.

She suddenly felt alone, as though balancing at the edge of a vast, crumbling, dangerous cliff. 'Don't you dare laugh at me. It wasn't just me kissing you in that carriage. You kissed me back. I know it.'

Max was serious as he reached forwards and cupped her face with one hand. Etta shivered as her skin tingled under his touch and found herself leaning towards him.

Perhaps it was the way the moonlight barely lit the scene, perhaps it was the anchoring effect of his touch, or perhaps it was the way he looked at her. The fear melted away and

Etta felt daring. She couldn't be afraid any more, only slightly audacious.

'Fine. Well done, I kissed you, and looked a fool, and now you found my diary. Perhaps I'm an idiot. But don't think I don't see the way you look at me.'

'How's that?'

'Like . . . like I'm raspberry trifle.'

Max grinned at her, his thumb lightly stroking her cheek. 'Well, I do love Mrs Baggins' raspberry trifle.'

Etta groaned, partly in memory of the evening's pudding but mostly in relief at not being outright rejected. 'Oh my god, I know, right? Jesus. It's even better than the Marks and Sparks version. I swear that's ginger cake at the bottom, you know.'

He leaned towards her; all of a sudden he felt terribly close. His hand left her face and gripped her waist.

'I didn't understand the half of that, but do you know, I think you might be right? There must be something truly magic about it,' he whispered into her ear, right before he kissed her.

It was unlike any kiss Etta had ever experienced in her life. At first chaste and tentative, it seemed to quickly deepen as every feeling slowly unravelled. It felt to her as though tendrils of lust – and even perhaps, something stronger – were uncurling from a tangle inside her and winding themselves around Max.

He suddenly pulled back, looking as dazed as she felt.

'Etta . . . we shouldn't . . . Just by being here alone, I have wholly ruined you. Tonight. That night in the carriage – it should never have happened. It's not fair. We shouldn't kiss.'

'I can't *not* kiss you, Max.'

He groaned and stood up suddenly, pulling her to her feet. 'You can't be seen here with me. If we were caught . . .'

'I'm so cold. It's very cold out here. Come in for a moment and help me get warm. You won't need to marry me, I promise.'

'I – we shouldn't.'

Indecision crossed his face. She could tell he was weighing up his impulse for chivalry against desire.

'It's *so cold*, Max.'

Etta led him inside and up the back stairs to her bedroom door, tugging him in by the hand. He closed the door behind him and looked down at her, his eyes dark with uncertainty, but also with longing.

God, how desperate was she? Very, very desperate, it seemed. 'Warm me up. Then you can go home to your bed.'

At the word 'bed' Max seemed to lose all restraint. He swept her up into his arms, kicking off his boots, and sat her on the edge of her mattress, pulling her into a deep kiss that seemed to make every hair on the surface of her skin stand on end. Then every thought left her body, an overwhelming need to remove every piece of fabric taking over.

She pulled open his shirt, running her fingers over his hard chest.

'Muscles! So many muscles. What have you been doing?'

'Boxing,' he mumbled into her hair, before groaning as she slipped her hands into his breeches. She realised she was moaning too, delighted with what she found. He pressed against her for one brief, delicious moment.

Then he was moving lower, tugging at her chemise, his hands at her ankles, her knees, her thighs. Etta groaned with pleasure as she felt his fingers right where she needed them most.

'Oh good god!'

Etta leapt back. 'Oh no! I'm so sorry. Is it that I couldn't shave? I had no idea where I could even get a razor.'

'What? Shave what?' Max blinked, then shook his head, as though coming back to himself. 'Etta, I have defiled you!'

He started pulling his clothes back on, eyes wild and anxious.

'My lack of control was abominable! Why, I have acted in the most ungentlemanly way . . .!'

'Because I asked you to!' Etta stumbled over the bed towards him, laying a calming hand on his shoulder as he yanked his boots back on. 'Because I wanted you to. Didn't you want to as well?'

'Of course I wanted to!' Max turned to her, boot in hand. 'It is all I have wanted from the moment I pulled you out of that cellar. But I am a gentleman, Henrietta. A gentleman does not ravish a lady – not under any circumstances.'

Oh god, Etta thought. So there was a male version of the Ladies Do Not list. Of course.

'Nobody has to know, Max. Nobody has seen us. It's absolutely fine.'

But his mouth was set in a firm line as he pressed her back into her bed, tucking in her sheets.

'No, Etta. This has gone far enough for tonight. We shall speak tomorrow.'

He gave her one last, lingering kiss, then tore himself away and rested his forehead on hers.

'Tomorrow,' he said again, almost to himself, and then left.

Etta sighed, then blew out her candles. Hopefully, by tomorrow, Max would have chilled the fuck out. But who knew? She didn't have a contemporary copy of the Gentlemen Do Not list handy. She'd read plenty of Regency romances, but it looked like Georgette Heyer rules applied here: chaste kisses and gently pulled curtains over secret trysts and midnight romps. Unless she was missing something, there was an awful lot of historical inaccuracy going on in her favourite reading matter.

Chapter 32

2023

Hetty hovered over Jemima, who was hard at work at her pristine sewing machine surrounded by swathes of fabric. 'Oh, I love you, Hetty, but do shove off. You're standing in my light again.'

'But are you truly certain she'll like it?'

'Of course she'll like it. Here, put these pins away. They're rattling away on the table like buggery and it's doing my head in.'

Hetty held the tin of pins emblazoned with a cartoon of an orange-haired boy and white dog – Jemima called it her 'Tintin Pin Tin' – and bit her bottom lip anxiously. 'They didn't really have colours like this in 1817, you know.'

Jemima sighed, stopping the machine to turn a corner. 'So you've said, dearie. But then again they didn't have sewing machines either, did they?'

Hetty was chewing her cheek now. 'No, and they truly are most ingenious. Aunt Jemima, I can't tell you how thankful I am. Really, it's so lovely of you.'

Jemima stood up and shook out the bright orange and

yellow fabric. The shot silk shone brightly, like the sun. Like Stella, Hetty had thought when she bought it. Her own dress was two shades of blue, like moonlight across a winter lake.

A distant door slammed. Jemima finished examining the fabric before wandering towards the stairs up to the main house. 'That'll be Aggie back from the shops, my lovely. You go and see her and wait for your girlfriend to arrive and I'll give this a quick press.'

Hetty wasn't sure how this would go. Would it be too soon into their . . . friendship . . . to give Stella a gown? Stella had suggested that the videos should be done in period-appropriate clothing, but she hadn't agreed to appear in them with her.

But Aunt Jemima had assured her that making two period morning gowns of completely differing sizes was little different to just the one. If she was to be trusted, of course. It was sometimes very hard to tell when her aunts were being serious and when they were not. Aggie had laughed uproariously when Jemima had said it, but Jemima had, after all, got to work and made both dresses.

She went upstairs to find Aggie and Stella. On hearing voices, she peeked carefully around the door frame to the kitchen. Stella was already there, carefully examining a mug of tea. It was a promotional one from the 2019 Knitting and Stitching Exhibition. Across the kitchen Aggie was stirring her own chipped mug, emblazoned with a faded Legend of Zelda logo. Two more cups sat on the counter, clearly waiting for Hetty and Jemima. Stella stared at them, as though wondering who'd get the Portmeirion one and who'd get the 'Colonoscopists Like It From Behind' one.

'So, dear, getting on well with our Hetty, then?' Aggie

asked. She was immaculate in a twinset and pearls, newly arrived home from the supermarket, and was pulling bottles of gin out of a carrier bag. 'Showing her the ropes?'

'The cables, really,' Stella said.

Aggie grinned. 'And does she know her USB from her HDMI yet?'

Hetty knew Stella wasn't going to be fooled. They'd googled Lady Agatha Bainbridge together in one of their first classes. 'I'm surprised you haven't taken her on yourself. Major investor in Apple, aren't you? I heard you knew Steve Jobs himself.'

'Oh, but Hetty has so much to learn and I have so very little patience,' Aggie said lightly. 'And much better she learns from someone her own age. Ah, here you are, Hetty. Do go and show Stella Jemima's artistry.'

Hetty smiled nervously and guided Stella back down the narrow steps to Jemima's many workrooms.

'Taking me down to the cellar to murder me, eh?'

Hetty turned, looking concerned, then saw Stella's face. 'No, but I wanted to show you something. A present, from me and my aunt Jemima.'

The next thing she knew, Stella was pinned into a bright orange shot silk, which she declared was 'the most beautiful dress I have ever, ever seen'. She stood on an old box in a cellar stuffed with piles of fabric, with Jemima fussing around the hem.

Stella was laughing to herself.

'What?' asked Hetty, feeling a ripple of anxiety. 'You don't like it, do you?'

'No, no, Hetty, I love it. I really do. It's just . . . I was trying to keep things slow. Court you like an old-fashioned lady. And here I am in a silk ballgown.'

Jemima tutted, mouth full of pins, and muttered something incoherent.

Hetty beamed. 'She's saying it's a morning dress, not a ballgown, and she's quite right, you know. But morning gowns are not traditionally crafted from silk, Jemima, as well *you* know.'

Hetty and Stella looked at one another, and then all of a sudden they both burst into laughter from the strangeness of it all.

Jemima gave up. 'Good god, off with it, then, if you're both going to roll about laughing. I'll have it hemmed in half an hour, girls.' She started carefully removing the dress from Stella, who carefully stepped down from the box she'd been standing on. 'Thank goodness you left your jacket behind last week, Stella, or I'd have had no chance of getting the size right.'

When they were safely ensconced in the love seat in the sitting room and they started discussing the videos, she was elated to see Stella's eyes shine with mirrored excitement. Hetty had no idea about things like 'short form videos' and 'social strategies', but Stella clearly did.

Her Substack was doing well – Hetty's writing was described by one reader as 'archaic but very sweet' and by another as 'just like reading a Jane Austen novel'. She couldn't remember how to tell how many people were actually reading it, despite Stella's detailed explanation. And when that had happened, she had forgotten about early entries that included her rapturous first impressions of computer class and her gorgeous teacher, which had been rather embarrassing, so she didn't want to ask again.

When Stella wasn't teaching computer classes, she

dedicated most of her time to finishing a degree in something called 'Marketing and Communications' that had clearly had nothing to do with either markets, physical trading, or public speaking. Hetty worried that her life was so much easier than Stella's seemed to be, but Stella didn't seem to mind. Stella was remarkably relaxed about most things. As Hetty poured tea, she realised that without even noticing it the world had become a far, far brighter place and she was pretty sure that Stella had a big part in that. She wanted to freeze this moment and stay in it forever.

Despite having little knowledge of the technicalities behind her Substack and Instagram page, it felt so good to be making connections with people online. She found herself engaging in the most wonderful conversations in the 'comments' sections.

Stella had warned her to expect negativity whenever strangers were able to talk to her on the internet, and she was right. But she had also been right about the benefits of being online: Hetty had met the most amazing people, too. Some of them were becoming quite regular correspondents, recommending books, websites and even offline events she might like to attend. It seemed that people had far more options when it came to making friends in 2023.

And though she had no idea how these new Instagram videos would work, they would be fun to plan. It didn't matter what she did, when she was doing it with Stella.

'So where do you come from, Hetty? I realised last night that I hardly know anything about you,' said Stella, cracking open a bottle of wine.

Hetty was surprised out of her reverie. She had been dreading this moment.

'Oh, well . . . I grew up in the countryside, with my mother and brother. But they're . . .' Hetty grimaced. How to explain this? '. . . not here now.'

Stella looked up from filling their wine glasses to clutch Hetty's hand.

'Oh, Hetty. I'm so sorry. Don't worry, I won't interrogate you about it.'

She felt awful. Then again, was it truly a lie? After all, surely her mother and brother were long dead by now? At the thought of it, real tears sprang to Hetty's eyes.

'Never mind. No, really, never mind.' She blinked them away, accepting both Stella's hand and her wine glass. 'What about your family?'

'I've got a brother called Elliot, and then there's my mum.' Stella bit her lip ruefully. 'My mum's – well, she's very old fashioned. The most old-fashioned woman you've ever met, probably.'

'Oh, I sincerely doubt that,' said Hetty.

'No, really. She's very religious. She wouldn't like this at all.' Stella looked away. 'But then, what she doesn't know won't hurt her, right?'

'Right,' said Hetty, thinking about all the things Stella didn't know. Hopefully none of them would hurt her either – because the thought of hurting Stella was unbearable.

Chapter 33

1817

Max was long gone by the time Etta went down to breakfast. A note slipped under her door had read simply: *We must talk – later.* It was unsigned. She supposed anything more would arouse suspicion with the servants, but it was thrilling to see his elegant, masculine handwriting nonetheless.

At breakfast she discovered that on his way out, Max had invited her family to go and see a balloon ascension that morning – and he'd promised a surprise.

Etta had expected the huge striped balloon and the crowd of awestruck spectators, but as their family's carriage drew up to the crowded park just outside London and Charlie offered her his arm, she spotted Max there with something – someone – unexpected.

She was tempted to be jealous, but there was no mistaking the tall, dark-haired woman sitting next to Max. She stared first at the stranger, then at Max. 'You never said you had a sister.'

Both Max and his hitherto completely unmentioned sibling grinned, Max apologetically and his sister in amusement.

'Oh, that's exactly what I'd expect from the both of you,' said the woman, looking between Max and Charlie fondly. 'Out of sight, out of mind. I daresay neither of you remember the time you went through my desk and ruined my best watercolours either. Or the time Charlie put all my dresses on and got caught by Nanny.'

'You must be misremembering, Lizzie,' Charlie said, bowing neatly in greeting.

Max grinned. 'Miss Bainbridge – let me remind you of my older sister, Lady Elizabeth Mackinnon.'

'Delighted to meet you again at long last,' said Max's sister. 'It's fair enough, you know, since I'm tucked out of the way in Scotland with my husband most of the time. We can't have seen one another since you were perhaps six years old, when I went off to Finishing School in Switzerland. I've come to London to our house here for my confinement, though. Do excuse me for not getting up.'

Etta noticed for the first time that Lady Mackinnon was indeed heavily pregnant as they shook hands. 'Gosh, I'm surprised you've come so far away from home. I suppose there aren't any hospitals nowadays, are there?'

The other woman looked at her curiously. 'No, not for—well, I shall see our doctor, of course. Besides, I wanted to see the balloon. I'm most interested in aeronautics.'

Etta felt her brows rise involuntarily. 'Are you? Most women I meet around London seem most interested in ribbons and glaring at me in the park.'

'Ha! Oh no, not I. Gosh you were completely right when you told me how amusing Miss Bainbridge is, Max. Well done.'

Etta looked questioningly at Max, but Charlie was calling

him over to inspect the balloon. Before Etta could say another word to him he was completely out of earshot. He seemed to be dissuading a determined Charlie from attempting to climb in the balloon basket. Etta wondered what he was thinking – if he was regretting what had happened last night.

What was the etiquette for this kind of scenario? Her mother's copy of *Debrett's* had left her as clueless as she'd been before she picked it up that morning.

Max's sister turned back to her. 'Call me Lizzie – everyone else does.'

'Only if you call me Etta.'

Etta couldn't deny she was massively pleased to find herself a new friend who was anything but insipid. Etta quizzed Lizzie on everything aeronautical. Even in 2023, Lizzie would have known a lot. She was livelier than her brother, but shared the same deadpan humour that Etta loved about him.

Huh. *Loved about him*. Interesting word to think of there. She tucked it away for later.

'So, you're quite a favourite with my brother, then?' said Lizzie, her voice ripe with gossip. Etta couldn't help smiling in return. Lizzie nudged her. 'I warn you, you're in for a rough ride. He never does what he's told. My father wishes for him to marry someone very traditional, like Miss Maria Marley.'

Etta snorted. 'Why, does your father not like him very much?'

Lizzie's eyes widened, and Etta briefly worried about having gone too far; then her new friend laughed, openly and loudly, just like her brother.

'Not right now, he doesn't, but the old curmudgeon's bound to come around. He's all bark but no bite – Max always gets what he wants in the end.'

'I'd love to meet your father. I bet he's one of those old guys you can charm the pants off just by being a little too honest,' said Etta.

She heard Lizzie cough on her wine. 'Um, not quite, I'm afraid. It's better to handle our father with kidskin gloves, we've found.'

Etta was unconvinced. Older people loved her. She'd spent a summer in her teens volunteering at a care home and always homed in on the battle axes.

After the balloon set off – most impractically, Etta and Lizzie agreed, compared to the intriguing idea Etta had floated of a powered winged craft – they all headed off for lunch at a nearby inn. Max had thought ahead and booked them a private parlour, as well as a large spread of cold meats and cheeses. Delighted, she plonked herself down next to Lizzie and started making herself a sarnie, chatting to her amazed new friend about the infinite sandwich-related possibilities the breadth of Max's spread had opened up. This was the life.

And yet . . . a tingle of nervousness rattled across her skin. She couldn't stop thinking about the feel of Max beneath her, her hands against his body, her mouth against his. She had all but handed herself to him on a platter. She hoped she hadn't gone too far.

When Etta went to the ladies' room, she felt Max's eyes on her and wasn't too surprised when she emerged to find he'd followed and waited for her in the corridor.

'Miss Bainbridge, we need to talk,' he whispered. He looked cautiously around before pulling her into a dark corner. She gripped onto his arms to keep from tripping. 'Last night. I am heartily ashamed of my behaviour. Of my complete lack of control. I must reassure you that of course

I'm going to ask your brother for your hand as soon as is prudent.'

Her fingers stilled on his arms and she suddenly felt cold with panic. She stepped back from him.

'You're going to ask him if you can marry me?' she whispered. 'That's a bit . . . intense . . . isn't it?'

'But you – you absolutely must of course marry me . . .!' She could see fear begin to overtake him as, for the first time, he appeared to question himself. 'Etta, we . . . coupled . . . or as good as.'

Etta was starting to feel claustrophobic. Heat was flooding through her, creeping under her skin. Yes, he was hot as hell. Hotter, even. And of all the people she'd met in 1817, Max was undeniably her favourite. She liked him a lot – more than she was comfortable liking anyone. But she hadn't really known him that long, had she? To marry him now . . . And because he felt he had to, out of obligation!

She hadn't even given him a full test drive in bed yet, for god's sake. What if he was all bark, no bite? Etta bit her lip, remembering his hard chest and dark eyes. She could always teach him, she supposed. That would be fun.

All the same, this had not been part of her plan. She'd had a five-year plan, back in 2023. It had been recommended to her in some book or other, so she'd bought a sunflower-patterned notepad in Paperchase specially. The plan was to meet a nice man at a party or a pub. An architect or graphic designer – someone vaguely arty, but not a vegan. Maybe they'd share a blinding flash of eye contact then awkwardly look away. She'd meet his Home Counties parents at the end of Year One. Then perhaps in Year Three they'd share a one-bed flat in Ealing. The hope was that by Year Five the graphic designer/architect would be a senior partner in his architecture/design agency, and they'd move out to Essex or Sussex or something ending with 'ssex' and have a lovely little two-up, two-down with Farrow and Ball painted walls and Scandi floor lamps.

Getting married to an extremely rich and privileged Regency nobleman she'd only known for a few weeks had not featured in the sunflower notepad.

'Etta, please say something,' said Max, trying to decipher her expression.

'Eh-uh,' said Etta, feeling like Jeremy Paxman ending a particularly vicious round of *University Challenge*. Oxbridge vs Lincoln, perhaps. Without another word, she turned and left.

If she was still in 2023, Etta would simply have been able to book herself an Uber and cry into a pillow for the rest of the day, but in 1817 she had to sit quietly through lunch, then claim to have a headache so she could retire home. Her mother and brother clearly knew something was up between her and Max, but also seemed to recognise she needed some time to think about it.

'You rest, my dear, and all shall be well. Nothing needs to be decided in a hurry, after all,' her mother said kindly, as she pressed a lavender bag into Etta's palm and kissed it.

Both of them were being remarkably generous, Etta realised, if they knew anything about what was going on. It was 1817, after all, and now she thought back through the last weeks – or was it months, even? – she guessed that she had been spending a lot of time with Max. They had to know there was more to it by now.

And what would be so bad about being married to him anyway? On the face of it, he was rich, generous, kind and definitely seemed like he'd be on board the 'equal rights' train. She was sure being married to Max could be wonderful. But like so many heroines of the romantic novels she adored, she couldn't just marry someone 'because we coupled'. It would feel transactional. Like he was doing her a favour. Ugh.

She thought back to his face. His expression as he said goodbye to her after lunch. He'd looked how she felt. Awful. Was marriage to her really that terrible a proposition?

Chapter 34

2023

'Right, ladies and gents. Today's the day: online shopping. We've done our online safety, so now you know when *not* to put your credit card deets online. Today, let's find out when you *can*.'

Hetty had been looking forward to this class, and not just because she and Stella were meeting up after. Jemima had finished altering Stella's dress, so technically they could start making their videos. However, Stella had decreed one evening wouldn't be enough to film more than a few short videos – Hetty had no idea why not – so that was something for the weekend. Instead they were going shopping – offline shopping.

Hetty had to admit that while her aunts had done an excellent job of finding appropriate clothes for her, they certainly didn't help her fit in with other women her own age. Etta's wardrobe wasn't quite in her style either – stretched finances were probably the reason she'd had such a limited selection of plain dresses which Aggie had informed Hetty were 'quite suitable for the office'.

But there was no office for Hetty – and an alternative way to spend her time was yet to be discovered. Stella said her Substack was becoming increasingly popular and as a consequence her Instagram following had grown. If that continued, she might be able to do some 'commercial partnerships' or make 'ad revenue' by 'influencing consumers'. So making these videos would not only be a nice way to fill the hours, but also 'commercially savvy', whatever that meant. She wasn't entirely sure on the details, but Hetty was more than happy to leave it all to Stella.

As they wrapped up their lesson and headed down the street together, Hetty's shiny plastic card sweaty in her hand along with her phone, Stella bumped her elbow against hers.

'Right, so where's your bag, Hetty? And what's your budget?'

'Bag? Like a reticule? I don't have one. Or a budget, in fact.'

Stella winced. 'Skint, eh?' She laughed at Hetty's confusion. 'No money?'

Hetty bit her lip. 'Gosh, no, no need to worry about that. Money's different nowadays of course, but Aunt Aggie showed me how to see how much I have on my phone.'

Hetty handed over her phone, the screen showing a sum that would have deeply shocked anyone in 1817.

Stella nearly fell over. 'Hetty. *Hetty!* What the *actual hell*? Who *are* you?'

It was a vast sum in 2023 too, then.

Stella wordlessly marched them both to a reassuringly staid-looking pub, collapsed into a chair and set about ordering a stiff drink on her phone.

Her heart seemed to be beating loudly. It was going to be

a difficult one to explain. Hetty looked at Stella's serious face and felt a rising sense of fear. How much could she safely divulge without returning to being Mad Hetty Bainbridge? For the first time in some weeks she recalled her bracelet, safely stowed in her jewellery box.

'Please say something,' pleaded Hetty.

Stella seemed to regain her power of speech. 'I'm trying to make sense of everything. You're in your twenties, but don't know how to use a computer and you barely even know how to use a phone. You dress like an old lady. You talk like, I dunno, Jane Austen. I've been trying to take everything at face value, to go with the flow, but honestly . . . You have nearly a *hundred grand* in your goddamned *current account*.'

Stella took a deep breath and sat back in her chair. 'Explain.'

Hetty burst into tears.

In the end Hetty couldn't bring herself to lie to Stella, so a garbled version of the truth had come out between tears. Stella sat next to her, looking dazed, and full of questions.

'You come from 1817. Okay. Right, okay. We can revisit that later, because we're right in the middle of a Wetherspoons and people are . . . looking.'

A server appeared with two vodka and Cokes and, surprisingly thoughtfully, a box of tissues, illustrating Stella's point.

'What I'm getting from this is that you're not exactly used to having a hundred grand in your current account either.'

'I have more,' Hetty sniffed into a tissue. 'Aunt Aggie says this is for me to spend on "essentials". The rest is invested with an accountant.'

'With an accountant. Right.'

Stella rubbed her temples; Hetty watched on anxiously.

'It's just . . . I've never dated a rich chick before. My last girlfriend stole half my savings, in fact. That's why I wanted to take it slow. I might seem easy going, but I find it hard to trust people. This is all a little crazy . . .'

'For me, too,' said Hetty. 'If you like, I can give it away? Aunt Aggie said much of the interest payments goes to something called the Trussell Trust, which helps to feed people?'

'Really? That's pretty cool.'

'Yes, and she said the family funded part of a university, too. And a hospital. The Kent Wing? To be honest, it was a lot of information to take in and I'm not sure I understood it.'

'I just – oh wow. It's not easy to get my head around.'

'I thought . . . I thought it would be good?'

Hetty felt like the world was falling out from under her. Her face must have betrayed her, because Stella reached over and gave her a hug.

'I need some time to think about everything. About what I believe,' said Stella. 'I'm just not used to it. To the idea of people having this much money. It's . . . It's a lot.'

Stella left her then with the rest of the tissues and a promise to text her later, but it had felt off, like something had changed between them. So now here Hetty was, lying on her bed, crying so hard her head ached, with Jemima smoothing the hair away from her wet eyes.

'I don't understand, Aunt Jemima. I know it's a lot to take in. But, you know, in 1817, all anyone wanted was to be rich.'

Jemima sighed. 'It's the same nowadays, my love – or at least it is most of the time. But Stella has always struck me as an imaginative type – give her some time to process everything. I'm sure she'll come around. And anyway – would you really want anyone who only liked you for your money?'

Hetty sniffled. No, she supposed not. 'How do I make her come back, Aunt Jemima?'

'You can't. That's for her to decide.'

Chapter 35

1817

Etta played out her ill-fated conversation with Max a million ways: all the things she could – should – have said. She longed to tell someone what had happened between her and Max and as she stood next to Clarissa Best in a ballroom a week later, she was sorely tempted. Clarissa had been a good friend to Etta so far, but she had not one shred of gossip to her name. She knew her timid friend would be way beyond outraged by even the hint of a midnight tryst.

No, Clarissa was one more ally than Etta had had back in 2023 and she was determined to keep it that way. Clarissa might be kind, but she would undoubtedly draw a very solid line at as little as demure handholding, never mind third base. Etta was stone-cold certain that the merest hint of any 'coupling' with Max would rock Clarissa to her very core.

So instead, Etta and Clarissa were giggling over a particularly dreadful hat – green, orange and purple – when Lady Best kicked off. Time and time again, Lady Best would drag her daughter to a ball, then nearly as soon again leave as she insulted or was insulted by someone or other. Being insulted seemed to be Lady Best's favourite occupation: she was marvellous at it.

Her imperious tones cut through even the noise of the busy ballroom. 'Why, Mrs Blackwell, I do declare! I have seldom been forced to witness such boldness as this!' Her tone ascended in pitch like a roller coaster cranking up a particularly unpleasant track. 'To sully the Best name in such a manner as this! The audacity! Clarissa, let us go at once!'

'Oh no, not again,' Clarissa cringed. 'Etta, I'm so sorry.'

Etta grimaced. 'Leaving me on my own again, are you? Abandoning me to my terrible fate?'

Clarissa looked guilty as sin. 'Oh, Etta. I'm so, so sorry . . .'

Etta bit her lip awkwardly, inwardly appalled that her friend hadn't realised she was joking. 'Don't worry about me, I'm just having a laugh. Come on, let's do a discreet circuit to your mother and you can drop me off with Max's sister, Lizzie, and that other preggers lady next to her.'

A slightly turned-about Clarissa blinked and nodded, curtseying to Lizzie, then departing to follow her mother's imperious (and very loud) exit.

'Evening, Lizzie. How are you doing?'

Lizzie sighed. 'Oh, you know. Still terribly, terribly pregnant.'

'I suppose it must really suck to have to stay sober at a party as boring as this one.'

Her friend looked at her quizzically. 'Sober? Do you know, I do prefer not to drink alcohol. But how did you know?'

Etta blinked, taking another drink off a passing tray, then blinked once again as Lizzie's heavily pregnant companion took one for herself. Etta watched as the woman downed what she absolutely one hundred per cent knew to be fortified champagne.

It felt like every time she thought she was used to 1817, she was brought back down to earth. She paused, weighing up what to say next.

'I had read, lately, in . . . in a magazine? A periodical . . . I read that it was, um, safer, for pregnant women not to drink. Alcohol, I mean.'

Mrs Something-or-other – was it Henley? Who knew? – eyed her up while rubbing her belly smugly, almost resting her glass on her bump. 'You mean, in case one imbibes too freely and falls?'

Etta took a deep breath. In for a penny, in for a pound. 'No, I mean, that it can cause the baby to be born with foetal alco— sorry, um, intellectual difficulties. Of the mind.'

Mrs Henley – it was definitely Henley – scoffed. 'But what else must one drink, dear? Lemonade? Milk? How dull! And besides, I've already delivered Henley of a son. What more could one want?'

Etta bit her lip. She saw Lizzie watching her sympathetically, and they shared a Look.

Etta took another glass of champagne, then excused herself. She needed a break from all this . . . 1800s stuff. She wanted to find Max. She was long, long overdue a conversation with him. But right now, there were other pressing matters to consider. Like her bladder, which was full of champagne and telling her very loudly to make a quick exit.

A crowd was gathering in one corner of the ballroom – right in front, in fact, of the most direct route to the ladies' loos. She ambled over tipsily, somewhat dreading the amount of time it would take her to free herself from her skirts.

The effete Mr Smythe was the centre of the crowd, Etta saw, as she fought her way through to the chamber pots. He was clutching a pair of gloves and seething with anger, Miss Marley hanging from one elbow, looking equally furious.

'Sir, I demand satisfaction! Your insult to myself and Miss Marley will not stand!' he declared pompously.

The impeccably dressed blonde man Smythe was facing off against looked slightly pale, but louche nonetheless.

'Dearest Smythe. All I said was that you and she are made for one another, being much of the same character,' he replied, gesturing between Smythe and Maria Marley. 'What could be wrong with that?'

'That character which I believe you have been impugning in every club in the city?' raged Smythe.

'Look, Smythe, if you must traipse around being Friday-faced—'

Maria Marley had turned as puce as her hair ribbons. 'SMYTHE!' she shrieked. 'You heard him, Smythe! Insulting the two of us. And in front of everyone here present!'

Etta had had enough. She'd never get herself to the bogs if this continued, even if intervening would probably save the idiotically weak and ultimately very drunken Smythe's life.

Smythe pushed out his chest like a pigeon, raising his gloves as if to strike. 'Swords or pistols then, Lord Bramley?'

'Rocks!' called Etta, holding out her fist. Every eye in the house swivelled towards Etta as her voice rang out. She swayed slightly as she tried again. 'No, no, not rocks, then? Urgh . . . Paper!' She flattened out her hand.

Silence prevailed. Smythe and Maria were visibly stunned, as was their opponent. Smiling, the other man – Lord Bramley – seized his opportunity, stepping forward with his fingers spread.

'Scissors beats paper, I believe!'

'Oh, I swear I'm terrible at these things,' said Etta. 'Shall we play again? I know we haven't been formally introduced, but I do usually win.'

Maria Marley just really couldn't help herself. 'Probably because people let you win, Mad Hetty Bainbridge.'

'Probably,' Etta replied, 'but I win myself so much pocket money that I really couldn't care less.'

Chuckles arose from the crowd and Maria snapped out of her rage and visibly shrank back as though slapped.

'Come, Smythe. These people are beneath our notice.'

'Or above,' chimed in Lord Bramley, winning himself an elbow in his ribs from Etta.

'I don't know who you are, but I need you alive,' Etta whispered. 'The enemy of my enemy, etcetera.'

The gentleman turned to her, smiling cheekily 'Miss Bainbridge, please do not labour under the impression I could not deal with one such as Smythe.'

'You must excuse me. The only thing I'm labouring under is the weight of my bladder. Good evening, sir.'

Her new chum choked back laughter and though somewhere in her vicinity, she also heard the distinctive tones of Max Stanhope, the call of the wild was too much: she made her escape and when she returned, he was nowhere to be found.

Chapter 36

1817

Etta didn't hear from either Max or her new friend Rock Paper Scissors Guns Swords again right away; when she did first hear of them, it was indirectly. But also directly, in so far as the woman who plonked herself down in the chair next to Etta's at the huge annual party at Lady Dinklage's house was nothing if not direct.

They'd arrived early and Etta had found a corner to hide in while the room filled up. This had turned out to be an excellent way to tune into the gossip mill, and she was quite dismayed to find out she was right in the middle. After just half an hour sitting behind two middle-aged women, she'd learned all about how she'd brazenly seduced the eligible Lord Stanhope with her Wild Ways. And even the renowned rogue Lord George Bramley seemed to be rather taken by her – they'd been seen laughing together at Lord Grimsby's ball, hadn't they?

She'd watched *Bridgerton*. Of course, there was no Lady Whistledown in her version of 1817. Nobody had said a word to her about these whisperings – not even Clarissa

Best – so she'd been completely in the dark. Hearing it now was deeply unpleasant – had Clarissa known and kept her completely ignorant about all of it? Etta couldn't work out if this decision was merciful or not.

But given they were A Thing, she probably was going to have to make a decision about her future with Max soon – if there was even still a decision open to her.

Thankfully she was interrupted from the gathering storm cloud of her thoughts by the sound of rustling skirts. A rose-scented, delicately-braceleted arm wrapped across the back of Etta's chair.

'So, I hear you rescued my brother George from a drunken skewering by Smythe the other night. Ta muchly, I must say,' the woman said.

Etta looked at her new dark-haired companion with mild surprise. A red-haired woman immediately appeared on her left. 'Oh, don't worry about Tessa. She's always so terribly forward. I'm Melissa, by the way. Melissa Bramley.'

Etta blinked. 'Nice to meet you, I suppose. You're welcome . . .?'

Melissa grinned. 'Oh, don't be all uppity. We know we should have made friends with you ages ago, but Dear Clarissa is such a stick-in-the-mud. Besides, everyone said you were mad.'

Her first instinct was to defend her friend, but less than a moment's reflection told her the redhead was right. Clarissa was a wonderful, loyal friend – but the woman in front of her was possibly the jolliest person she'd ever laid eyes on. She was infectiously jolly. Almost—

'Painfully jolly, isn't she? Oh, don't glare at me, Lissie. You know it's true,' said Tessa.

Etta turned to Tessa and raised an eyebrow. 'Not you, though?'

Lissie laughed behind her, in reply. 'Oh no, not Tessa.'

Tessa coughed, pointedly, and turned to Etta. 'Miss Bainbridge, Tessa Bramley.'

She dipped into a half-hearted curtsey.

'It's lovely to finally make your acquaintance, Henrietta,' said Lissie, dipping to mirror her sister.

'Lissie! You know that's too informal. Miss Bainbridge—'

Etta had seen enough. 'Etta. Call me Etta. It is bloody brilliant to meet you both.'

Both sisters seemed to let out a collective sigh of relief. Tessa was the first to recover. 'Thank goodness for that,' she said. 'We have a reputation, you know.'

'Yes,' Lissie added. 'For being a little . . . raucous.'

Etta sat back, so she could smile at them both at the same time. 'Raucous is good. I can handle raucous.'

At that, Lissie jumped up and grabbed Etta's hand, hauling her up, too. 'Well, there we are, then. Do you know,' she added mischievously, 'I very much think we should go and check out Lady Dinklage's orangery.'

'Oh, yes,' Tessa said, as they walked briskly toward the nearest door. 'Mustn't forget to peruse the orangery.'

It didn't exactly require a superior intellect to understand that something interesting awaited Etta in Lady Dinklage's orangery, but as she followed Tessa and Lissie and caught a familiar scent wafting on the air she quickly knew this was wholly new territory.

The glass of the orangery was opaque with smoke – marijuana smoke. She stood in the doorway and took in the scene. Cushions were piled in the central walkway, with about half a dozen women and men her own age sitting on metal garden chairs or reclining against the raised beds. They were passing around a brown pipe – an old-fashioned sort of thing she vaguely remembered some uncle from her youth carrying – with the unmistakable scent of weed on the air. So this is what had been behind all of those closed doors.

It was reminiscent of her school prom, except with muslin instead of net and much, much better hair.

Lissie grabbed her hand and hauled her down to a cushion right next to her brother, who looked up and grinned at her lazily. 'Ahh, Miss Bainbridge. Welcome to the club. I see you've met my sisters. Are you familiar with this unique herb? Lady Dinklage's late husband was rather fascinated by botany, so we never fail to attend her soirees.'

Etta adjusted her skirts thoughtfully. Now she came to think of it, there really was no reason weed wouldn't be smoked in Regency England, was there? Sure, Georgette Heyer didn't exactly dwell on it, but then there was an awful lot the historical romance genre hadn't prepared her for.

Etta sighed, the desire to fit in perfectly complemented by the urgent need to let loose. 'Pass it over, then,' she said.

Lord George Bramley raised an eyebrow thoughtfully, but handed the pipe over. 'I think you'll make a nice little addition to our group, Miss Bainbridge.'

She lay back on her cushion as the high hit, looking around her.

'So you're telling me you've all been hiding in orangeries getting wasted while I've been sitting at the side of the ballrooms watching stuffy people dancing and getting ragged on by Maria Marley?'

'But that's not all you've been up to, is it?' asked Tessa.

'I hear you're practically engaged to our good friend Lord Stanhope.'

Lord Bramley winked. 'Shame.'

Etta couldn't remember the last time she'd smoked weed – university, probably, back before everyone had gone back to their respective hometowns to work remotely or marry their childhood sweethearts. Lady Dinklage's marijuana was not the same oregano-laced stuff they'd sold in Manchester's Piccadilly Gardens, for sure.

She blinked, trying to focus. 'Lord Stanhope. He's perfect. Seems too good to be true. Not sure I'm a good enough girl for him, though. And, well, marriage . . . Should you really marry someone you haven't known all that long?'

Etta refused the pipe as it made its way round again. Lissie giggled and handed it to the woman next to her before hugging Etta impulsively.

'Oh, I'm certain you are. And don't we all marry strangers, anyway?'

Lissie had a point there. Tessa joined in the hug, clearly off her face.

'Etta, darling. You really must marry him, you know. His sister adores you, all the gossipy old tabbies of the *Ton* are talking and besides, he can't keep his eyes off you.'

A loud and very pointed cough drew their attention. Etta looked up to see the subject of their discussion looming attractively over them.

'Ah, Miss Bainbridge. I see you've befriended the Bramley clan,' said Max, looking rather resigned.

He waved away the pipe offered to him from a grinning Lord Bramley. Etta was surprised by how relieved she was to finally see him.

'George,' he nodded in acknowledgement. 'Always good to see you and your delightful sisters.'

Etta felt momentarily jealous as Tessa and Lissie smiled at Max, but then turned to find him looking at her.

Tessa's voice cut through her haze. 'Oh, is it, Lord Stanhope? Seems like all you can see is our new friend Etta.'

'Yes, tell us, Stanhope. When can we wish you happy?' drawled Lord Bramley.

'Just as soon as Etta tells me so.'

Etta and Max entered a stare-off and she couldn't look away.

The rest of the group started gossiping about a supposed secret liaison between Maria Marley and Smythe, but Etta felt as though the whole world was melting into nothingness around them. Only Max mattered now.

Max's expression became serious and he dropped his voice. 'When will you tell me so, Etta? The Bramleys are right – the tabbies are talking. Besides, I have ruined you.'

'No,' Etta whispered, the marijuana making her feel elated and honest all at the same time. 'You haven't ruined anything. Everything is absolutely perfect.'

'Then marry me.'

'Why? Because I have to?'

They were nose to nose, but Max suddenly seemed to recollect their surroundings and hauled her up to her feet.

'I think I'd better return you to your mother, Miss Bainbridge. Spending too much time with these reprobates and their mysterious herb will do nothing to help your reputation and will likely addle your mind.'

Lord Bramley laughed. 'See you at White's, then, Stanhope? I'll expect to read the engagement announcement before the end of the week.'

Max jaw was clenched tightly as he led her back through to the ballroom. 'Miss Bainbridge, I am sorry that I have put you in this position, I really am. I should never have let things escalate as I did. But you must accept my hand in marriage. You truly must. When may I ask your brother?'

Etta sighed. She knew he was being noble and well-mannered and chivalrous and all the things a young lady in 1817 would be lucky to find. Marriage with him would promise financial stability, and high societal standing, and plenty of hot carriage snogging. But he was also using a few too many *musts* and *shoulds* for her liking. Being strong-armed into a marriage of convenience was not on the table for her.

He was looking at her expectantly, but her mind was a jumble of competing thoughts.

'Will you give me Christmas to think about it?' she said eventually. 'I didn't really expect to be getting married any time before thirty. It feels . . . weird, I guess.'

'Thirty?' he repeated, appalled. She saw anxiety in his eyes and realised suddenly how intensely vulnerable he looked.

'It's not that I'm totally against it. It just feels so quick,' she added.

Max rocked on his feet. 'I've barely slept this past week. If anyone finds out I've compromised you . . .'

'Compromised!' repeated Etta, stifling a laugh. The whole thing seemed so absurd to her all of a sudden – she felt giddy with it.

'Etta, this is serious. This is your reputation we're talking about. This is about the rest of your life. If anyone at all in this room, even a servant, had even an inkling of what has passed between us—'

'I know, I'm sorry, I'm sorry. It's just rather surreal, that's all,' said Etta.

She supposed that her whole reality now was surreal, but somehow over the last weeks she had stopped questioning it. Was she really in a ballroom right now, in 1817, rebuffing a male supermodel's marriage proposal?

The old ladies on the Tube had asked her if she wanted a holiday in Regency London, but this had become so much more than that. Marriage was meant to be a lifelong commitment, wasn't it? Was that what was holding her back?

She opened her mouth to give him a proper answer, but no words came out.

'I'll write to you over Christmas,' said Etta quickly. She could see her mother weaving her way towards them through the crowd. 'That's all I can promise. For now.'

Lady Bainbridge's amused voice cut through the air as she took Etta's arm. 'Enjoy the orangery, dear? I know Lady Dinklage is particularly proud of it.'

Christmas seemed to come around so much sooner than everyone had expected and before she knew it, Etta was whisked off back to the countryside to spend Christmas at Bainbridge House. Almost every upper crust family had fled London for the festivities, and the Bainbridges were no exception.

As a rule, Etta loathed and despised Christmas. Every schmaltzy advert and themed chocolate bar and sad piece of office tinsel had been agony. In the past, she had spent the day itself in lonely misery watching Christmas specials over a bucket of leftover KFC. Not once since her dad had died had Christmas seemed like an even remotely good idea.

But Christmas back at the estate was unlike anything she had ever witnessed. In costume dramas she'd always wondered how miserable it must be for the servants to have to slave away while the poshos had fun, but in actual fact everyone was equal parts merry and productive.

While kitchen staff prepared huge spiced boiled hams and mulled vats of sweet wine, which made the entire house smell a million times better than any peppermint third-hand Secret Santa Yankee Candle (Etta couldn't say she missed those at all), she and her mother got to work draping boughs of rather prickly local foliage around the hallways.

There was no tree, but Etta was fine with that – the only Christmas tree she was used to decorating was the one in the office reception, because putting one up in her studio flat had always seemed like the ultimate exercise in futility. Besides, she'd thrown away the family decorations the first Christmas after Dad had gone. There was only so much pain she could take, and seeing her long-gone mother's family baubles was so far across the invisible line she'd drawn for herself that it might as well have been on the horizon.

So Christmas with her new family was something new, and unbelievably welcome: she was finally ready to start again. Some of the traditions were really quite wonderful, too: putting together baskets of expensive goodies for the people who lived on the estate was a highlight. She had loved sitting in the morning room with her mother, close to a roaring fire, parcelling up packages of her mother's favourite robust tea leaves, bundles of dried fruit, and hanks of sugar loaf. Even Charlie had joined in, despite it being, as he'd attempted to put it, 'really just for the girls, surely'.

Her brother might be a bit of a feckless idiot, but he

took his duty to the people on his estate very seriously indeed – the last Lord Bainbridge had drummed it into him very thoroughly, but Charlie was also a very kind and generous man. It had been good spending more time with him, too.

'So clever of you to think of pinning the ribbons instead of cutting them, Henrietta. Ribbons really are extortionate these days. I think I might ask Nanny whether she has any receipts for dyes, too, although I might not ask you to copy them out – I know you've been practising, but your handwriting is still really quite dreadful.'

Lady Bainbridge turned a beady eye to Charlie, who was attempting to untangle ribbons and failing miserably.

'Charles, I believe that means the duty falls to you.'

Charlie groaned, but didn't attempt to remonstrate.

'If that means Etta can deal with these bloody buggering ribbons – sorry for cursing, Mother, but they really are the outside of enough – then I'm all for it.'

He earned a rap on the head with a roll of parcel paper as he passed by, but Lady Bainbridge was in a good mood.

'You know, Henrietta, this is the best Christmas I think we have enjoyed for perhaps a decade or more.' She wiped away a stray tear. 'It really has been wonderful, these past few months, having you back with us.'

Etta gave her mother a hug, feeling her own tears welling.

'I know, Mama. It's been wonderful being here, too,' Etta said.

'Just. . . Please don't leave us again, Henrietta. I don't think I could bear it.'

'I won't,' she promised, remembering the bracelet now buried deep in a box, along with Hetty's long-forgotten notebooks, and hugging her mother even tighter.

It could stay there forever, as far as she was concerned. It really had been perhaps the best thing that had ever happened to her – The Switch had been incredible, and Christmas was a highlight she'd never seen coming. Every season was better than the last.

But one thing played on her mind more than anything, like a deep current running through every festivity. Etta knew Max was waiting for her to make her decision, and it was time. She'd asked Bessie if there was a way to deliver his present over to his house nearby and had bravely put a note in one toe as she carefully wrapped the slippers in tissue paper – the brightly coloured embroidered tigers shining against the navy velvet in the candlelight.

Chapter 37

2023

Stella's text came at midnight: *Been thinking about the videos. Wld be funny to get you to react to stories from Reddit. I like this one.*

There was a link, which Hetty clicked. It jumped straight to the words: 'Sounds perfect for you – you've already fallen for her, right? She's a winner with or without the cash. Who cares if she's a little cray-cray? I say stick with it and see how it pans out.'

There was another underneath: 'Seems like OP is freaking out more about the money than the whole Regency thing. Controversial but I don't see any problem in having a rich GF haha.'

Hetty scrolled up.

My millionaire girlfriend (21F) told me (23F) she's a Regency lady and I think I believe her?

The title, really. I met this woman at a class I run at an adult learning centre and she's so unique. Sweet, cute, and very caring. Plus totally gorgeous.

The only problem is she says she's from the 1800s and weirdly I kind of believe her? She dresses like an old lady and has a really posh voice. She hasn't got a clue how to use computers or her mobile phone which is how I met her. She got her aunt to make me a dress as well for this short form video idea we had and it's exactly like something out of Bridgerton.

She came to computing classes and she legit didn't even know what a credit card was. Then today I saw her online banking and she's got a hundred grand in her bloody current account and no idea how much it is.

I was already kinda freaked out that she lived with her two super rich aunts in some central London mansion and now it turns out she's super rich herself. I'm from a council estate FFS. Not even sure how I'd introduce her to my family.

Is it weird that I want to carry on with our relationship? I kind of don't mind about the whole Regency lady thing but I'm not sure how I feel about dating someone so completely different to me.

Hetty clicked on 'View all comments.' It was a mixed bag, but all the top-voted opinions were things like 'Stop moaning about your super rich pretty girlfriend' and 'Does it really matter if she's a bit mental if you like her? Because it sounds like you really do.'

Her phone vibrated with another message from Stella: *Happy Christmas – hope you had a nice time with the Aunts.*

Sorry I freaked out. Shall we take two on that shopping trip? I'm off work tomorrow. See you outside River Island at 10?

Hetty collapsed backwards onto her bed with relief. It had been a long, worrying Christmas without Stella, however cosy it had been sitting around eating Aggie's enormous roast lunch and drinking Jemima's home-brewed spirit she called 'Damson Gut Rot'. They'd still been drunk on Boxing Day.

She hit the green button next to Stella's name, seeking her voice: needing to know for certain that everything was going to be okay.

'Hetty?' Stella sounded even more exhausted than Hetty. 'You know nobody calls people on the phone, right?'

'Why does it let me, then?'

'Fair enough.'

Hetty heard Stella moving and realised she must be in bed. She felt a rising blush touch her ears. 'So . . . You've changed your mind? You'll still court me?'

Stella huffed with laughter.

'Court you. . . ! Hetts, I never made my mind up in the first place. I've never met anyone who makes me feel like this. But you tell me you're from 18-something—'

'1817.'

'Okay, 1817. So you're by far the strangest girlfriend I've ever, ever had. Even stranger than the girl who kept frogs, and the girl who used to steal wallpaper, and even the girl who couldn't have sex unless she was watching a live recording of Metallica's 2003 Summer Sanitorium tour.'

'My goodness, that's a lot of suitors . . .! All those women. . .' said Hetty.

'Yes, and not one of them was from the 1800s, Hetty.' Stella broke off, sighing, then continued, 'But you really are from then, aren't you? I've barely got my head around that. You're, like, two hundred years old! You come from a place that didn't even have cars! And your main concern – your primary worry, in all of this, Hetty – is my dating history?'

Hetty sank back against her headboard, fisting her hand in her pillow. 'Well, I don't have one,' said Hetty in a small voice. 'A history, that is. Nobody has ever courted me before. Marriage has never been on my horizon before.'

'Marriage?' Stella snorted. 'Oh, Hetty. You're getting a bit carried away, aren't you? And anyway, marriage is a bit old-fashioned, isn't it?'

Hetty didn't know how to respond, but Stella had started laughing.

'Don't worry, Hetts – it's an adventure. And the only way to go on an adventure is one step at a time. One foot in front of another.'

'That's the wisest thing I've ever heard, I think.'

Stella laughed again. 'I know, right? I got it off Reddit.'

Hetty had slept like the dead. The next morning Aggie taught her how to use the map app on her phone and keyed in River Island, a worryingly modern-looking, sharp-edged shop that was far larger and more intimidating than Hetty would have liked. The Christmas lights were almost dazzling, tourists occasionally jostling her as they made their way from one attraction to the next, but Hetty was already getting used to it. The busyness didn't bother her when it was Stella she was waiting for.

She stood nervously on the opposite side of the road away from the main thoroughfare, simultaneously excited and fearful of seeing Stella again.

But when Stella appeared she immediately wrapped Hetty in a huge hug. She melted into her, oblivious to her sincere apology, gratefully sliding her chilled hand into Stella's delightfully warm one as they crossed the road.

'I'm so sorry, Hetty. Like I said on the phone, I didn't mean to freak out. I just . . . I dunno, I don't know any rich people. Or Regency ladies, obviously,' Stella said. 'But then I remembered that you're just Hetty.'

'No, I'm sorry. I should have told you earlier about everything. I was just . . . scared. That you'd . . . I don't know . . .'

Stella laughed and completed her sentence. 'That I'd freak out, exactly like I did?'

'Well, yes, I suppose . . .'

Stella's hand squeezed hers. 'I don't know if I fully get the whole Regency thing, but it explains a lot. And it gave me a great idea for our videos, if you're up for it?'

They'd been planning to riff off Hetty's diaries, but Stella had noticed a fascinating online trend for reading – and reacting – to online horror stories of relationships and situations gone wrong. The idea of staid old Hetty reading the very worst of Reddit while dressed in her fancy shot silk gown in the middle of the aunts' eclectic sitting room clearly spoke to Stella's sense of the ridiculous. Hetty had to agree, having spent twenty horrified minutes browsing Reddit the night before.

As Stella had rightfully pointed out, though, Hetty couldn't spend the rest of her life veering between Regency ballgowns and the full-length dresses her aunts had picked out for her. They'd served her well while she'd adjusted to her new surroundings, but it had only taken one session of people-watching in a café for Hetty to realise she was dressed very conservatively indeed compared to her modern peers.

But it was one thing seeing other people wearing short skirts and showing their middles. Though Hetty was not at all averse to seeing anyone's middle, it was another thing completely to wear a crop top herself – especially as the winter chill set in.

Hetty stood in the brightly lit changing room staring at herself. Stella had given her a heavy armful of clothing to hang in the changing room and was now sitting on a chair outside the curtained cubicles waiting for her patiently. The pile had contained a variety of dresses – they'd decided to stick to dresses for now – and Hetty's eye had immediately been drawn to a tiny, stretchy, silver one.

It was completely unlike anything Hetty had ever seen or imagined. She'd wrestled it on and then stood wrapped in awe at her own body for several minutes. She could hardly believe such a thing could be considered clothing.

'You okay in there?' came Stella's worried voice.

Hetty paused. 'I'm trying the glittering silver one. I'm – I'm not sure I've got it on correctly, frankly.'

'Are you decent? Come show me.'

Hetty might as well have been naked, she thought, as she bravely stepped out from behind the curtain. Her arms and torso were covered – the dress had a high, wide neck and long sleeves – but the vast majority of her long, strong legs were completely on display. Nobody but Bessie and Mrs Cummings had seen this much of her body before.

Hetty felt air on her legs and struggled not to cover herself with the curtain, but then dared to look up from the floor and saw Stella's face.

Stella was looking at her as though . . . well, as though she were the brightly shining moon, dazzling in the night sky, clothed in glittering stars. Which fitted, since Stella was still – would always be – the sun. They gazed at one another for a few long seconds before Stella finally spoke.

'That's it. You're definitely coming out with me and the boys for New Year's Eve.'

'But I already came out, surely?'

Stella rolled her eyes. 'Out-out.'

'Oh.' Hetty nodded knowingly, knowing nothing at all. 'Out Out. I see.'

'No, you don't.' Stella laughed. 'But you will.'

Chapter 38

1817

Max was, as so often the case when he travelled in this direction, 'on the lam' as Etta's dear deceased father would have put it. According to Charlie, Max's own father had nearly exploded over Christmas lunch when Max had once again rebuffed his recommendation of a bride for him: the beautiful but highly toxic Miss Marley. The story was, Lord Kent had tried a different approach: an apoplexy.

Etta had always wondered what an apoplexy was, and after questioning Charlie closely it turned out it meant Lord Kent was having one of his infamous tantrums. The Marquess was perfectly fine: apparently he knew it, and Max knew it – even the butler knew it. Lord Kent had apparently kept peeking at him under his eyelids as he moaned and groaned and clutched his chest. Consequently, Max had been able to slip off to Lady Bainbridge's New Year's Eve soirée in his waiting carriage as planned.

Yes, her note had said. Just *Yes*.

The truth was, she had made her decision the same night she'd asked him to give her more time. Maybe before that, even. Long, long before that. She couldn't quite honestly say she'd fallen in love with him at first sight, but there had always been something about him – something right, something that slotted into place right back in that cellar. She might have been busy freaking out at the time, but even then there had been . . . comfort. He just radiated comfort – not just physical, but in every possible way. He just fitted.

Ultimately, it felt like it had been the old ladies from the Tube that got her over the line, in the end. *Roll with it*, they'd said. They'd also mentioned a marquess, hadn't they? And they seemed to feel pretty positive about how things ended up. Even without the instinct, deep down in her stomach, that was telling her it was what she needed, she could reconcile the logic to herself that way.

Being a *Roll with it* kind of person didn't seem like a bad way to live – though, admittedly, Etta was pretty high when she'd come to that conclusion. Still, she'd decided to go all in. The Regency life had its challenges, but even discounting how she felt about Max, overall the last weeks had been a blast. She'd had more fun in her short time in 1817 than she'd had in her whole life in the entire twenty-first century.

Sure, there were no mobile phones. No endless rows of chocolate bars and popcorn, no quick flights to the continent, no TV reruns of *Judge Judy*, no sweatpants. But Etta was used to spending her evenings doing something more productive than googling unaffordable weekend breaks while stuffing her face in front of CBS Reality until the logo had permanently burned itself onto her TV screen. She'd read more in the last couple of months than she had in the couple of years before that, she'd played pianos more beautiful than she'd even dreamed of touching in her old life, and she'd been to more parties than she had in the whole three years she'd spent at university. Her dresses might not have any give in them, but they made her feel like a queen.

And let's face it, Max Stanhope in his tight capris and neat cravat was infinitely superior to the last six Hinge dates she'd been on in 2023 – in fact to anyone she'd ever dated in her life.

He was looking dashing as ever tonight in his evening attire, ostensibly listening to one of the local gentry talking about crop yields but in reality watching Etta out of the corner of one eye. She felt beautiful in her favourite blue evening dress as she stared at him brazenly – completely unable to stop herself and unwilling even to try as she watched her prey held captive by his monotonous tenant.

Thankfully Charlie was there to swoop in and Etta watched in amusement as he completely failed to notice that Max wasn't alone. She moved around a column so she could earwig on their conversation.

'Stanhope, old fellow! On the run from Dearest Papa, are we?'

She saw Max grin, as the worthy local squire and his wheat harvest finally sodded off. 'How on earth did you guess?'

Charlie gestured to a nearby footman to top up their glasses. 'It was in my waters, Maximillian. In my waters. Don't worry, there's always a room for you here in the family quarters. Stay after dinner, play some billiards.'

'Don't mind if I do,' said Max.

Etta stepped forward.

'Enjoying the champers, old girl? Looking rather snazzy tonight, I must say,' said Charlie.

Etta simply raised an eyebrow, watching Max finish his

glass. Yes, his suit was smart – he really did have excellent taste – but as ever, all she could focus on was his face. He was smiling at her – a wide, genuine smile that she knew he never showed to anyone else – and any other thoughts just melted away. She just had to be near him.

They were called in for dinner and she gratefully found herself seated next to Max. When her mother winked at her, she knew it was no coincidence.

Max touched her hand gently under the tablecloth as Charlie gave a rambling, completely unprepared speech to the table about welcoming in the New Year – a family tradition, apparently – and leaned towards her subtly.

'Thank you for the slippers. And the note.'

Etta bit her lip. 'Did you – did you like them?'

'Oh yes. They were quite unforgettable.'

Of course they could hardly share any intimate feelings over dinner, especially since half the table seemed to be watching them. They were both delighted, though, to find Lady Bainbridge had served her signature raspberry trifle.

'The problem with your mother's trifle,' Max told Etta wryly, 'is that there's never enough of it.'

She laughed. 'Oh, but I know where Cook keeps her secret extra trifle, so it's not a problem for me. She always makes an additional bowl or two for the pantry.'

'I wonder if your mother would consider handing over the family recipe?' Max watched Etta's face, and she understood that he was asking if she had changed her mind.

She carefully replied, 'Yes, I believe she would.'

He raised his glass. 'Well, cheers to that.'

She merrily clinked her glass against his, her heart soaring, and they drank together.

Lady Bainbridge's attention was caught from across the crowded table. 'A toast? What are you toasting to, Etta?'

Max grinned. 'Your trifle, madam.'

The whole table ended up drunkenly toasting Lady Bainbridge's trifle, much to her pink-cheeked mock consternation, before the ladies left the gentlemen to their port.

They'd all gone to bed late and drunk. Etta tried to sleep, but she ended up snoring on her back and woke herself up. Groggily, still half-drunk, she stood up to use the chamber pot.

She'd been having a wonderful dream about raspberry trifle. Trifle, and Max. She'd been smearing it on her tits while he sucked it off. She shivered at the thought of it. Etta remembered the look on his face as he'd gently kissed her hand before bed and wondered what he was up to now. She knew he planned to ask Charlie formally for her hand in the morning, so he was probably as asleep as she'd have liked to have been.

Her stomach rumbled loudly, and she went over to her mantelpiece to look for the beautiful, delicate little carriage clock her mother had given her for Christmas. She'd had it etched with the words 'Time to wake up' in gorgeous but hard-to-read copperplate lettering and Etta had cried when she'd unwrapped it. She couldn't deny it – she was undeniably happy here. Life was good, full of family, love, great champagne . . . She was definitely still rather tipsy.

It was 3 a.m. Everyone would be asleep by now – servants and all.

Etta remembered what she'd told Max about the trifle Cook always squirrelled away in the pantry and made a snap decision. She might not be able to log onto her smartphone and get a kebab and some cheesy chips delivered, but she sure as hell could put a dressing gown on and find a spoon for that trifle.

Lighting a candle from her dwindling fire, she crept downstairs still thinking about her X-rated dream. She thought back to their illicit encounter after he'd caught her in the garden. About how he'd looked as he moved against her. How he'd felt.

Imagine waking up to that every morning, she thought. To his smile, his ruffled hair, his long, muscled body. As she padded through the moonlit kitchen, she remembered how he'd carried her that first night and wished he was there to carry her again. God, she'd had so much pudding wine with that trifle and it was already drenched with sherry. Oh well, a little more couldn't hurt.

The only spoon she could find was a huge one that Cook used for, well, cooking, but it would do. The servants had clearly had trifle for dinner too, but luckily there was a good half-bowl left. She greedily dug her spoon straight in.

My god, it was good. She'd always thought the M&S raspberry trifle was the best, but the addition of a layer of ginger cake instead of lady fingers was pure genius. She didn't miss the jelly at all, preferring the thick layer of sweet yet sharp jam-like raspberry coulis there instead.

She was just a spoon in when she heard the quiet sound of feet on the stone flagstones and looked up, too drunk to be afraid. There in front of her was the subject of her trifle-related fantasies, looking rumpled with hair flying in all directions and his shirt untucked into his knee-britches.

Max stopped, swaying slightly. 'Miss Bainbridge,' he

croaked, sounding like he too had been fast asleep only moments ago. 'Trifle.'

She giggled and put on her Lady Best impression. 'Why, Lord Stanhope. Have you come to trifle with me?'

He sighed. 'I should have known you'd be here, Etta. You've invaded every corner of my thoughts and now here you are, invading the delicious, delicious trifle, too.'

Etta laughed as he made a grab for the spoon and hopped away. 'No, it's mine, all mine! Bad man! No trifle for you! . . . Oh!' She had overloaded her spoon and, firm as it was, some trifle had fallen off.

They both looked down at Etta's nightdress. A cold dollop of cream and custard had landed on her left nipple, which had immediately peaked beneath the thin fabric.

His eyes widened. 'You really should clean that up.'

'Why don't you clean it up for me?' she replied saucily.

To both of their surprise, Max lowered his mouth to her nightdress-covered breast and sucked off the custard. He pulled back suddenly, eyes dark with lust and longing.

Etta looked at him appraisingly, then, without breaking eye contact, brought the spoon to her right breast.

'Etta. I'm not sure I can control myself if you . . .'

'Then don't.'

She slowly and deliberately dropped custard on her nipple. His eyes darkened even further and she knew she had him.

He stepped forward again, looked her in the eyes one last time, then kissed her. 'You'd better not get custard on my shirt, Miss Bainbridge.'

She leaned backwards across the table as he sucked on her second nipple. Instinctively, her legs opened to accommodate his and she felt his hardness against her core. She writhed as he returned to her first breast, needing more. The wet fabric pressed against her body as she felt his tongue and fingers moving across her hard nipples.

He pulled back to adjust himself, looking down at her in the moonlight. She felt completely open to him, dizzy not just with wine but with lust, and yes – yes, love. It coursed through her – rivers and rivers of love.

'Oh, Etta,' he whispered tenderly. 'What shall I do with you?'

It was a rhetorical question, but one she knew how to answer. The spoon lay abandoned next to her and she fumbled for it before sitting up.

She raised her skirts to her knees, feeling braver and more beautiful than she ever had before, then went to smear the last of the trifle . . . who knew where?

His mouth quirked into a wicked grin. 'I'll take that, thank you very much.'

He took the spoon from her and gave her a quick kiss, pushing her back onto the table, then disappeared. She felt hands on her ankle, and then her knees, and then up the insides of her thighs. Then she felt the cold touch of metal, cream and custard on the most intimate part of her.

Then, finally, his tongue, sliding up her body, and again, pushing inside, exploring her. Oh my, but Max was good at this.

He started slowly, judging her body by her sounds and movements. She soon lost herself to the feeling of his tongue, his fingers until her orgasm swept over her. She felt it all the way to her toes.

Max came up to kiss her neck, his hand gripping himself through his trousers as he desperately tried to keep it together.

'More. Max, more.'

'I can't. Not here. Not on this table.'

He went to lift her up, but she protested and wriggled free. He began to groan, frustrated and desperate, but she held up the empty spoon and tapped him on the nose.

'You'll be needing those arms to carry that trifle bowl.'

Chapter 39

2023

Stella and Hetty slid into a cab just after 9 p.m., which was only slightly before Hetty would usually be sliding into bed. She yawned.

Stella raised a finger. 'Ah, I got this. Figured this might be a late one for you.' She shook a can of M&S espresso martini and handed it to Hetty, who looked at it in confusion.

'What . . . How do I . . .?'

Baffled, she saw Stella staring at her with equal bemusement.

'You really, actually, do come from the past, don't you? I'm still not sure whether to believe you, but one way or another you're definitely not from *here*.'

Hetty smelled the heady, familiar scent of lemon and mint as Stella leaned over and opened the tin can for her. 'Drink – it's alcoholic, if you're up for drinking tonight?'

Hetty sniffed at the can. Coffee. She took a sip. Strong, tipsy-smelling coffee. She pulled at the hem of her scary, exciting silver dress. Yes, she was indeed up for drinking tonight. She worked her way through the can as Stella prepared her for the night ahead with an agenda.

'So it's gonna be noisy, Hetty. *Loud*. And proper crowded, but don't worry because you've got your phone. Oh, and I've brought you earplugs in case it gets too much. We're going to the pub first so you can meet the lads.'

'Which lads?'

Stella laughed – truly Hetty's favourite sound in the world – and grabbed her bag as she paid the cabbie and handed Hetty out.

'Oh, I don't know what they're going to make of you. I hope you like them, Hetts.'

This evening Stella came up past her shoulder, much taller than usual in tottering golden shoes. Her bright yellow dress was far smaller even than Hetty's, and Hetty was both awed by and admiring of her audacity. She couldn't help looking, even though her eyes didn't seem to know where to look – Stella's eyes, her legs, her smooth arms, her breasts . . .

Stella caught her finger under Hetty's chin and brought her face up to her own. 'Enough ogling the goodies, you. Come and meet my favourite people in the whole wide world.'

Hetty was glad of Stella's briefing as, hand in hand, they left the freezing cold darkness of the street and headed into the brightly lit, stiflingly hot pub. She smelled mixed perfumes as Stella hauled her through crowds of chattering, laughing people – but none of the heavy, clinging scents of sweaty humans she'd experienced on her few trips to 1800s London as a child.

And strangely, instead of panic, she felt a buzz of excitement. She felt like part of something.

And she supposed she *was* part of something, now.

Stella introduced her to three men. The first was in the most beautiful makeup Hetty had ever seen, kissing another with long brown hair in a corner, while the third rolled his eyes at them and grinned.

'Alright, Jimmy?' said Stella, embracing him.

'Will be when these two stop snogging each other's faces off,' replied Jimmy. He nudged the other two and they all stood there expectantly.

'So come on then, Stella, hurry up! Introduce us to the Famous Hetty Bainbridge before we all die from curiosity.'

It was not 1817 now. Hetty felt a thrill of ecstasy run through her as she was hugged by each man in turn and truly felt, for the first time, concrete evidence that she could be herself in this world.

She squeezed Stella's hand, her heart burning up with joy, and impulsively raised it to her mouth and kissed it. Stella's arm wrapped around her middle and together, as a group of wild renegades, they made their way to the nightclub.

Hetty jumped up and down to the thumping beat, not caring about the noise, or the sweat, or the dazzling lights. Only caring for Stella and her friends, jostling against her in the crowd. She and Stella drew closer and closer with every move, until it seemed to make much more sense if their arms twined around one another.

'Groove Is In The Heart' was being wailed by the singer over a frenetic rhythm – 'MY FAVOURITE REMIX!' Stella yelled – and Hetty couldn't agree more. She couldn't ask for another – not another place, not another time, certainly not another person.

The DJ's voice echoed across the room, as if by magic, Hetty thought, and the crowd started the countdown to a new year. A new life, Hetty thought, being hugged by each of Stella's friends in turn and then feeling her body tingling all over in minty, lemony welcoming arms, her face burning as plump lips brushed her cheek.

On the few occasions she'd attempted to wade through novels – my god, how she'd hated the predictably trite morality of her time – she'd always wondered what happened after the happy-ever-afters. Did the heroine settle down into marriage, risk the dangers of childbirth, manage her household? How on earth could she ever adapt to normality after the supposedly life-affirming adventure of, for example, being kidnapped or very nearly ravished by an evil villain?

It had never occurred to her that perhaps the heroine would go on to dance and drink and revel in the joy of life. That the *after* part might be the best part.

As the song ended and they made their way through the crowds to the frankly disgusting privvies, Hetty smiled back at Stella's shining face and kissed her hand. Was this it – after the happy-ever-after? She never wanted it to end.

Chapter 40

1818

Etta woke up groggily as she heard the grate being cleaned. Her aching body reminded her immediately about the night's rather epic activities – it turned out his ginormous bank account wasn't in fact the largest thing about him – but Max had snuck out into the guest bedroom before the servants had risen. They'd been drunk, but not too drunk that she didn't recall quite a bit of wild trifle sex. Etta had been very surprised to find Max had had a condom – it turned out that yes, such things did exist. He'd been momentarily taken aback that she knew what it was and what to do with it, but he hadn't complained as she'd hopped on top of him. She'd been startled by the soreness – she remembered a moment too late that her new body hadn't been through a test run – but my goodness, it had been worth it. It had been worth it the first time, and the second time, and most definitely the third time.

She sat up, wanting to catch the maid before she left and found her staring – first at Etta, and then at the empty trifle bowl sitting on her bedside table. *Damn.*

'I'll send for Bessie and have hot water brought up immediately, Miss Henrietta.'

Etta knew instantly that this gossip was going to be far too good to charm her way out of and lay back on the bed with a sigh as the woman silently exited the room, trifle bowl under one arm. This was going to be all over the servants' quarters well before breakfast.

Etta and Max walked arm in arm by the small lake on the estate after what had to be the most awkward morning meal of her life. She gazed up into his eyes and found him staring steadfastly at her.

'We cannot delay any longer, Etta. We must make our engagement public. I do not wish to – trifle – with your affections any longer.'

Etta felt herself burst wide open with laughter, Max joining her. He was so funny. She kept forgetting how much he made her laugh.

'They'll all be talking, you know,' he continued. 'My valet found custard all over my nightshirt. We'll be infamous.' He passed her a small, flat wooden box from the inside pocket of his jacket. 'I got you an engagement gift. Take a look.'

'Oh my god, Max. Where on earth . . .? You must have had this made, surely?'

She ran a finger over the misshapen tiger brooch, staring at her from its perfect little box with all three eyes shining in the sunlight.

It suddenly all sank in. She really had made her decision – the biggest of her life. She was going to do it. She already knew she felt All The Feelings for Max Stanhope, but now she knew he loved her back: he understood her as no man in her own time ever had. And she was quite certain she wanted to go all in, stay here and marry him.

They walked back to the house together in comfortable silence, holding hands, and she knew her life would never ever be the same again: not because she was living two hundred years before she'd been born, but because of the burgeoning love she felt for the man beside her.

Back in the morning room, Etta's mother was almost as taken with the tiger-face brooch as Etta was. 'Oh, darling, it's so delightful! Goodness, where on earth could one even purchase such a thing? Maximillian, I believe this must truly be an heirloom piece.'

Charlie came barging in, eager to see what all the fuss was about, and broke out into almost hysterical laughter. Doubled over, tears in his eyes, he rolled himself onto a nearby sofa.

'Good god, Etta. Max given you a gift, has he? I wonder which unfortunate jeweller was tasked with that commission?'

Etta watched as Max pinned it onto her dress, beyond delighted. 'How did you know, Charlie? I thought it was an in-joke?'

'I told him about it at the club,' said Max, 'in case you were wondering for even a moment that he might have been seen dead in the British Museum.'

'You should wear it at the Baxter ball when we get back to town, sis.'

'I think not, Charles.' Their mother's voice was steady and clear. 'Unless the two of you have come to an agreement?'

Etta looked at her guiltily, then nodded.

'Finally!' She clapped her hands together. 'Oh, my dears, I am delighted. Maximillian, you will follow me to

Lord Bainbridge's study immediately. We shall make the announcement and read the banns when we get back to London, I think, after the Baxter ball. The village church is far too parochial, and I should like to give my only daughter a good send-off.'

Charlie had already settled back onto his sofa and reached towards a newspaper, feet up. Unfortunately for him, his mother grabbed it first.

'Charles! You are forgetting that it is your study.'

'No need to hit me with a rolled-up newspaper, Mama! Coming, coming!'

Rubbing at his sore head, Charlie reluctantly followed, and the door was resolutely shut. The only person not required was Etta, it seemed. Now agreed in principle, the paperwork was someone else's business. She had never felt further away from the office.

Etta sighed, thinking of all the responsibility now solidly off her shoulders, and settled in with one of her brand-new first edition Jane Austen novels. She hoped Hetty was having as much of a lovely time as she was.

Chapter 41

2024

It had been a proper bender, Stella had declared as she'd dragged herself out of bed to brush her teeth. They were both still fully dressed, having collapsed giggling long after night had turned to morning.

Hetty glanced at her phone as it buzzed at her with a message from Aggie: *Awake yet?*

She smiled as she replied, then got up. God, her head felt awful. She wandered to the loo, took two aspirins and started to remove her makeup as Stella grinned at her, bumping shoulders as they passed.

As Hetty finally relieved herself on the ugly green toilet, she heard Stella meet her brother Elliot in the hallway and his panicked voice as he whispered to her, 'Ooooh, you're in trouble, Stell. Mum's back early. She knows you've got someone here.'

She heard Stella's reply. 'Elliot, you'd better not fuck this up for me. Hetty is everything. *Everything.*'

Hetty felt the happiness playing across her face and pierce right through to her heart. This was it. This was her happy ending.

'Ugh, gross,' said Elliot. 'Okay. I'll help you with Mum. Maybe she'll be all right if you're going out with a posho.'

Then she heard a sharp, older voice echo from the kitchen. 'What posho? You look like you've both been caught trying my wigs on again. Elliot, washing up. Stella, we need to talk. Now.'

Hetty knew what she was doing was wholly beneath her, but she closed the toilet lid and, without flushing, crept to the closed bathroom door. She was vaguely aware things were tense between Stella and her mother – tense enough for Stella to check with her brother before bringing Hetty home last night. But he had been wrong: their mother was home after all.

She heard the creak of springs as Stella plonked herself on the sofa.

'Mum, I'm really sorry you don't have the nice, slim, well-behaved straight little church girl you wanted, but—'

'You're going to have to get out,' Stella's mother interrupted her, her harsh voice cutting clearly through the bathroom door.

Hetty's breath caught in her throat. She silently opened the door a crack and her heart broke at Stella's expression. She looked like she was drowning, or floating in space without oxygen, or falling. Perhaps all of those at once, Hetty thought, as she stared at the back of Stella's mum's perfectly coiffed head.

Hetty registered a low groan behind her and turned to see Elliot across the hallway peeking out from his bedroom door. He looked at Hetty, wincing, as if to brace her for whatever would come next. The look on Stella's face didn't bode well.

'This is a house of God – you can't bring women here.

I've spoken to the pastor. It's wrong. If you want this . . . lifestyle . . . then you're not welcome any more.'

Hetty felt a tear crawl down her cheek, a mirror version of the one travelling down Stella's perfect, dewy skin. She expected Stella to say something – to defend herself in some way, but she stayed silent. But the older woman wasn't done.

'I'm going out and I expect you gone by the time I get back. You've got half an hour. Give me your keys.'

Hetty watched Stella rummage through her bag and produce her keys, which her mother immediately snatched from her hand.

'This isn't easy for me, Stella.'

'Seems pretty easy to me,' she said, finally finding her voice.

A loud gasp escaped Hetty as Stella's mother roundly slapped her. The woman turned at the sound, stared for a long moment at Hetty, then strode out of the flat.

Stella sank down into a chair, so alone, so small, and Hetty could almost hear the cracks as her love's heart slowly shattered. She lowered herself next to Stella, putting a hand on her arm.

'All will be well, in the end, you know.'

'No, Hetty, I don't know.'

Hetty sighed and turned Stella's chin. They shared a long look, before Hetty spoke again.

'Perhaps it's my turn to look after you now.'

Stella nodded, the tears flowing freely down her cheeks as she spoke. 'You know what, Hetty? That would be lovely.'

Chapter 42

1818

Etta looked around confidently as she entered the Baxter family's ballroom, hoping to find Clarissa who she knew would be back from her own Christmas celebrations. She knew she wasn't supposed to be spilling the news about her engagement until it had been formally announced, but surely it wouldn't hurt to tell her closest friend?

The feisty Bramleys had called Clarissa a stick-in-the-mud and, yes, it was true that she was quiet. But she'd been there for Etta right at the beginning, when nobody else was prepared to give her the time of day and Etta wouldn't forget that. Though she wasn't sure how well Clarissa knew her new mates the Bramleys and couldn't even begin to imagine a world where she'd approve of their weed habit, she hoped an introduction to some lively new acquaintances might help Clarissa come out of her shell a little. She set herself to the task.

Etta found the Bramleys first and grinned as George was simultaneously elbowed in the sides by both of his sisters.

'Yes, yes, of course I'm going to ask Etta – sorry, Miss Bainbridge – to dance with me. God, no need to break any ribs.'

Lissie and Tessa both waved goodbye knowingly as Lord Bramley rolled his eyes and pulled Etta into the dance that was just beginning.

There wasn't much time to talk during the dance, but George was much struck by her brooch. 'That's the tiger from Marley's godawful exhibit at the British Museum, isn't it? I'm assuming it was specially made?'

Etta grinned at him as he valiantly tried to contain his laughter. 'Yes, and before you ask I know that's not what tigers look like. It's – it's a bit of an in-joke.'

'An expensive in-joke, for sure. Need I ask the name of the admirer who undoubtedly commissioned it?'

'I don't like to count my chickens before they're hatched – or, I should say announced – but I imagine you have already guessed.'

George laughed as the dance ended. 'The whole of London must know by now, Miss Bainbridge. I can't be the first to wish you both happy?'

Etta took his arm and they headed together towards his sisters. 'And yet you are. He hasn't spoken to the vicar yet to have the banns read, anyway.'

'Oh, he will – or he'll face the end of my scissors. Perhaps even my rock. So, what next, Miss Bainbridge?'

Etta bit her lip thoughtfully, wondering if there was an orangery, but felt the call of the wild. 'Sorry, but I need to powder my nose. Try not to murder Smythe while I'm away, will you?'

Lissie grabbed her hand. 'Come on, let's all go together.'

They headed into the hallway towards the room dedicated to the usual grim chamber pots.

'You know, you really should get to know Clarissa Best,'

said Etta. 'I know she's super quiet, but really she's been very lovely to m—'

Etta stopped short, her praise crumbling to dirt and ashes in her mouth. She heard Lissie and Tessa gasp next to her, but all she could see was Clarissa. Her quiet, stolid friend Clarissa, her mother in the background instead of the foreground for once, pressed up against Max. Her Max. Kissing him full on the mouth.

'What the hell. What the HELL?'

Etta heard the words coming out of her mouth without being quite sure where they were coming from. A smug Lady Best stepped forwards.

'Ah, Hetty, the Misses Bramley. And my daughter. Lord Stanhope, how very dare you compromise my unmarried daughter?'

Lady Best sounded anything but outraged. She looked, in fact, like the cat that got the cream.

'I see only one way forward from this, Stanhope. Whatever you may have had going on with the Bainbridge girl is surely rendered meaningless by your ungentlemanly behaviour towards my daughter. Ladies, you may wish my daughter happy.'

Etta barely had time to register the shame on Clarissa's face as she turned and ran, leaving Max, the Bests, the Bramleys, the world behind.

Chapter 43

2024

Hetty and Elliot manoeuvred Stella out of the XL Uber, hauling bin bags full of her brightly coloured, glittering clothes with them.

Elliot almost dropped everything when he got out. 'Jeez, Hetty, this is your place? Can I move in, too?'

'Well, I suppose . . .'

Elliot laughed at Hetty's tentative response. 'Nah, don't worry. I've got to stay behind and sort out Mum. God, what a mess.'

Jemima had clearly seen the group of them from the window; before Hetty had time to formulate a response, the cavalry arrived. They were hustled in, Aggie standing guard over the bags while Elliot brought them in as Jemima put the kettle on and opened The Good Biscuits.

'No need to explain, Hetty, dear. Shove her stuff in the Blue Room. Actually, no. The Yellow Room. Blue's too sad.'

'Blimey, how many rooms have you got?'

Elliot was staring around the entrance hall in wonder, his

eye caught by a taxidermied animal. 'And what the hell's wrong with that tiger?'

'Top of the stairs, second left. Off you go,' said Aggie, ushering him up the stairs with Stella's bags.

They heard him calling, 'Bloody hell, Stell, there's an *en suite*!' as they took Stella into the kitchen.

Hetty gripped Stella's hand as Jemima brought over a mug of tea in a delicate blue and pink china mug with gold lettering – 'Trans Rights Are Human Rights' – and a large box of tissues.

'Thanks,' Stella sobbed. 'I'm so sorry.'

'No,' Aggie said, visibly angry. 'I'm sorry, dear. There's no need to explain – Hetty texted ahead. You'll be staying here, of course, for as long as you want.'

Stella collapsed into tears. Hetty could just about make out her response. 'I can't – you can't—'

Hetty gripped her hand harder. 'Stella. My aunts rescued me. I think you're much easier to rescue than I was.'

'Too bloody right,' growled Aggie.

'Now, now, Aggie. Calm down.' Jemima put her hand on Aggie's shoulder. 'Stella, Hetty's right. This is a place of refuge. Our home is your home, for as long as you like.'

Stella moaned, her head in her arms. 'I never thought – I never thought she'd actually throw me out. It's 2024! They literally let us get married in churches now!'

'Her loss is our gain,' said Jemima. 'Now come on, you drink your tea and we'll show you around the bits you haven't already seen.'

*

Hetty was sitting with Elliot tucking into a Full English when Stella came down the next morning, bleary-eyed from crying, and didn't immediately notice her entering the room.

'So you're telling me she just . . . she just eats loudly *for a living*?' Hetty enquired, horrified. Elliot shook with laughter as Hetty continued, insistent. 'But that's quite terribly indecent! And you're saying this is viewed by *millions of people*?'

Elliot choked with laughter. 'Yeah, yeah, but Hetty, that's not even the grossest thing out there. That's, like, so, so far from awful. Oh! Hey, Stells.'

Stella grinned at them both. 'Showing Hetty the worst of the internet, then?'

'Oh, mate, I have no idea where you found this one. She's hilarious.'

'Been rizzing her up, have you?'

Elliot laughed. 'The opposite, I reckon.'

Hetty turned to Stella. 'Stella, your brother has been telling me all sorts of things and truly, the world really is a *very* different place now.'

Hetty got up as Stella padded over to the coffee machine and plucked a capsule from the tarnished, battered silver vase they lived in. 'Hetty, if you break that bracelet on me now, I swear to god . . .'

Without even realising it Hetty put her hand on Stella's shoulder, feeling electricity but also warmth spreading through her. 'You know I would never, Estella.'

'My brother told you my full name, then? What else have you learned about me?' Stella turned and suddenly Hetty found that her arms were wrapping around Stella's waist, as though they had a mind of their own.

'I've learned I don't want you to leave. Ever,' Hetty whispered into Stella's ear.

'Gross,' said Elliot, pushing them aside and making off with Stella's coffee. 'Come on, lovebirds, I've got the perfect format for your new bestselling social media offering.'

Stella sighed as Hetty put another pod into the machine and found a chipped mug – 'Hungry Like The Sloth' this time.

'Go on then, Smelliot.'

Stella's brother paused, toast halfway to his mouth. 'I say we get you two in your fancy dresses and you can outrage Hetty some more for me. But this time, we film it.'

Hetty looked at the two of them assessingly. It was the second time this idea had popped up. She had learned that it was a popular format, the whole 'agony aunt/reacting to terrible Reddit stories' thing, and it was true that her reactions would be, well, authentic. The world was indeed an interesting place.

'Aunt Aggie said she bought us both a ring light and some microphones for the sitting room. Come and have a look,' said Hetty.

Stella rubbed her temples and sighed. 'Oh, bugger it, why not? I need distracting, anyway. Are there any sausages left?'

Elliot smirked. 'Didn't think that was your bag, Stells.'

'Sod off. I love you. I'm not doing this on an empty stomach.'

Chapter 44

1818

Etta aimed for the terrace, desperate for some fresh air and perspective. Sadly, it was not to be.

'Miss Bainbridge! What a delightful and immensely accurate brooch!'

She stopped dead at the acerbic tones of the walking vinaigrette Maria Marley, accompanied of course by the loathsome Smythe.

'Not now, Maria.'

Miss Marley stepped back, face full of mock surprise. 'Oh no, *Hetty*, don't tell me now's a bad time? Are we not, indeed, to *finally* wish you happy?'

Etta had had enough, and then some. She wheeled away from the terrace doors and stared her adversaries right in the face.

'And what about you, the gruesome twosome? I think you're *perfect* for one another. Both obnoxious, sour-faced bitches who don't know a tiger from a . . .' Etta trailed off. 'Um, a thing that isn't a tiger.'

Miss Marley and Smythe were looking at one another

as though struck by some kind of unfortunately non-deadly lightning bolt.

Etta sighed. 'Oh god, that's it, isn't it? Don't tell me. Even Maria Marley and her pompous little sidekick get some kind of ridiculous happy ending.'

Smythe had taken Miss Marley's hand in his, as they looked at each other like two amorous honey badgers deciding whether to fight over or share a tasty meal of raw rattlesnake meat.

'Ugh, enjoy. Don't bother sending an e-vite to Chez Bainbridge. It's too much to hope you'd elope, isn't it?'

Maria Marley's voice came in a whisper. 'You can buy me something cheap from the rag merchant, Hetty, if you can afford it.'

Etta rolled her eyes as she walked off. 'Pistols or swords?' she growled to herself.

She retreated to a corner, plate full of chocolate eclairs and heart dripping with misery. She was more than fed up, and she couldn't even leave yet – her mother was deep in conversation with one of her usual gang of confidantes.

'Why the sour face, young lady? Eaten something you don't like the taste of?'

She looked up in surprise. A frail, but stern-looking man was making his way over to her, his face twitching in disgust as he glared at her. She dropped a half-eaten pastry back onto her plate. Suddenly, she'd had enough.

'Oh, I'm afraid I'm no longer accepting applications to the Etta Bainbridge fan club. It's been disbanded, due to me being a deranged lunatic out to ruin everyone's lives.'

The man was so stunned he dropped his cane. Etta automatically bent down to pick it up, absently placing it into his surprisingly firm hand as she continued.

'If you're looking for tips on how to be an outrageously horrific bitch, you'll need to submit your application to Clarissa Best instead. She's overtaken even Maria Marley in the Gorgon stakes.'

The older man snapped to attention, all confusion replaced by anger almost equal to Etta's.

'Best? Best, you say? Agatha Best's daughter?'

'That's the one. Although she'd be better named Agatha Dirt-Worst, I'd say.'

Etta watched the man shudder in distaste, noting she was clearly not alone in that opinion.

'What's the old harridan's brat been up to? The apple never falls far from the tree.'

She paused, the burning edge of her rage slightly spent, realising she should probably avoid completely destroying her reputation.

'Oh, don't worry. You can tell me. I've never liked that godawful woman. Besides, if Agatha Best's got anything to do with it, we'll all know soon enough.'

'Man-stealing,' Etta explained. She could feel her anger rising again just at the memory. 'She was my friend, but she took Max Stanhope – who is, you know, the most handsome, cleverest, *the* most amusing man in the country – she took him into the hall and she kissed him just when she knew people would be walking there. And I just caught them, along with her mother, and, oh, the bloody Bramleys. There were multiple witnesses.'

'Oh, there were, were there? And I suppose you, young lady, wanted him for yourself?'

Etta wiped an angry tear away. 'Of course I did! Who wouldn't? He's the most fascinating, kindest, the most – I don't know, *comfortable* man I've ever met.'

'And heir to an ancient, prestigious marquessate, of course.'

'Look, he can't help being a posho, can he? Poor sod.'

She picked up her plate again, dejectedly stuffed half an eclair into her mouth, and kept talking.

'Look, I gotta go. My mother has finished her conversation and I need to ask her to call our carriage. Sorry for unloading onto you. I bet this'll come back and bite me in the arse just like everything else.' She handed the stranger her plate. 'Try one of these. They're delicious. Besides, I'm sweet enough already.'

Chapter 45

1818

Etta didn't sleep that night. She lay transfixed by the note Bessie had brought her in Clarissa's fine, swirly handwriting:

Etta,
 I will not apologise for what you saw last night. I must be married, and quickly, before my youth fades. The time we have spent together with Lord Stanhope and the courtesy he has shown to even one such as you tells me he will be a kind and decent husband.
 I know you may find yourself unable to move past this, and that we can no longer be friends after my engagement to Lord Stanhope, but I hope you will one day find it in you to wish me happy.
 Clarissa

So that was it, then. The only man who knew and could understand her full story was gone forever.

The man she loved. There was no doubting it now. Her whole heart and body screamed out for him.

But Max was as trapped as she was, if not more. He had been caught with Clarissa and she'd had them drummed into her enough by now to know that Regency rules dictated he would have to marry her even though the double-crossing bitch had duped them both. Lady Best would no doubt ensure *everyone* knew about the pathetic smooch in the hallway.

Etta rolled back over in bed and stared at the wall, crumpling Clarissa's rage-inducing note in her hand. She'd never really had a long-term relationship, but she'd had lots of short ones and had never had any problems ending them. Breaking up with someone because they had been caught in a hallway kissing someone else and now must marry them wasn't really a 2023 problem.

It had been a while since she'd even thought of 2023. It was almost hard to believe she'd ever been a single woman, completely independent. Hard to remember the wild period of travel she'd been on after Dad had died, when she'd skipped a month of lectures and just caught the first flight to Paris with a backpack and caught train after train around Europe, grieving not only the dad she'd had but the dad she'd *wished* she'd had. But her grief had followed her.

Etta sat up in bed, the solution obvious. She didn't have to feel how she felt; she didn't have to endure this. The solution was right in front of her: the bracelet. Just break the damn bracelet!

She scrambled over to her knicker drawer, but it was nowhere to be found. Ten minutes later she'd emptied out every trinket box and drawer in her room.

She was panicking, she knew. And the panic just swept over her again and again as she realised what a trap she'd been caught in all these months. She might have been having fun at parties, wearing pretty dresses, playing the piano as much as she liked and sparring with Maria Marley, but if she thought about it, she didn't actually have any autonomy in this age, did she? She couldn't marry the man she loved. She couldn't vote, she couldn't have a bank account, she couldn't even go on a bloody walk without a chaperone! She was chattel.

But she was still Etta Moore underneath it all, wasn't she? She didn't need to break some stupid bloody magical bracelet to escape. She had feet and arms and a brain of her own. And she could still speak French, right? She surveyed her room. There were no bars on her four-poster bed. No chains on her legs. What, precisely, was stopping her?

She had more to pack this time – her dress wouldn't fit in a backpack, that was certain – but maybe this time her grief wouldn't fit in her baggage. Maybe that, at least, she could leave behind.

As she sat in the crowded carriage later, stuffed between a sleeping elderly woman and a younger man awkwardly desperate not to touch her, Etta felt a large pang of guilt. It was far, far worse than the time she'd stolen a Mars bar after school as a child. Then, she'd felt so much guilt she couldn't eat it and had buried it in a plant pot instead. Her dad had found it six months later.

This was definitely her darkest day. Etta had stolen from pretty much everyone.

She'd known she'd need money, but not how much – she so rarely spent any that she still wasn't sure how it worked. So for that, she'd ransacked Charlie's study and her mother's dressing table.

She needed clothes – normal clothes, not the soft, thin clothes of the rich. So, she took a trip to the laundry and pilfered some of the servants' clothes. Etta had felt like the worst kind of criminal as she crept around the house before dawn. It was by far the most dreadful thing she had ever, ever done in her life. She felt almost as detached from her actions as she had during her first few days in 1817, when she'd still thought she was living in a dream.

She cried over her letter to her mother, as the reality of what she was doing started to creep over her. She listed the people she'd stolen from, the money she'd taken, so that nobody else would cop the blame. Her tears had blotched the paper, making it hard for her pencil to write. Etta wrote around the teardrops. She wasn't from 1818, she reminded herself. She was from 2023, and she had lived alone for years. This was barely real. The lady she was writing to was not her mother; the rich man whose desk drawers she'd extracted a bundle of weird, large bank notes from was not her brother.

Max was not her fiancé. This whole world, her happy ending – it was all a fantasy. A dream that had gone bad. It was time to wake up. If she couldn't return to 2023, then she could at least leave London – and she planned to do just that at first light.

Etta rubbed her eyes wearily, remembering the worst part, which had been writing to Max:

Lord Stanhope,
  Let me be the first to congratulate you on your engagement.
  Goodbye,
  Etta

She hadn't been able to help herself, but she knew her curt little note – written several times until she'd finally produced one without wet patches – would worry him. Well, good. Perhaps he shouldn't go around letting dull-as-ditchwater, double-crossing bitches kiss him in corridors.

She had been travelling for most of the day; she hoped they would be at Dover soon. She wondered whether anyone would guess where she was going. Probably not, since Hetty couldn't speak French. Etta, however, could. She was rusty, but she'd got an A at A-level. She'd be fine. Surely, she'd be fine.

Probably.

Chapter 46

1818

Max was just tying his cravat when a servant interrupted his valet with the news that Lady Best was waiting downstairs. He'd spent a restless night. It was bad enough to be unexpectedly mauled by a young lady the very night before his interview with the local bishop, but to be caught by Etta mid-maul was far, far worse.

Of course, it was fixable. Nobody but Etta and the Bramleys had seen, thank god, but even though it was most certainly not his fault he was going to have to take Etta a huge bouquet of flowers for even letting himself be trapped in such a scenario. He'd searched for her in the ballroom with more obvious desperation than was decorous, but she'd been nowhere to be found. He didn't blame her: the situation had looked dire, to say the least.

But now Lady Best was at his door, which meant the situation was even more dire than it had looked last night. He sincerely hoped she wasn't about to make a scene, because there was no way on earth he was going to become in any way attached to her and her dull, duplicitous daughter.

He sighed, resigned to a difficult conversation. 'Tell Lady Best I shall be with her shortly—'

But he was interrupted by a booming noise from downstairs. Max froze, his hands still against his collar. The unmistakable sound of his father's voice echoed across the hallway:

'Lady Best, you will remove yourself from my house *immediately* . . .'

Max waved his valet to one side and crept down the hallway, feeling like an errant schoolboy. He didn't have to listen hard in order to hear the Marquess's livid tirade, but he felt an irresistible urge to see how his victim was taking it.

'Years ago, you attempted to entrap me into marriage with your foolish self. Now, decades later, you attempt it again with your idiot harpy of a daughter.'

Max peered down the grand stairs into the hallway. Lady Best stood indignantly on the tiled marble floor, her daughter cowering behind her.

'Sir, I did not come to speak with you. I came to speak with your—'

'Son, I know. You came to harass my son. Well, I can tell you here and now that if my son ever, *ever* has the *latent idiocy* required to propose to you, your daughter, or *any member* of your family, I shall immediately disinherit him.'

Max couldn't help but smile. It seemed his father was finally back in full health. Perhaps the opportunity to ream out his old enemy had helped him regain his *joie de vivre*. The Marquess certainly seemed to be enjoying himself.

'But your grace, your son was clearly caught—'

'By whom, I might ask?'

'Well, by—' Lady Best began to bluster, her defences clearly worn down.

'Miss Henrietta Bainbridge, perhaps?'

The older woman swelled slightly, buoyant with what she clearly considered to be good news. 'Yes! Mad Hetty! And the Bramleys. They were there to witness the terrible affront on my daughter's virtue inflicted by your son! Ask them!'

She was interrupted by a shout of derisive laughter from Lord Kent. 'The Bramleys! Ha! My Miranda's family! You chose badly, if you thought to choose my deceased wife's kin. The Bramleys couldn't be more trustworthy allies of the Kents.'

Lady Best faltered. 'Well . . . I might have mentioned it to several ladies before we left the ballroom, and surely Miss Bainbridge will have told others . . .'

'I don't care who she might have told. Nobody, I imagine, if she has any sense at all. And not a single member of the *Ton* would believe any cock and bull story about my son marrying your daughter. Ha! A Kent, deign to marry a mere Miss Marley? Over my cold, rotting corpse!'

Lord Kent was in his element now, Max realised. His father had needed something to get really, truly cross about for some time – and he was very glad it wasn't him, for once.

'At any rate, madam—'

Max decided it was time to make his presence known. He coughed and made his way down the stairs. His father swivelled to look at him, still glaring.

'Got a cold, boy?'

'No, sir,' said Max smoothly. 'I just wondered why you and Lady Best were discussing my fiancée out here in the hallway.'

His father replied instantly, brandishing his stick energetically. 'Because I will *not* taint my library with the likes of this harpy.'

Max fought the desire to laugh aloud. 'Well then, Lady Best. Since my father won't receive you in his library, and I won't receive you at all, I can only suggest that you leave.'

'But my daughter . . .'

'. . . will remain unwed indefinitely, if she continues to try and ensnare unwilling men using dirty tricks,' finished Max.

Clarissa stepped out from behind her mother, eyes flashing. 'How dare you! Any number of people might have seen us in that hallway . . .'

'And yet you know as well as I do that they did not, Miss Best. Good day.'

Max beckoned to the butler, who opened the front door.

Lady Best narrowed her eyes. 'This won't be the last you hear of this, believe me.'

The Marquess took a deep breath, struggling to contain himself, but Max made his reply as he walked them to the door.

'If you mean that your future granddaughter will be accosting my future son, I sincerely hope I am there to send her packing in half such a grand style as my father. But if you mean to bother *my fiancée*, Miss Bainbridge, I strongly recommend against it.'

His father's voice rang out from behind him. 'And I look forward to any opportunity to tell the Prince Regent about your erstwhile husband's debts to me. And his prostitutes. And, of course, *his syphilis*.'

Max winced. So too did Lady Best and her daughter, who hurried away without another word.

He turned to face his father. 'Changed your mind about Miss Bainbridge, then?'

'Into the study, boy. We do not discuss ladies in the hallway.'

Grinning widely, Max followed Lord Kent into his large, wood-panelled study and poured two large glasses of brandy.

'Go on, keep pouring. I'll be needing three fingers after all that nonsense.'

Max raised an eyebrow and passed his father a small glass, refusing to pour any more. The Marquess's doctor had been quite clear and they both knew it.

Max cleared his throat. 'So, I see your opinion of Miss Bainbridge has undergone a miraculous transformation since we last spoke.'

'I saw her last night, after she caught you kissing that awful harpy. That girl is no more mad than I am.'

Max was halfway through taking a large swig of brandy that caught in his throat.

His father looked at him disdainfully. 'Yes, yes, I realise that does make her ever so slightly mad. What on earth were you doing, anyway, getting caught with that damned awful girl?'

'It's hardly my fault, Father! She lay in wait and leapt out at me!'

'You should know to expect these things by now, Maximillian. You're a prime catch on the marriage mart.'

'Unless, of course, you disinherit me. I seem damned if I do and damned if I don't. Not Miss Bainbridge, not Miss Best . . . Who will you have me marry, dare I ask?'

Lord Kent eyed him warily over the rim of his brandy. 'I think we are both well aware that the estate is entailed.'

'Yes, I spoke to Ponsonby about it the moment I came of age. But the question stands.'

Lord Kent harrumphed. 'Well, the Bainbridge girl is a better catch than I expected her to be.'

Max sat back, triumphant. 'I'm glad you like her. It will make things all the easier when I begin to prepare her rooms in the west wing. Providing, that is, that you still take objection to me having my own house?'

His father eyed him carefully. 'Damned waste of money.'

'Good. Then I shall prepare them immediately.'

'Yes. In blue. The girl looks good in blue.' His father paused. 'And throw her a ball, too. A big one.'

Max grinned. 'Shall I invite Lady Best?'

His father slammed his empty glass down onto his desk. 'Don't push it, boy. Now leave me. And get Hammond to fetch for the family jeweller. I'll buy her a wedding necklace. No, damn it. She deserves a full parure for marrying a scoundrel like you.'

Max set out to the Bainbridge townhouse to finalise the paperwork. If Etta persisted in being angry with him . . . well, he'd find a way to bring her round.

Etta sat on the edge of the docks, hugging her bag forlornly. For the first time, it all felt terribly real. Her lovely Regency adventure was finally over – and there could be no question that she was not in a dream now. The taste of bile in her throat told her, once and for all, that this was no Georgette Heyer novel. This was her life now. And she'd not even got the bloody bracelet.

Whether her subsequent dizziness was from the journey, her sudden grounding in reality, or just from the general atmosphere of the Dover docks, she would never know. The whole area was absolutely packed with people, loading and unloading ships big and small.

The hustle and bustle was overwhelming. She drew her

cloak around her tightly as she found herself being ogled by any number of disgusting-smelling sailors who seemed determined to whistle and catcall any woman nearby.

When she wasn't pushing past rough, malodorous men trying to cop a feel, she was being glared at by sex workers who clearly felt she was potential competition.

A sign pointed her to a small ticket office, fronted by a sniffling, stern-looking man.

'How can I help you, miss? A servant, I suppose. Hope you're not here for a ticket for your mistress. We're sold out.'

Etta's heart fell through her chest. 'To Calais?'

'That's right. Nowt for a se'ennight, miss.'

'But can't you make an exception? My – my mistress is terribly important.'

The man snorted derisively. 'Aye, and that'll be why she sent a little slip of a girl like you and not a manservant. Off you go.'

'But—'

'No ticket, no crossing. I can book you a place for a week on Tuesday, or nothing at all.'

A week? She had plenty of cash, but almost certainly not enough to put herself up in a strange city for a week.

Etta clutched her bag to her chest as she looked for a way out of the crowd, forcing her way past a mass of people boarding the ship she'd just been denied entrance to and dodging a large crate being hauled aboard.

She took one last look at the boat, already packed with passengers, then walked some way through the streets of Dover. She could feel the rounded cobbles pressing painfully through her boots and decided to keep going until she found somewhere to sit and think – it was already so late, the sun beginning to disappear behind the low rooftops.

Thankfully she soon came across a small church, its doors unlocked, and gratefully crept in to sit in a pew at the back.

The vicar was nowhere to be seen, so Etta slumped in her pew, tipped her head back and took a long breath, grateful to be alone.

She rested her chin on her fingertips and decided to do a brief audit of her belongings before she went to look for something to eat. Opening her bag, she rifled for her purse that she'd stuffed deep inside.

Of course, she couldn't find it.

She upended the bag onto the pew. Its contents went everywhere, scattering in the darkness. A few coins rolled out, but nothing else. No purse, no paper money, and her ring and necklace were gone.

Well, she was now, as 2023 her would say, Proper Fucked.

Chapter 47

2024

Hetty adjusted her dress. It was a little tight around the bosom, but when she looked up she caught Stella peeking at her decolletage and didn't mind one bit. She just smiled right back.

'Stop staring at each other's tits. God,' Elliot said. He palmed his face, exasperated, as Stella and Hetty wiggled eyebrows at each other.

They each had a wine glass in front of them, because this first one was bound to be a little difficult, right? It had been such a very long week and the wine was so very good.

Hetty grinned at Stella, her very favourite person in the world, and everything felt exactly right.

Stella shone at the camera, ignoring her brother.

'Welcome to Two Fancy Ladies. I'm Stella, and this is Hetty. Hetty, what are you?'

Hetty laughed. 'A Lady of Distinction, born in Regency England.'

'Right Outta Regency. Must be nice, you'd think, but takes some adapting to get your head around 2024, doesn't it, Hetts?'

'Cheers to that, my love.' Hetty clinked glasses, registering Stella's blink of surprise before swiftly revisiting her words. Oops. 'Um . . . In for a penny, in for a pound?'

Stella was staring at her, the edge of a smile playing on her lips. Beautiful, Hetty thought. So beautiful. She took a large gulp of wine.

Elliot coughed. 'The first comment, sis?'

Stella snapped her fingers, as though waking herself up. They were slightly drunk, to be fair. Even Stella had been pretty nervous about this, since the success of Hetty's Substack and linked Instagram account had meant any kind of live video was bound to have a pretty large audience.

'And that's our producer, my baby brother Elliot, isn't it, *my love*. Say hi, Elliot.' Stella grinned, her foot nudging Hetty's under the table.

Hetty's heart soared as Elliot grumbled off-camera.

'Let's kick off. The most common question on your Instagram, Hetts, is about the bogs. Where did you go Number Two in 1817?'

'Number Two? What's that?'

Stella grinned and told her.

Hetty's reaction – a fine mist of red wine right into the camera – was a meme before Elliot had finished wiping the tripod down.

Stella grabbed Hetty's hand and pulled her away from her latest newsletter and over to the sofa. 'Come away, Hetty. I've got something to show you.'

Hetty looked at the phone Stella handed her in confusion. 'It's our video. I thought – you'd already shown me this, no?'

Stella pointed to a little number on one side of the screen.

'Two M? What does two M mean?' Hetty asked.

'Two million, Hetty. It means two *million*.'

Stunned, Hetty sat back in what was most definitely the least ladylike position she'd adopted in her life. 'Do you mean to tell me, Stella, that *two million people* have watched our videos?'

She looked over at Stella, whose grin seemed to soak up the whole room. 'No, they liked it. That's just the number of people who liked that single video.'

'How many people didn't like it, then?'

'No, silly! What I mean is, loads more people actually saw it. And then two million of those people pressed a little heart-shaped button saying they liked it. *Two million*.'

Aunt Aggie was bringing in a tray of tea. 'It means, Hetty, my dear, that the two of you will need to choose an agent. Do let me introduce you to my good friend Marina.'

Chapter 48

1818

When Max arrived at the Bainbridges' residence, he knew immediately that something was horribly wrong.

Servants were coming and going through the large front doors at full speed, and Max followed a lost-looking and very upset Monsett to a much more upset Lady Bainbridge. The woman was clutching Etta's maid Bessie to her bosom, the both of them wailing.

Max turned to the panicking butler. 'Monsett. I realise this is most irregular, but—'

Charlie rushed over, looking more hassled than Max had ever seen him or perhaps anyone. 'Never mind that, Monsett. Max, come with me now. Now! Mother?!'

A deep foreboding was sweeping over Max as the panic of the household seemed to infect him. Charlie led them straight into his study, looking suddenly twenty years older than he had just moments ago.

'Etta has gone missing,' Charlie croaked, turning to comfort his collapsing mother.

'Missing?' repeated Max, the beginnings of dread

unfurling within him. He instinctively poured each of them a large glass of brandy and turned to Lady Bainbridge, heart in his mouth.

'How . . .?'

'Monsett has heard back from several of the footmen he sent across the city, and it seems Henrietta caught the stagecoach towards Dover,' Charlie explained. 'A clerk at the ticket office was able to give a detailed description.'

'But – but why?' asked Max.

An anguished voice rose from Lady Bainbridge's hunched figure. She jabbed a finger in Max's direction. 'You.'

Charlie's mouth almost vanished into a hard line as Max's face collapsed. His voice came out in a tone he barely recognised. 'Surely she couldn't truly believe . . .?'

'Well, she did,' said Lady Bainbridge, handing Charlie a tear-stained note, which he read with increasing consternation.

'Am I reading this correctly? You are engaged to Miss Best?'

Max felt his chest crackle with rage. 'Do you seriously believe,' he drawled incredulously, 'that I would prefer an insipid damsel who attempted to trap me into marriage to your sister – the woman with whom I have been deeply in love for many, many months?'

Lady Bainbridge raised her head, watching carefully as Max continued, 'Do you, Charles Bainbridge, my childhood friend of two and a half decades, really truly believe that the Stanhopes would ally themselves with harpies such as the Bests? That we would . . . It was an awful scheme by the awful Best woman, but my father and I have seen that off. It is your sister whom I want to marry. With whom I am in love.'

'Says here you were spotted kissing Miss Best by the Bramley girls,' Charlie interrupted, still cynical.

'Oh, and you think I was in on that, do you? That my reputation can't survive a mere kiss? And the Bramley girls will be all over London with it? The Bramleys?! I've known George Bramley since Eton, and so have you. My own *mother* was a Bramley. I'd trust the Bramleys with—'

'Enough, Maximillian. Henrietta clearly has no idea how society works. How unequal the balance is between men and women. As proven,' Lady Bainbridge raised her eyebrows, 'by her highly inappropriate closeness with yourself these past few months.'

Max drank some of his brandy, the wind stolen from his sails somewhat by the surprisingly humbling glare of an outraged Lady Bainbridge.

'While your reputation as a man will easily survive Miss Best's attentions, you must be aware we have all spent months making sure Henrietta knows that hers would not. And we all know Henrietta sees women to be the equal of men – as, of course, we are.' Lady Bainbridge slammed her empty glass down on a side table. 'But not equal in the eyes of society, sadly.

'I cannot travel to fetch my daughter, of course, unless we all want a wash of rumour to be across half of London before the end of the day,' she continued, putting her handkerchief to one side and picking up Hercules. 'Which means that I will be having stern words with the servants while you two go on a trip and my daughter "lies abed with a cold".'

Charlie puffed out his chest. 'What, Mama, you're happy for me to be left alone with this charlatan? I can't promise he'll remain unharmed.'

Max and Lady Bainbridge looked at one another for a

split second, before turning to Charlie with eyebrows raised. Charlie stood glaring at the two of them until his mother finally broke the silence.

'Now is not the time for levity, Charles. Off you both go.' Lady Bainbridge stood up. 'Maximillian, I do not expect you to return without my daughter.'

Max nodded solemnly, as Lady Bainbridge and Hercules swept out of the room. He turned to Charlie. 'We must leave immediately.'

Max had his best horse readied straight away and he and Charlie hadn't looked back. Etta had taken more than enough money to get a fair distance if she wanted to, but the coach was slow and they had an excellent chance of catching it before she left the country.

The two of them rode all night. They needed to rescue Etta – and now. Max shuddered to think about what could happen to her.

They made it to the docks and interrogated the clerk, but it seemed no woman of Etta's description had boarded the regular crossing. As they left the office, their attention was drawn to a young man sitting on a mooring post.

'Messieurs!' The man removed a blackened pipe from his mouth and looked up at them, yawning. '*Vous êtes Anglais?*' he asked. 'You are English, *non?*'

'Yes?' Max said, at the same time as Charlie demanded, 'Yes, but my god, how can you tell?'

The man shrugged. 'The clothes. You English lack a certain . . .'

'*Je ne sais quoi?*' Max interrupted, more than ready to move on.

'*Non*, I am not knowing either. But it is –' the man waved at them judgementally – 'unpleasant.'

Charlie looked outraged. 'The bloody cheek! Did you stop us just to remark on our sartorial choices, my man, or did you have something worth saying?'

The man scratched his nose in perhaps the most French gesture either of them had ever seen, then shrugged. 'I thought, per'aps, you might be looking for the mademoiselle without a ticket?'

Charlie dropped his hat, necessitating a dismount from his horse. 'Bugger.'

Max ignored him, his attention focused solely on the Frenchman. 'You saw her? Blonde, thin, freckles? Which way did she go?'

'*Oui*, the hair, her face, same colour, *non*? Fascinating.'

'Which. Way. Did. She. Go?' Max ground out, as Charlie hoisted himself back onto his restless mount.

The man gestured towards a building across the docks. 'That way, into the church.'

'Much obliged, mon-sewer,' Charlie yelled, as they simultaneously broke into a canter.

Chapter 49

1818

Etta opened her eyes and looked around. Oh yes, the church. She was safe, and she was dry, and she was angry. Very, very angry.

She stretched, feeling a rumble of hunger wrack her stomach, then counted her meagre possessions again. No money, no food, no hope. She was going to have to go crawling back to London somehow – probably a long, dangerous walk, with no Google Maps and with no food or water either.

She felt no small amount of self-pity, but even more anger. With herself, yes, for her rash decision-making. But also towards Max.

How dare he? How very, very dare he? He'd managed to avoid getting caught having a midnight tryst and insane drunken trifle sex with her, but he couldn't avoid being seen snogging Clarissa Bloody Best in a corridor?

It was her own stupid fault she was here in this freezing cold church in Dover, she knew. She'd acted rashly and running away had never solved anything. But it was his bloody fault, too.

Etta got up, her back cracking in pain as she lowered her sore feet to the cold church floor, and looked around to see *him* right there in the church doorway: the architect of all her woes. She leapt up from the pew, ready to take Max to task, but the world swirled around her, blood rushing to her head, sadness overtaking her rage. He was handsome. So very, very handsome. And so very, very not hers.

It was the last thing she thought before her legs went from under her.

The first face she saw when she opened her eyes was Charlie's. 'Good god, she's dead! Don't die, don't die!'

She was lying on the ground, Max's coat under her head. She recognised the smell of him, comforting, against her face.

'She's not dead, Charlie – she fainted. Here, she's coming round.'

Charlie grabbed Etta into a hug, pressing her against him.

'Don't worry, Charlie, it wasn't your fault. I'm sorry for leaving you. I was so upset, and then I was robbed and didn't have any money to get back and . . . well, thank god you've found me, is all.'

Max looked relieved and almost tearful. Surely not?

She waited for him to say something – anything – but he just knelt there, completely still, staring at her.

'And you!' With a lot of effort, Etta raised an accusatory finger in Max's direction. 'You . . . You . . . *Cheating bastard!*'

'Let's get you home, Etta,' said Charlie, helping her to her feet. 'And you don't need to worry about marrying Max, or seeing him again, if you don't want to.'

At this, Etta turned her face away and began to cry herself, her world collapsing all over again as she remembered everything. 'I can't marry him anyway, Charlie. He's engaged to Clarissa Best. He's the only person alive in this world who understands any of it, and he's gone and ruined *everything* by snogging the face off that . . . that . . . horrible friend.'

Charlie patted her arm awkwardly. 'Well, about that . . .'

'I bloody well am not marrying Clarissa Best! Not that harpy! How could you think that?' Max's voice rang out too loudly in the empty church, and he checked his tone. 'I'd rather die!'

'Go tell everyone and their dog then, since the whole bloody world was there with me watching you stab me in the back!'

Max looked incensed. 'I can hardly help it if the awful girl launched herself at me when I was making my way back from the privy, can I? Doesn't mean I have to bloody marry her!'

'Because you're a man, I suppose,' Etta said in an accusatory tone.

'Yes, and in this case I'm extremely glad of what you will no doubt consider a grievous double standard.' Max paused, clearly trying to calm his temper. 'Anyway, my father forbade it.'

'He did?' Etta eyed Max suspiciously, feeling a beat of hope thump in her chest. 'So he knows about her, then?'

'She had the audacity to turn up to our house.' Max frowned. 'You should know he hates Lady Best. He chased her and Miss Best out of the house. He's off buying you a parure as we speak.'

'What the hell is a parure?'

The two men looked at her appraisingly.

'Full set of diamonds, sis,' said Charlie. 'Tiara, necklace, earbobs, you name it.'

Etta couldn't believe her ears. 'Why on earth would he do that?'

Max bit his lip. 'It seems you made quite the impression on him at the refreshments table of the Baxter ball.'

'On your father?' Etta gasped. 'Oh god. I didn't realise that was him . . .'

She hardly knew how to continue; she dropped her head into her hands and sobbed.

'Well, now the lot of you are trying to buy me!'

'No, my father is. I can't promise you anything more than my unending love and devotion, Etta.'

She staggered, still unsure on her feet, but Max was there to steady her; she felt his hand cupping her chin as he forced her to look into his eyes. She looked up to see him staring at her earnestly, Charlie fading into the background.

'Will you, Etta? Will you forgive me?' He took a breath. 'Will you love me, as I love you?'

Etta stared back at him, her eyes dark with emotion, hair floating wild in the breeze of the draughty church. They drew closer together until there was barely an inch between them.

'I will give you anything. Everything I have is yours.' Max's voice broke, as he stroked her cheek with one hand. 'You must know you already have my heart, but you can have it all. My house, my vote in the Lords. Hell, if you're really set on going to France, I will travel with you there – or anywhere else you wish to go. Please.'

A tear ran down his cheek; she reached up to wipe it away.

'Do you really love me?' she asked. 'Do you really want to marry someone like me, Mad Hetty Bainbridge?'

'No. There is no Hetty Bainbridge. I want to marry *you*, Etta. You have made my world brighter with every part of you. I cannot live without you: your outrageous remarks, your remarkable music – even that ludicrous tiger.'

Etta sobbed. 'Then yes, of course. I can't live without you either. Please take me home, Max. I love you.'

Before she knew it, she found herself being enthusiastically folded into the most passionate kiss of her life. She tangled her fingers into Max's hair, willing the moment never to end, before a light cough from Charlie brought them both crashing back to earth.

Max leaned against a nearby pew with a light groan of relief. 'Thank god for that. Oh, Etta. My Etta.' He wrapped his jacket around her carefully and then paused thoughtfully. 'Do you think Mrs Baggins will share the trifle recipe after this?'

Etta beamed and leaned forwards, giving Max one last, brief kiss loaded with promise. Life had never felt so bright.

Charlie made a noise of mild disbelief behind them. 'What the hell is it with you two and that bloody trifle? Honestly.'

Chapter 50

2024

Now they'd been assured of their happy ending, there was something they were both putting off. Stella knew it, Hetty knew it – and they both knew they knew it.

The rush of media interest over their videos had distracted everyone from highlighting the fact that Hetty and Stella had been spending every moment together. Except those Stella spent at her job, though somehow it was often more convenient for Hetty to write her online diary from the empty corner desk.

The aunts had exchanged mischievous looks but said nothing as they left the two curled up together on the sofa every night watching films. Hetty pretended not to notice Elliot poking Stella in the ribs every now and then as he set up the camera for videos. Perhaps he wasn't looking his new guest bedroom-shaped gift horse in the mouth, but he didn't mention her mother either – for that Hetty knew Stella was grateful.

But now they'd been invited onto a major American talk show, and they were being flown first class. Elliot had a dissertation to hand in. The aunts said they couldn't make it either, and though they'd never confirmed or denied anything, only one hotel room had been booked for them.

Hetty had thought about it constantly. Of course she had. 'What do you think our room will be like?' she asked, looking at Stella timidly, before getting confirmation that the Americans did still drink tea.

But Stella had just smiled flirtatiously, which had done wild things to Hetty's insides.

Elliot's subsequent revelations about Americans microwaving their hot water had distracted them all seconds later, but not before Stella had time to register Hetty's reddened cheeks and bitten lip.

Excitement for their upcoming trip was tempered by the constant, angry calls Stella was receiving from her mother. The previous evening she'd actually thrown her phone across the room in frustration and Elliot had to go out and get the screen fixed.

Therefore, they were all surprised by the silence that day, which Hetty tentatively brought up.

'Your mother seems to have been rather quiet tonight, Stella?'

Stella didn't look up from the novel she was reading. 'Oh, I blocked her number. I know the urge to triumphantly win back another "lost soul" will quickly trump the embarrassment of having a morally redundant daughter, and hearing about either of those options sucks.'

Hetty knew that Stella was trying to sound blasé about it all, but she wasn't quite pulling it off.

'That's a lot of words to use just to say our mum's a cow, Stella,' said Elliot.

'Oh, I've had more than enough time to think about it. She tries so hard, but she's trying the completely wrong thing.'

'My mother was like that,' Hetty said quietly. 'She tried so hard, but I just wasn't the right kind of daughter for her. I could never provide what she wanted from me.'

Stella nodded. 'I don't want to live a life where I can't be myself,' she said blankly.

'Me neither,' said Hetty. 'And I've got you to thank for teaching me that. But I'm still sorry,' she added. 'I wish we could get through to your mother. I wish you could be in each other's lives.'

'I'm sorry too,' said Stella. 'And I wish you could have been yourself where you came from, though I can't pretend I'm sorry you're here now instead.'

They were briefly silent, as Stella's hand found Hetty's across the table. The air crackled between them.

And then Elliot coughed, and Hetty went back to asking a barrage of questions about aeroplanes. They were going to be interviewed for television, a mind-boggling thought too big to fit in anyone's heads – but Hetty was more concerned about the idea of hurtling through the sky in what sounded suspiciously like a baked bean tin.

Although Stella was trying to move forward, Stella's mother and her pastor had other ideas. As her mother's phone calls were no longer getting through, they came knocking a few days later. Unfortunately for them it was Aggie who opened the door. Even worse, Jemima was at home.

It would have been terribly poignant and dramatic, Hetty imagined, had it not ended up with Hetty comforting Stella on the sofa while they listened to Lady Agatha Bainbridge schooling the unwelcome visitors on the history of lesbianism and women's rights in the UK with Jemima spurring her on.

Stella sobbed against her shoulder and Hetty found she too was crying. She hated to see her confident, happy-go-lucky love so battered down.

One last angry shout echoed across the hall. 'I hope you're happy, Estella!'

Stella sobbed again, as the slamming door made the pictures actually rattle on the walls.

Hetty took a steady breath, unsure how to proceed.

'I know it can be hard to find happiness. I was terribly sad, before I came here, but then I met you, and now Elliot, and all the acquaintances I've made online. You have all helped me immensely.'

She paused, taking Stella's hands in hers.

'And, well, I also take the most ingenious tablets every morning. They seem to have helped, too. Perhaps – perhaps they can also help you?'

Stella smiled through her tears, squeezing Hetty's hands back.

'Oh, Hetty, bless your heart. There aren't any pills for this sadness. I think it's just going to take time to heal.'

Hetty dabbed at Stella's wet cheeks with a tissue and squeezed her hand.

'Will you . . . Will you perhaps spend that time with me? I care for you so very deeply, Stella. I truly will do everything in my power to help you – how you have helped me.'

Stella took a deep breath and managed a genuine smile. 'Oh, Hetty. Oh yes. And – well, I care for you back. Very deeply indeed.'

And there it was, Hetty realised: the happiness she'd travelled two hundred years to find.

Chapter 51

1818

In unspoken agreement, the travel-worn trio went in search of food. In no time at all, they were drawing towards an impressive-looking, bustling pub. Etta suddenly felt extremely shabby in her mud-covered borrowed dress: she wasn't entirely convinced there was going to be room at this inn for them.

Max and Charlie had also clearly realised this as they entered the yard. She saw an ostler point to her and start asking questions. Max approached him and said something in an angry voice. The ostler went off, giving her a cynical once-over on the way. Max offered her his hand as she got down from his horse and brushed down her skirts.

'So, old chap,' said Charlie, 'you got us rooms, then. How on earth did you explain Etta's appearance?'

Max raised an eyebrow. 'I told them she had been kidnapped.'

'Kidnapped?' Charlie asked.

'Couldn't think of anything else to explain her lack of baggage, maid, or clothing. Charlie, they didn't have two rooms available, so we're going to have to share.'

Charlie gaped at him. 'Share? With my damned sister?'

'If your mother wants us to marry in your family church, I don't see any other option.'

Hetty looked down at her crumpled, mud-strewn dress. 'What about my clothes? I can't wear this dress. I'm filthy.'

Max smiled, guiding her inside. 'Don't worry. I've hired a carriage to take us home first thing tomorrow. We'll smuggle you in through the back entrance.'

As Max's breathing evened out from the floor beside them and Charlie and Etta settled awkwardly, top to toe, into a small, lumpy bed, Etta realised she could hear sniffling by her feet.

Charlie tossed and turned next to her. 'God, Henrietta, stop moving the blankets. You're making my feet cold.'

His voice sounded hoarse, almost like . . .

'Are you crying?' asked Etta.

'Never you mind.'

She sat up and got out of bed, shuffling around to his end.

'You might as well tell me, you know. A problem shared is a problem halved.'

'Not this one,' said Charlie, but he sat up nonetheless and adjusted the ridiculous bedcap he'd borrowed from the landlord of the inn. He paused, and Etta waited while he wrestled with himself. Finally, he spoke.

'I feel terrible, old girl. We've treated you appallingly, haven't we? Me, really. I've been a complete blighter. You weren't mad at all. We just didn't – we didn't give you a decent chance at things.'

'Charlie . . .' Etta put her hand on his shoulder. 'I don't think I tried much either, did I?'

'No, but we – Mama and I – we shouldn't have just given up on you like that.'

'You didn't, though, did you?' said Etta, a faint smile playing on her lips. 'I seem to recall this all started with you strapping me into that chair in the cellar.'

Charlie brightened at this, taking his head out of his hands. 'I say! I do believe you're right there!'

'Don't go thinking it's all down to you,' Etta warned. 'No way am I letting you—'

'. . . Write a paper for the Royal Society? Gosh, I daresay I could actually get in! Imagine that?'

Etta's grip on his shoulder tightened painfully.

'Or not,' Charlie continued, chastened. 'Just glad you're all right and tight, old girl.'

'You'll be dressed to the nines from now on, Etta,' said Charlie, as she pulled at her dirty, travel-stained dress in the carriage the next morning. 'Stanhope's full of juice, aren't you, old fellow? Should actually get him to take you to Paris and get you rigged up in all the latest fashions.'

'I'll take her anywhere she wants to go, and she can wear anything she likes.'

Charlie rolled his eyes. 'I'm not sure how I'm going to manage this. Like April and May, you two. Very unfashionable, this sappiness.'

Etta yawned, then grinned. 'What happens in Dover stays in Dover, Charlie.'

'Too many secrets going on at the moment,' Charlie grumbled. 'Not sure how we're going to keep track of them personally.'

'I suppose the secrets are rarely written down for history, only the gossip.'

Max looked thoughtful. 'Yes. I suppose when we look back, we'll only have the newspapers, the tuppenny gossip sheets and the satirical comics to look back on. How depressing.'

'Oh, don't you worry. I've been keeping a diary.'

They entered the house through a back door and were let in by an emotional Bessie. 'Oh, miss, such a note you left me. I thought we'd never set eyes on you again!'

Max eyed Etta suspiciously. 'Just how many notes did you leave?'

Her maid was looking sheepish as she pulled a glittering chain from her pocket. 'I hope you'll forgive me, but I didn't think you'd want to leave just yet, miss. I hope you don't think I've done you wrong.'

'No. I think you've done me the greatest favour possible,' said Etta, clasping Bessie's hands. 'Bessie, you'll be coming with me to live with Max, won't you?'

Bessie looked deeply offended that Etta would have considered any alternative. 'You wouldn't leave me here, would you? Not take your lady's maid?'

'Well, no, but I wasn't sure if—'

Bessie gasped. 'That I'd not want to become lady's maid to a marchioness? Begging your pardon, my lord. I know he's not corked it yet, but . . .'

Max sank further into the background as a wailing Lady Bainbridge appeared and immediately clasped her errant daughter to her bosom. 'Henrietta, you must never leave me again!' She paused, collecting herself. 'Well, I know you are to be married, but . . .'

Etta hugged her mother back. 'Don't worry, I shan't go

too far away, I promise. Only the next country estate along, remember.'

Lady Bainbridge hugged her again, impulsively. 'Oh, Henrietta. Come, we must plan your trousseau. And the Bramley girls will want to see you, too. They visited this morning and were most concerned not to see you.'

Etta spared one final loving look for Max as she followed her mother obediently.

'Yes, Mama, but . . . What's a trousseau?'

Chapter 52

2024

Over the years, Hetty Bainbridge had ridden horses, travelled by coach and even been in a sail boat on the family lake with Charlie. She had never, of course, flown.

And yet here she was, huddled next to Stella, clutching her hand tightly as she surveyed her unfamiliar surroundings. She was sitting in a large metal tube with large combustion engines attached. It was nightmarish – and what was worse, she was 'only' flying to New York in this terrifying contraption.

Oh, but her life was now so diverting, she thought, wondering how Etta was getting on.

Now that she'd gone through them herself, Aggie had shared the rest of Etta's diaries with her and Hetty had decided that Etta must indeed be happy. How could she not be, with such a fairytale ending? Hetty had felt deep, deep relief: the bracelet was here to stay. She'd wrapped it carefully in one of Aggie's silk scarves and placed it back in the box they'd found it in. She'd had enough time travelling for one lifetime.

Her ancestor – or her descendant, depending on how one

looked at it – had gone on to do truly outstanding things. And now it was her own turn.

She gazed out of the window and was horrified to see London quickly vanishing from under her. The skyscrapers seemed akin to dollhouses.

Tingles shot through her hand as Stella squeezed it. 'You'll be okay,' she whispered.

Hetty turned to look at Stella, whose face was closer than she'd expected. 'Do you think so?'

'I know so.'

Stella's breath seemed to caress Hetty's face. Right at that moment, all Hetty could think of was her cushiony, pillowy lips. Time seemed to slow. They moved closer and Hetty's heart beat harder than ever. This was going to be it. Her first kiss, and with the most beautiful, perfect woman she had ever set eyes on.

Except it wasn't, because suddenly there was the ping of a bell and around them, seatbelts unclicked as the plane levelled out. The moment was gone.

Hetty felt her shoulders drop in disappointment, but Stella was smiling.

'Don't you worry,' she whispered. 'You've got the rest of our lives to kiss me.'

Paper 1, Question 1:
Lady Henrietta Stanhope, Marchioness of Kent

Born in London in 1796 as Henrietta Bainbridge, Lady Henrietta Kent was one of England's first suffragettes. Campaigning alongside her supportive husband the Marquess of Kent, she travelled extensively across Europe and India, as well as other British colonies. Her writings were instrumental in the growth of suffrage across Europe and were first discovered along with her diaries in 2023 by her descendant, social media influencer and scientist Dr Hetty Moore, and her wife Stella.

Describe the impact of Lady Kent's work on modern feminism.
[16 marks]

Extract from AQA History GCSE paper, 2040

Acknowledgements

Congratulations! You have reached the boring part, and are bothering to read it. I shall reward you, dear reader, by attempting to make it interesting – I shall tell a strange and unbelievable short story in which a dull civil servant decides to write a romantic comedy and spends the next several years boring everyone half to death about it.

My mum and dad kick this story off by teaching me to love books, particularly Georgette Heyer, Katie Fforde, Terry Pratchett, and Douglas Adams. Thanks for letting me read any book I could reach – I found out where the romances were hidden very early on, and it feels like it paid off.

Thanks, next, to Tactile Games, a Danish games company who employed me in the height of the pandemic off the back of a fan letter I wrote to them and an interview in which I had a freshly shaven head. John Sutherland in particular gave me confidence that my bizarre writing might in fact be commercially viable.

My writing for Lily's Garden let me sneak into the Romantic Novelists' Association – a group of remarkable people who do not, contrary to expectations, sit around on chaise longues all day wearing pearls and smoking cigarettes from long holders. Thank you all for the remarkable chance to show my writing to publishers and agents, and special thanks to Virginia Heath who picked up the pieces after my first eye opening industry one to one.

Next I must of course thank my agent. Mine answered a hastily scrawled email I now understand is known in the publishing industry as a 'query'. My rather unorthodox subject line was something like 'Argh argh argh somebody wants to publish my book'. Marina, I am so glad you opened it. Thank you for waiting for me to finish it, too, for your help making it ready, and for subsequently finding someone willing to actually print it. You are exceptional, and I would send you flowers every day if I could.

This book was largely written in the café attached to my daughter's dance class, and edited during her 11+ tutoring – thanks to Miss Katie, Miss Lorraine, and Miss Diana at the KAS Academy for the lattes, and to Lou Kershaw for the cups of tea and ice lollies.

Thanks also to content design, a profession so perfectly aligned to my own skills that it allowed me to spend plenty of time on this book while working a 9 to 5 job. If I never have another novel published in my life, I shall be happy to continue in content design. I am of course now contractually obliged to write a second book, however, so do keep an eye out.

Can you believe that I have lost friends over this book? Thanks so much to the various agony aunts who've helped me through it, including Philippa Perry, Katie Fforde, Marta Suarez, Miriam Firth, Kay Ashton, Vanessa Robertson, Margaret

Nicholls, my wonderful in-laws Charlotte and Helen Gaskell, and many others who I've no doubt forgotten.

Then, of course, on to my publishing editor Kate. Thank you for getting it, when I was worried nobody would. This book is better because of you. The same goes for my copy editor Sally, whose eagle eye has been beyond valuable.

Finally, we must never forget those closest to us. This book was written during a time of immense pressure and stress, and involved great sacrifice not just from me but from my husband James and daughter Libby. You can find them in my hero's stoic patience and my heroine's beautiful freckles.

I have my own happy ending, now, which may only be just a beginning – but what happy ending isn't? All I have ever wanted is to have a book of mine on one of my many shelves. If you have enjoyed it, even better. So, my final acknowledgement is to you – for taking a chance on something (and someone) new.

Oh, and who is Nana Joan, the woman to whom I dedicated this book? She is the woman to thank if you prefer wild time travel comedies to cosy small town romances. I enjoy both, but she preferred the former. We miss you, Joan.

Dear Reader,

We hope you enjoyed reading this book. If you did, we'd be so appreciative if you left a review. It really helps us and the author to bring more books like this to you.

Here at HQ Digital we are dedicated to publishing fiction that will keep you turning the pages into the early hours. Don't want to miss a thing? To find out more about our books, promotions, discover exclusive content and enter competitions you can keep in touch in the following ways:

JOIN OUR COMMUNITY:

Sign up to our new email newsletter: http://smarturl.it/SignUpHQ

Read our new blog www.hqstories.co.uk

𝕏: https://twitter.com/HQStories

: www.facebook.com/HQStories

BUDDING WRITER?

We're also looking for authors to join the HQ Digital family! Find out more here:

https://www.hqstories.co.uk/want-to-write-for-us/

Thanks for reading, from the HQ Digital team